KING RICH

Joe Bennett

FOURTH ESTATE

Fourth Estate

An imprint of HarperCollins*Publishers*

First published in 2015
by HarperCollins*Publishers* (New Zealand) Limited
Unit D1, 63 Apollo Drive, Rosedale, Auckland 0632, New Zealand
ABN 36 009 913 517
harpercollins.co.nz

HarperCollins*Publishers*
Unit D1, 63 Apollo Drive, Rosedale, Auckland 0632, New Zealand
Level 13, 201 Elizabeth Street, Sydney, NSW 2000, Australia
A 53, Sector 57, Noida, UP, India
1 London Bridge Street, London, SE1 9GF, United Kingdom
2 Bloor Street East, 20th floor, Toronto, Ontario M4W 1A8, Canada
195 Broadway, New York, NY 10007, USA

A catalogue record for this book is available from the National Library of New Zealand.

ISBN 978 1 7755 4055 7 (pbk)
ISBN 978 1 7754 9092 0 (ebook)

Cover design by Darren Holt, HarperCollins Design Studio
Cover images: Man by Bert Loewenherz/ Getty Images; background images by shutterstock.com
Typeset in 12/18.5pt Bembo by Kirby Jones
Printed and bound in Australia by Griffin Press
The papers used by HarperCollins in the manufacture of this book are a natural,
recyclable product made from wood grown in sustainable plantation forests. The fibre
source and manufacturing processes meet recognised international environmental
standards, and carry certification.

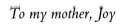

To my mother, Joy

Chapter 1

A woman is screaming. The hotel doorman, a Sikh, has forced a metal bar between the doors of the lift.

'Be peaceful, madam,' he shouts through the crack, 'be peaceful.'

'Can I help?' says Richard. He says it before he knows he will say it. Without looking up, the doorman indicates the bar. Richard's bad hand protests as he seizes it.

Another aftershock. The floor of the hotel lobby rolls like the sea. Bottles and glasses crash and scatter. The woman's screaming becomes a continuous wail.

'Heave, sir,' says the doorman. The doors of the lift part a few inches. Richard can see the woman's hair. She is kneeling on the floor of the lift, as if praying. She looks up, her face wrenched by terror, her teeth bared like a baboon's.

'Hold on, sir,' says the doorman, seizing a chair and wedging it into the gap between the lift doors, just before Richard's strength fails.

'We are coming, madam. We are coming. You are all right. You are all right.'

He puts his hand through the gap above the chair. The woman reaches out.

Richard heaves on the bar again. The doors open a fraction wider. The doorman pushes the chair deeper into the gap, twisting it. The chair back snaps. The gap narrows again. The woman whimpers.

A cough rises in Richard's chest. Rises and keeps rising. He is seized by coughing, bent double over the bar, all strength gone. There is only reflex, only the primal urge to live. He crumples to the floor, knees to chest, foetal. A racking, panicked shudder and the blockage shifts. Richard lies gasping, drained, weak as cotton thread, his vision blurred and dotted with darting lights. Another brief bout of coughing.

When he looks up a man in uniform is helping with the lift. The doorman's turban, royally purple, shaded with plaster dust, has begun to unfurl at the back. They have the doors a foot open, a planter wedged into them. They are reaching in, handing out the woman. She is blubbing and limp. The doorman bends, scoops an arm under her knees, another beneath her back and lifts her like a bride, across the lobby and out the revolving door, as another aftershock, a smaller one, sets the long lights swinging.

'You all right, Granddad?'

Still lying on his side, Richard nods.

'Come on, I'll help you out,' and the man in uniform – fireman? policeman? – offers a hand.

Richard shakes his head, gets to his knees, looks up and tries to smile. 'I'm fine,' he says. 'I'll follow you. Go on. You're needed out there,' and he gestures past the lobby restaurant tables, some overturned, some still bearing the abandoned remains of meals, past the bar and the smashed bottles and the fallen ceiling tiles to the revolving door and the street beyond. Through a cracked plate-glass wall he can see a scatter of rubble, of fallen facade, a half-buried car. 'Go on, I'll be fine. You're needed.'

The revolving door graunches as the man forces his way out.

Sirens are sounding outside, but in the hotel there is calm. Behind the bar the optics are still fixed to the wall and the glass-fronted fridges are stacked. Richard flips the cap off a Steinlager, still cold and beaded, and drinks. He feels the stuff seep into his tissues. Bottled God, someone called it. Bottled God. He drinks again. The jangle of the moment softens a little, its sharp edges dulled.

Through the tall glass he can see people walking quickly, dusted with plaster, others uncertain where to go. It's like an ants' nest kicked. He ought to be out there, ought to be helping. He slides beers into the pockets of his coat, goes to the revolving door, glass and crockery crunching underfoot, and pushes. The door shifts a foot, then sticks. He pushes but it doesn't shift. He pulls but it doesn't shift. Except for the sirens all is quiet. It seems that everyone has left the building. The guests, the porters, the receptionists, the chambermaids and waiters and bar staff, the duty managers who have so often emerged to move him on, to threaten him with the police, have fled. Richard retreats into the hotel.

'Exit' says a green sign above a door, with a picture of a stick figure running. Beyond the door the carpet stops and Richard is backstage on luxury. A staircase of bald concrete with painted metal handrails, zigzagging up, self-replicating and unadorned to the top of the tallest building in the city.

Down here they must have run, not twenty minutes ago, perhaps five hundred people fleeing the swaying building, down this shaft, the building's spine. He remembers a middle-aged woman in a hotel robe lurching onto the street, with wet hair and bare feet and veins on her legs like great purple worms. Her eyes were wild, her breasts pendulous. She just stood on the pavement gasping until a younger woman went to her and led her away around a corner.

Richard sets a foot on the first concrete step. He pauses after the first flight, breathing, looking down at his left hand on the metal rail. How old it looks, a reptilian claw.

One more flight, another pause for rest. When he pushes open a door, concrete reverts to carpet and the mezzanine lounge. A pot of tea still standing on a low table. He lays his palm against its metal flank. It's faintly warm.

An unbroken glass wall gives a view of High and Cashel. Half a dozen men are clearing rubble off a green car. Its cabin is staved in, crumpled. He can see where the rubble fell from, the Edwardian pediment three storeys up. Half of it is still up there, held by some temporary balance of forces. Urn shapes, fashioned from plaster or concrete or stone, placed there by men on wooden scaffolding, to fall, a century later, as murderous rain.

A man signals to the others to pause, reaches in through a gap in the rubble, reaches into the car, bends his head and shoulders into the gap to reach further, emerges, says something to the others and they move off down High Street and out of sight.

Richard draws a beer from his pocket. As he flips off the cap with the handle of a teaspoon, his forefinger rasps against the cap's crimped edge. The skin tears. He swigs at the beer, then studies the white tear of skin, watches the old thick blood slowly well beneath it, to form a bulb, a little grape, a droplet that courses suddenly down the side of his hand. He sucks at the tiny wound, tastes his dim metallic blood, presses the finger against the flank of his coat to stem the leak.

There is no one in the street. Sirens are wailing a few blocks away but here, nothing. The air is granular with dust. An hour ago the street was lunchtime crowded. People with duties, matters on their mind, and in almost every skull a sense of the day ahead, the day mapped by need and habit, the afternoon of work, the journey home, the shopping, dinner, the evening of television or family or income tax return or fixing the motorbike, or mowing the lawn in the long summer light. All of it gone, erased in a moment, all the certainty, the sense of future time, the sense of control of an accustomed passage through the valley of the days; the whole social edifice fallen like the pediment opposite, now not even rubble, just gone, wiped by a single shrug of the rocks below. Richard drinks from his beer.

A few blocks away a plume of black smoke. From time to time knots of people hurry by on the street below, stepping round the litter of rubble, looking around at the sights, unwilling tourists of destruction. A woman appears on high heels, dressed for the office, a cell phone clamped to her ear. As she turns the corner of Cashel and High she stops abruptly, stops both walking and talking, and stares at the staved-in car.

She goes to it, touches the bonnet, peers inside, puts the cell phone back to her ear, speaks briefly, then takes photos with the phone, five, six, seven shots, touring the car, crouching to get an angle. She stands a moment, undecided, then strides swiftly back the way she came.

And from the other direction, a little girl. Wild-eyed, lost, perhaps seven or eight years old in a simple blue dress and Richard goes to the window and bangs on the glass. The girl has stopped, is looking around. Richard bangs again. She looks up, sees him. He raises both hands, as in a gesture of surrender, telling her to stay where she is, he'll come and get her. She bursts into tears and turns to run the other way just as a man in a suit comes running round the corner and the girl sees him and runs at him and leaps into his arms and clamps her chest against his, her head over his shoulder, and wraps her legs around him, a baby ape, and father and daughter stand there fused and rocking.

The girl's head lifts from the father's shoulder and he wipes the hair from her eyes and, still in his arms, she turns and points towards the first-floor window where Richard drops below the sill and does not move. Until he hears the footsteps, heavy booted footsteps on the stairs.

Chapter 2

Paul and Annie lay under two duvets in the flat in Turnpike Lane, she on her side with her knees drawn up, he with his knees drawn up behind hers, his chest against her back, the pair of them like forks in a cutlery drawer. His left arm draped over her breast. On the radio alarm clock the pips for six o'clock and the cultured voice of a newsreader.

Annie's eyes popped open on the instant. Her legs swung off the bed. Naked, she stepped into the little sitting room and turned on the television. Pictures of people panicking in rubble-strewn streets. Of a collapsed building on fire. Of car-swallowing silt on suburban roads. Of sniffer dogs clambering over twisted metal.

She stood and stared, hugging herself in the cold, dark little room, her eyes fixed on the images of disorder from the other side of the world.

Paul appeared behind her and fitted a robe over her shoulders and wrapped his arms around her and pressed against her, an erection rapidly wilting in the small of her back. 'Oh my God,' she said. 'Look, it's River Road, that's our house, look, there, that one,' and she moved towards the screen to point at a weatherboard villa two beyond the split and broken one centre stage. But River Road became the mayor in an orange jacket saying things to a cluster of thrust microphones. Behind him a white pancaked building and parked fire engines, their lights flashing.

'You all right?'

'Yeah,' and she leant into him, her eyes still on the screen.

'I'll make some tea,' he said, detaching himself and turning on the lights and the gas fire on his way to the kitchenette. Christchurch yielded after two minutes to a flood in Bangladesh. She turned the television off and picked up the phone but paused for a moment. The sight of River Road had evoked a flood of disconnected bit-part memories of childhood, all coming in a rush – a one-armed greenish doll, statuesque herons in the shallows, doing nothing then suddenly, fiercely and profitably stabbing, her father coming home from work and throwing her up and catching her and rubbing her against his bristles, her first prick, huge and purple, dramatically and briefly revealed to her alone at the bus stop on Stanmore Road by a man with a beard, the sun, New Zealand's summer sun that seemed to bite an inch into the skin of your arm, your shoulders. Scones with raisins. Watching from her bedroom window her mother feeding a bonfire and the smuts rising.

Annie dialled a number, was surprised to get through.

'Are you all right, Mum?'

'Darling. So you've heard. I didn't know when I could decently ring you. Course I'm all right. Blenheim is a long way from Christchurch, or have you been away so long you've forgotten?'

Annie let this pass, along with quite a lot of isn't-it-terrible-poor-Christchurch stuff that followed, and that contrasted somewhat with her mother's excited, animated tone.

'We've got a meeting of the wine club in an hour and we're going to see what we can do to help, you know, in our own little way.'

'You're not going to send them wine,' said Annie.

'I shall ignore that comment, dear.'

'I saw River Road on the telly. It looked, well...'

'I know, dear, I know. Did you see old Bateman's place, miserable old sod that he was, but still... And that dog of his, great brute used to leap up at the fence and scare the living daylights out of me, and it wasn't as though it was much of a fence either, though I suppose it's long gone now, the dog, that is, thank God. Old Bateman, too, I'd guess.'

Huddling towards the gas fire for warmth, Annie gripped the edge of the little low table she had perched on. 'Mum, do you know if Dad's still in Christchurch?'

Paul put a cup of tea beside her, placed his great engineer's hand on the top of her head briefly. She didn't look up, intent on the about-to-burst silence on the other side of the world.

'No.'

'No he isn't or no you don't know?'

'No, I bloody well don't know and no, I bloody well don't care. And if you don't know by now why I bloody well don't care I...'

Annie only half listened to what followed, listened more to the tone of it, the building self-righteousness, the indignation, the self-pity, all fuelled by a sense of injustice that had swollen over the years through repetition and simplification into a story of black-and-white betrayal.

'All right, Mum, all right,' said Annie as she felt the pressure easing.

And after a couple of oil-on-watery I'm-glad-to-know-you're-safes she put the phone down.

Paul's frame filled the doorway to the world's smallest and coldest bathroom. 'You all right?' She could hear the hopelessly inadequate shower already running, slopping against the plastic curtain that, if you didn't actively keep the best part of an arm's length between you and it, loved nothing better than to wrap itself around your flesh and cling.

Was that 'You all right?' an actual enquiry about her wellbeing or was it what you said when you knew it wasn't all right but you wanted the other person to agree to pretend it was all right so that you could get on with your own stuff such as having a shower and going to work, which, of course – Annie was nothing if not fair, a weakness – Paul had every right to do?

Or was it, more complicatedly, a role Paul was playing, knowing, unconsciously, or semi-consciously, that the right

11

thing to say on seeing distress was 'You all right?', without any particular concern other than to feel he was doing the right thing, thereby maintaining the notion, the semi-fictional scaffolding of partnerliness, and allowing them to move on to whatever the next scene in the play might be, and hoping it wouldn't be tears because then he really would be late for work. Oh God.

It rarely was with Annie. She smiled and nodded.

* * *

Because it had happened to people who spoke English and who were predominantly white and who had several proper television cameras and who lived in buildings that, bar the tin roofs, could almost be described as houses, the earthquake had registered on the Great British consciousness. So Annie's customers, several of whom were more or less aware of her provenance, did plenty to keep it front and centre of her mind all morning.

'You're from down that way, aren't you, Australia and that?' said an old dear in a coat apparently manufactured from carpet. 'No one you know hurt?' she added hopefully.

'Not that I know of, Mrs Penaluna. Now, you're to take two of these before breakfast and another two before tea, dinner, before your evening meal. It's all spelt out on the label. All right?'

'Yes, dear, and thank you. Not surprised you all come over here. Safer, like. I mean if it's not earthquakes it's spiders the size of a mouse. I seen them on the telly, hanging around in the lav. Turned my stomach, they did.'

Annie spent her lunchtime at the computer in the pharmacy office, where she found screeds of disaster porn, the most catastrophic images seized on and reiterated by every news-gathering agency in the globe. To most people the name Christchurch would mean nothing, but the pictures would grasp their attention, would form part of the day's intake, to be replaced tomorrow by similar images from somewhere else. Annie found more and better pictures of River Road, old Bateman's place slumped and all but split in two, the garden buried under what she was learning to call liquefaction. Had he really had a dog? She remembered no dog. She'd so wanted a dog when she was little, a cute puppy. Dad had too, but Mum was immovable. 'Filthy creatures.'

Up to two hundred people were feared dead, most of them in the two collapsed buildings downtown. But she could find no list of names.

Chapter 3

'I've got sixpence,' hums Richard as he waits, 'jolly jolly sixpence,

I've got sixpence, to last me all my life.

I've got tuppence to spend and tuppence to lend

And tuppence to take home to my wife.'

He has listened to the boots working their way down the building, can hear them now on the floor above, thumping along corridors. Doors open, voices boom. Down the stairwell they come again. Richard sees the base of the door swing open. Two pairs of boots, black, polished, fawn trouser cuffs.

'Anybody here? Hello? Hello?'

The boots pause for a reply.

'You do in there,' says a voice. 'See you in the lobby,' and one pair of boots turns and heads back through the door. The other man steps behind the breakfast bar and pulls open the door to the kitchen beyond, then lets it close again without passing through. Richard could reach out and touch the leather toe cap, could tie the laces together. He wills himself not to breathe, not to cough. The chiller door beside him opens, a hand and shirtsleeve reaches in, takes out an apple juice, then disappears from view. Richard hears the metal perforations yield as the man unscrews the cap, and the glugging of air through liquid as he drinks. The cap drops to the floor and spins and comes to rest a foot from Richard's face, then the kitchen door opens again and the boots walk through. From beyond comes the sound of more doors being opened and shut, then the boots return, the juice bottle clatters into a bin, and the boots head to the door and Richard hears them down the stairs. Voices from the lobby below, then the graunch of the revolving doors.

Only as he relaxes does Richard realise that he has clenched his right fist, has dug the nails into his palm. He waits a minute, two minutes. Distant sirens still, the wail of some sort of three-tone alarm, but no voices. Bracing a foot against the cooler, Richard half slithers, half crawls like a lizard out from under the counter. He raises himself onto all fours and stays there, slowly rotating his neck to ease the ache, then reaches up for the counter edge and hauls himself to his feet. The beer he takes from his pocket has warmed a little. He flips the cap off, not daring yet to go back to the chillers in the lobby.

In an upholstered chair set well back from the window he hoists his boots onto a coffee table and ranges his three remaining beers beside him. The afternoon sun picks out sparkles of plaster dust. The room warms. He closes his eyes.

Another aftershock jolts them open. The building groans and shudders. But already Richard's senses have attuned to a shaken world and he does not get out of the chair.

When he wakes the sun has dropped away to the side of the building. His throat is familiarly dry. The tap in the bar delivers a still-cold stream of water with which Richard sluices his throat and face.

In a dark corridor on the floor above half the doors stand open. By some instinct of caution Richard shuns the rooms nearest the stairs, goes as far as 107, pushes open the door. A wheeled suitcase with a grey ribbon tied to its handle lies open on the strapped rack. Underwear folded, socks, a laptop and a duty free carton of Rothmans. The bed is made. In the wardrobe two suits, four shirts. In the mini-bar, abundance. Baby bottles of Johnnie Walker, Stolichnaya, mixers, a full-size bottle of cabernet sauvignon. In the knee-high fridge Heineken, Steinlager, pinot gris.

Richard wrestles the pillows from the bedspread, stacks them, places a Scotch and dry and a packet of peanuts on the bedside table and flops onto the mattress with a little gasp. He drains a third of the tumbler. He tears at the foil packet but it resists. He bites the corner and pain sears through a right front tooth. Sickened, he holds still while the pain wanes, studies the packet, finds an indentation in the foil, tears at it with his crabbed fingers and the foil tears meekly, neatly open and he tips nuts into his mouth, keeping them to the left side. How deft the mouth is, how fast to learn. The nuts grind down to a salty paste, which he rinses away with an anaesthetic swig of Scotch. Richard sighs with the ease of it, the softness of the bed, the blessing of the booze. How many rooms are there? He pictures the building from the outside, the tallest in the city. He watched it being built. No need to compute. There are rooms for the rest of his life.

The Scotch, a frisbee-sized biscuit and half the cab sav later, the edges of the world softened, Richard heaves himself to the bathroom. As he pisses – a hesitant start, a brief jet, a pause, a dribble, another pause that he knows to be a delusory conclusion – he sways slightly and braces his bad hand against the wall above the cistern, his head against his bicep. He smells the ripeness of his coat. No eight-year-old girl, however lost or stricken with fear, would bury her face in that. On the shelf, shampoo and gels in little bottles and a stack of white towels. A wash bag in patterned leather, a razor protruding. A toothbrush.

Turned to maximum, the shower soon runs warm. Richard's coat falls to the floor, a bottle in the pocket thudding. He sits on the end of the bed to remove boots and socks, sits up too fast and has to pause to allay the dizziness. He stands to let his trousers and underpants fall, hauls his shirt over his head, grabs the Stolichnaya from the mini-bar, turns towards the bathroom and sees himself in the wardrobe mirror. He stares at the body. It is years since he saw it all plain. The breasts like empty piping bags; the belly slumped in corrugations; the sparse grey hair of groin and thigh as nest to that shrunken withered dick, the vastly pendulous lop-sided balls. The scrawn of thigh and the familiar red and purple uselessness of his left hand dangling like Hook's claw. 'Jesus,' says Richard and he raises the vodka to his lips. 'Holy Mary Mother of God.' He drinks.

He stays in the shower till his fingertips shrivel, laving his flesh with random miniatures of gel and shampoo and conditioner. He towels himself with a deep white fluffiness, sets a gin on the bedside table and slides between the sheets. The luxury is a cocooning wonder. Richard could almost cry at its embrace. The things money can buy. Softness. Comfort. Ease of the flesh. He is asleep before he can even reach for the gin.

Chapter 4

When she'd arrived in London Annie had fallen in love with
the Tube. She loved the scheme of the Tube map, giving her a
template for the city, a way of grasping its hugeness, its thirty-
times-as-big-as-Christchurch-ness. She loved being able to
burrow underground and then re-erupt into the light and air
wherever in the city she wished, from Hyde Park to Plaistow
in half an underground hour. What places, what impossibly
resonant names lay within its purlieu. And how it would have
delighted old Mrs Fernyhough. In her final week of teaching
after forty years at Avonside Girls' High she had offered a
battered copy of the *Albatross Book of Verse* to any girl in Annie's
class who wanted one. 'They'll only be gathering dust after I've
gone,' she'd added with undisguised bitterness.

As if in corroboration only half a dozen girls had taken up
her offer and Annie suspected that several of those had done so
only out of sympathy. But her own copy had gone everywhere
with her, had almost been enough to persuade her to a degree

in English, until her own innate pragmatism and her mother's forthright opinion persuaded her otherwise.

Still, with its blue boards and its impossibly thin paper, it was the one book Annie had brought with her to London, and it felt as if she was taking it home. At eight one morning shortly after she'd arrived, Annie had taken the Tube to London Bridge, had climbed up past the reeking bus station and onto the bridge solely to watch the crowd flow over it. She had not been disappointed. The head-down hordes on a grey London morning poured like something geographical. 'I did not know death had undone so many,' she murmured as they streamed past her and she felt close to the heart of something.

Eliot's lines had been the second and last that she'd pinned on her bedroom wall. Yeats had been first. 'I have spread my dreams under your feet. Tread softly, because you tread on my dreams.'

'That's nice,' her mother had said. It had been enough to blow some of the magic from the words.

With Eliot, it was 'Do you have to be quite so morbid, dear?', which was somehow better. All the same, after that Annie preferred to keep the book by the bed and memorise lines that sang to her, holding them tightly to herself like treasures, never opening the vault to her mother's thin gaze.

But now, of course, after a year in the city, as she marched towards King's Cross on a February evening after work, dark at half past five, head down and thinking of home, she knew she had joined the contingent of the undone. The crowd she was part of was sucked down the steps into the Tube station like water down a drain. The platform was six deep with the undead, the bright-lit train when it came already crammed to the window glass, flesh pressed against flesh, faces held fiercely in neutral, faking impassivity. The squeeze aboard. The whistle, the doors failing to close and whooshing back, twice, three times, then finally she and a thousand unknown souls were sealed inside. And with the lurch of starting, Annie felt the usual tremor of premonitory claustrophobia. What if the power were to fail and the train stop dead between stations, and she and the thousand strangers crushed together in the... She dismissed the thought, put herself mentally elsewhere, in River Road.

The images she had seen that morning had stirred so many older ones, bright with childhood.

She recalled her father lifting her out of bed one winter morning, saying, 'I've got a present for you,' and carrying her to the window. Still in his arms, she parted the curtains and saw nothing special, the trees, the river, the road, and she swivelled and looked into his face, and he wore a serious look and said, 'Look again' and then she saw them, the ducks, scores, perhaps hundreds of ducks, grey and brown, most still roosting on the bank, heads swivelled, beaks buried under wings, ducks to the edge of River Road.

'They've come to see Annie,' said her father, smiling, and he folded her tighter in his arms and kissed the top of her head.

'Can I feed them?' she said.

'Of course. It's what they're expecting. You mustn't let them down,' and in pyjamas, dressing gown and gumboots she'd gone out with her father into the frozen morning and woken the ducks with a hail of thrown bread, and soon she was wading through ducks.

'Did they really come to see me?' she asked over the toastless breakfast table.

'Sweetheart,' said her father, 'they have flown from every continent on earth to be fed by the Princess of River Road.'

Later her mother casually let it slip that the ducks came into town at this time every winter because the duck shooting season had begun. Annie thought she had already known that.

Turnpike Lane was winter dark. Lights refracted on the wet asphalt. People went bent against the weather. At the all-purpose Asian store the tiered cascade of fruit and vegetables announced implausibly that somewhere on the planet there was warmth enough for growth.

In a recessed doorway just beyond Poundland a youth sat in a nest of old duvets, a dog curled beside him. How, in this weather, how? The days would be bad enough but the nights! She found the thought of it, as always, untenable, painful to consider. At the same time she was aware that she had never done a thing to help beyond dropping a few coppers in a plastic bowl. The sympathy was instinctive in her. The practical charity, the active doing of good, was beyond her. It was fear, of course. Her admiration for the likes of the Sally Army was limitless. But it went unexpressed.

With an inward smile of relief she remembered it was Tuesday, Paul's squash night. She'd have the flat to herself, could curl in solitude on the sofa, the gas fire on, reading perhaps, drinking soup, watching soaps, whatever. The deliciousness of being alone, of not having to be anyone but unfettered self, dragged her past the little park with its winter-bald trees, like gesturing trolls, and its fenced playground with the stranger danger notices, and into Hampden Road.

The terraced houses on either side had not been generously sized when built a century or so ago. Yet every one of them was now split into two, an upstairs and a downstairs flat. In the shared front yard, effectively filling it, two bicycles belonging to the Laotian couple downstairs were chained together and to the drainpipe. Last summer Annie had put out a planter of azaleas. Someone stole the azaleas that first night. The planter within a week.

Even as she opened the door that blocked off the stairs to their flat, a door the frailty and shoddiness of which never ceased to affront and amaze her, that this thing should have been bought and sold as a door, a barrier between the safety of home and the hostility of a world beyond, this thing of hardboard tacked to a frame of what seemed to be balsa, a door that any weakling of a burglar could simply stick his fist through, she knew immediately that Paul was home. She sagged. First at the luxury of solitude snatched from her, and second at the thought that, well this could hardly be it, could it, could hardly be that much-mentioned brilliance, love. To come home tired to your lover, your partner, your soul mate, for God's sake, at the end of a dreary winter's day should be, according to the script, a tonic, a joy. With it there should come a sense of wholeness and unity, and a real sense of coming home, like sinking into a warm bed. Not a disappointment.

'Hello,' she said, as Paul appeared at the top of the stairs, gently smiling. She let him fold her in his arms and kiss the top of her head.

'Hello,' he said, 'how was your day?'

And maybe it wasn't as bad as all that, she thought, as she smelt the bolognese – it was more or less the only thing he cooked, but he cooked it well – and in the kitchen the table was laid and there were candles and a bottle of wine and, of all things, and suspiciously, napkins. She looked straight at him and he smiled his big schoolboy smile, which came out only when he knew he'd done something deserving of praise.

'I thought,' he said, 'after this morning, you know, the earthquake back home and that, I thought, well, you could probably do with something. You know, something nice.'

'Oh Paul,' she said, 'and on your squash night.'

'Squash was cancelled,' he said.

* * *

'No,' he said, as she made to clear the empty plates from the table, the little bowl of freshly grated parmesan, 'leave them. My treat tonight.' He refilled her glass – a Waipara pinot noir. He really had gone to some trouble.

As he filled the sink to wash up she admired his simple heft, the V of his back, the long strong thighs. Professional, level-headed, kind in a clumsy blokish sort of way, faithful – and she couldn't imagine him ever deceiving her if he wasn't – and endowed with a British passport, Paul was emphatically what her mother would have called 'a keeper'. Though Annie wasn't her mother.

'Don't you want to watch the news?' he said when she made to dry the dishes. In the sitting room she curled on the sofa in front of the cinema-sized screen. Christchurch led the bulletin still, the morning after the day before. The ghoulish cameras had had time to scour the city for the most affecting images, the fallen spire, the rubble-crushed cars, the survivors white with plaster dust, parents finding children, the hotel on a Pisa-ish lean, office workers being lowered from the windows of a tower block, houses with a side missing, the interiors open to the world, children sitting in Latimer Square near the smoking remnants of the building where their mother was entombed. An aerial shot of the east of the city showed how the Avon, the gentlest and prettiest of little rivers, willow-lined and duck-paddled, had half reclaimed its swampy floodplain. A hundred and fifty years of human effort had been shrugged off, without great effort, a mere flick of the earth like a swish of a horse's tail and well, we all know we are mere ticks on the earth's flanks, but to see this happen to somewhere she knew, the place that nurtured her, felt to Annie like something bitterly different, like a sense of certainty lost.

In interviews edited for maximum emotion, she heard the frightened weep and the excited burble, while those in authority spoke with a gravitas that masked their delight in being in authority in a disaster, in being listened to and looked to for information and orders. Thanks to television, she had a god-like view of the event that was unavailable to those at the heart of it. For them, Annie sensed, the grieving kids, the trapped and the freed, the suddenly homeless, it was just a present-tense mess, the here and now of being alive. And she felt impotent.

When the quake gave way to unrest in Tunisia – Bangladesh had sunk rapidly in the rankings – Annie turned the television off and sat staring at the blank screen, imagining what it must be like to be there right now, in River Road, the central city, anywhere in her home town. The frame of the sofa squeaked as Paul sat beside her. She leant into his chest and his arm encircled her and a paw cupped her shoulder.

'Thanks for the dinner,' she said, nestling, 'it was lovely. Just what I needed.'

'You all right?'

That standby line again, indicative of both his kindness and his bafflement. He seemed to have little idea what feelings she might have, and he clearly didn't want to know the detail, but in his own sweet way he cared, or, at the very least, he wanted her to be happy rather than sad. Which on the scale of emotional complexity was at the primitive end, but whoever said that complexity was a virtue?

She nodded and sank deeper into his hug. 'It's just... oh, I don't know...'

'You think you ought to be there,' he said.

In her surprise she turned to look into his face. He held her gaze without blinking

'So why don't you, then?'

'Now you're being silly. What good am I going to do? And what about work? And it's not exactly cheap flying home, you know.'

Paul shrugged and drew her back against him.

'But you're right in one way. I do feel, I don't know, sort of guilty for not being there. I mean it's home, where I was brought up. And it's like seeing your childhood smashed to bits.'

She looked away from him towards the blank screen, thoughts whirring.

'The first thing they teach you at engineering school,' said Paul after a pause, 'lesson one on day one, is that nothing lasts for ever. Nothing's permanent. Everything you build is going to fall down eventually. You're just delaying chaos for a bit, that's all. It won't last. Everything's ephemeral. In the long run entropy wins all the battles.'

'Really?' said Annie.

'Of course.'

'No, I mean is it really the first thing they teach you at engineering school?'

'It should be,' said Paul.

She laughed.

'Will you marry me?' said Paul.

She said and did nothing. Just stayed in his arms, both of them looking towards the black depth of the television screen.

Annie wanted to speak. She formed the start of several sentences in her head. She said none of them.

'Ah well,' said Paul after thirty seconds or so, and he plucked the remote off the arm of the sofa.

'Oh, Paul,' said Annie.

'No worries,' he said.

Later, in bed, in the attic with the sloping ceilings, the one room of the flat that Annie liked, and where there was only about one square yard of floor where Paul could stand upright, they lay side by side on their backs, less than an inch apart at the hip. Her skin could feel his body heat. He always radiated heat. He burned fuel at a prodigious rate. He ate and ate and yet was lean.

'Annie,' he said to the ceiling.

She waited for him to go on.

'What chance is there of you changing your mind?'

'But I haven't made up my mind,' she said.

'When will you?'

'I don't know,' she said, and she wanted him to seize her and kiss her.

'Goodnight, Annie,' he said, and he rolled the heat and bulk of his frame away from her towards the wall and the bed-base squeaked like a nest of mice. 'Oh, and I think you ought to go home for a bit.' Within ten minutes he was snoring.

Chapter 5

Sunshine wakes him, a shaft of it across his face. It takes seconds to assemble the explanation of where he is, how he got there, the broken city beyond. He lies awhile in the unaccustomed freshness of the sheets, just watching the light cross the room. He tries to reconjure the sense of wellbeing from last night. It does not come. The day is jangled, sharp-edged and unsatisfactory and he feels a remote uneasiness, a sort of precursor to dread, its cause undefined. And with it there's the familiar morning hollowness, and he gives in to it without a fight, without even thinking of fighting.

The beer is warm but it is beer. He sits with it at the window and lets it fill the hollow, draw a veil over the unease, push dread offstage. Beer is the friend whose hand you don't want to let go. He can see to the Port Hills, burnt late-summer brown. In the distance you would not know that anything had happened. But in the foreground below, rubble, crushed cars, shattered glass and no people. They must have thrown up some sort of cordon. He sees only a pair of soldiers patrolling on Cashel Street with guns. It is good to observe them unobserved, to spy. Later a police car slowly negotiates the rubble. Aftershocks come at intervals. The building seems to sway with each of them. At every shock Richard finds himself hoping for another big one. When he is halfway down the second beer he glimpses between buildings a contingent of men and women in hi-vis vests and hard hats passing along Manchester Street in the direction of Cathedral Square. They are talking excitedly.

Two Heinekens and a Johnnie Walker later the sun climbs out of sight of the window and Richard realises he is hungry. He slides into a pair of fluffy slippers like hooped poodles.

In the ground-floor kitchen vegetables and crockery litter the floor. On the hob, a fish fillet sits in a pan. A deep-fryer is cold and gelid, the basket of shoestring fries still buried in it. On the far side of the kitchen several sacks of washed potatoes and onions in bags of red netting. Inside a double-doored fridge the size of a master wardrobe there's a mass of meat, several beasts' worth of meat. Gas and power are off but Richard finds the little trolley that is wheeled into the dining room to make show-off dishes, instant wok stuff, flambéed crepes. And he would like to wheel it out into the bistro now, for the theatre of it, the self-amusement, but he does not dare to risk being seen.

A spark clicks at the turn of the dial and the gas flares fierce and blue. The frying pan he chooses is copper-bottomed, posh. From the fridge a fistful of bacon. The noise and smell of the sizzling briefly worries him and he turns the gas down a little, goes hunting for eggs, finds them, dozens of them, no, thousands, stacked on trays in a pantry that held them snugly. Only the top two layers are broken. He flicks the bacon onto a plate, cracks two eggs into the fat and hears a noise.

He turns off the gas, stands still, barely breathing. The noise again. From the back wall, the door there. A scratching and then, yes, a whining. He slumps with relief, breathes out. Goes to the door, puts his ear to it, then gently depresses the handle, opens the door a crack, peers out, then opens it wide.

The dog backs off in surprise. Its ears flatten. Its tail wags deferentially. It is wearing a worn leather collar. Richard looks around the hotel's delivery yard. Empty, flanked on three sides by tall blank walls, the fourth side leading presumably to Manchester Street. He fetches bacon from the fridge, holds it out for the dog. It approaches cautiously, takes the rasher, gulps it down but stays outside. Richard fetches more bacon, lures the dog in, shuts the door while it's eating.

He offers the dog the back of his hand to sniff, then strokes the soft fur of its neck. It's a mongrel of sorts, a bit of huntaway perhaps, a bit of lab, the sort of dog that all dogs would be in only a few generations if people just let them alone.

In the giant fridge Richard finds a flat cardboard box of steaks, porterhouse. He tosses two to the dog, fills a bowl with water and places it on the floor. The dog slurps greedily.

'And now, if you'll excuse me, dog,' he says, and the dog looks up and wags its tail. While Richard fries his eggs and eats at a bench of stainless steel, the dog tours the kitchen floor, finds plenty to keep it busy.

The tour done, it comes cautiously to Richard, who strokes the dome of the dog's head, feels the angles of the skull. The dog leans against his thigh. A registration disc dangles from the collar but no name tag.

'Friday, I'll call you Friday.' Richard chuckles and the dog's tail swings in response. 'Shall we go get a drink, Friday?'

To cross the floor of the bistro Richard loops the belt of his dressing gown through the dog's collar. 'I know you, Friday,' he says, 'you'll dawdle.'

But on the leash Friday becomes a trained dog, as faithful to Richard's pace across the floor as a guide dog, the leash never once going taut. 'Good boy, Friday,' says Richard when they are safely in the stairwell. 'Very good boy,' and he ties the belt back round his waist. 'Go on then, up you go.' The dog bounds ahead then turns and stops on the landing and looks back at Richard.

'Patience,' says Richard, smiling. He grasps the rail and as he sets his foot on the first step the dog barks. 'No, Friday, no,' hisses Richard. The dog falls silent but looks eagerly down towards him, ears cocked, tail going strongly as if this were the start of some ritual game.

Richard lays a foot on the next step. The dog barks. Richard stops. The dog stops barking.

'Here, Friday,' says Richard, 'come,' and to his surprise the dog trots back down the stairs and sits in front of him on the bottom step.

'Stay,' says Richard and again he unhitches the belt and loops it through the collar. He starts back up the stairs, hauling on the rail with his right hand and the dog keeps pace with him step by step, the pattern of all patience, and pauses beside him on the little landing between floors as Richard leans against the wall and regains breath.

Past the mezzanine to the floor where Richard slept, but he goes down the opposite corridor now in search of the sun, releasing Friday to bound ahead of him. He opens a door at random and the room is so bright that he has to close then shade his eyes. The fridge retains a hint of coldness and he chooses a Heineken over the red wine that he'd thought of having, pouring it into a tooth glass from the bathroom floor.

'Cheers, Friday,' and he raises his glass to the sitting dog whose tail sweeps back and forth across the carpet like a windscreen wiper.

With difficulty Richard drags the one easy chair over to the window and collapses into it, breathing heavily. The sun is warm on his legs and feet. The window looks out over roofs to the north and northwest. Through a gap between bank buildings he can see the broken steeple of the cathedral and the staved-in roof of a building beyond. There is smoke in the air though he cannot see where from. The distant Kaikouras retain a little cap of snow, glistening like dew.

Sensing calm, the dog curls in the sunlight, a paw tight against Richard's slippered foot. Richard feels privileged by the contact.

34

Another aftershock, and the dog is instantly awake and on its feet and looking round for the source of the attack.

'It's all right, boy,' says Richard, 'here, come here,' and he stretches out an arm as the building shakes and wheezes, and he smiles at the beast and makes coaxing, clucking noises, and as the tremor rumbles to its end the dog comes to him and accepts the offered stroking on the neck and chin, and rubbing of the silky ear between the thumb and forefinger. 'You'll be okay with me,' says Richard, and as he speaks he means it. And he's pleased to see the dog's tail rise a little and swish from side to side. '*Contra mundum*, Friday, *contra mundum.*'

Richard finishes his beer. With a gasp of effort he heaves himself out of the chair, fetches a small array of bottles from the mini-bar and stands them by the chair. The sun is warm through the glass. He can see only roofs and the broken spire and the distant mountains. He twists open the cabernet sauvignon, glugs at its deep, thick redness and stares out towards the pale sky of high summer. He can feel the welcome oblivion of sleep stealing towards him. And as it comes an image rises unbidden in his mind, an old familiar image, a tent in a stand of trees near the Grey River, and afternoon sunlight dappling naked flesh. Richard pushes the image away, forces it down.

He is woken by the dog's paw scraping his thigh. Drowsy, fogged, he pushes the paw away without opening his eyes. The dog whines.

'Shhh, dog, shhh.'

Quiet, and Richard is falling back into the luxury of sleep when again the paw scrapes his thigh with soft urgency and the whining restarts.

'What is it?' and he hauls himself up into the cruelty of consciousness. He feels a sudden stab of pain between his shoulder blades but it just stabs and goes.

The dog is prancing on its toes, eager for something. Richard listens for noise in the building – nothing. The dog whines again. Richard puts his right hand on the arm of the chair, twists his weight over it and levers himself up. The dog dashes to the door, but Richard's leg has fallen numb and buckles under him and he collapses back down into the chair.

'It's all right, boy, I'm coming.' He rubs the leg into life and heaves himself back up. The dog is already at the door and pawing at it. When Richard opens it the dog bounds towards the fire door leading to the stairs.

'Oh, bloody hell,' says Richard but he follows and on the stairs he again leashes the dog with the dressing gown belt to keep it from barking and down the stairs they go and the dog leads him across the lobby to the kitchen and then through the kitchen to the outside door and Richard opens it and the dog bounds across the yard and by the wheel of a delivery truck the dog walks twice in a tight circle, then squats like a weightlifter and concentrates.

Richard looks away out of engrained politeness. And to encourage the dog to relax and be thorough he makes a tour of the yard. There is little to see except the access lane leading to what he thinks must be Manchester Street, where a row of little shops, a convenience store, an old-fashioned greengrocer's, is fronted with a barricade of brick and rubble, all fallen from the Edwardian second storey. Richard is tempted to go for a closer look but even as he thinks of it a soldier ambles into view. Richard holds himself flat against the wall. The dog sees the soldier too. It stiffens and stares. It is about to bark.

'No, Friday, no.'

The dog looks across at him. The soldier has been joined by another, both of them brown-skinned, looking barely out of their teens and cradling weapons as mothers cradle babies.

'Stay,' whispers Richard to the dog. The soldiers look relaxed, do not seem to be expecting any action. Richard inches back along the wall. He is acutely aware of his fluffy slippers, his legs bare beneath the dressing gown. He reaches the end of the wall and turns into the yard and out of sight. He peers back around the corner. The soldiers are still there. The dog is looking his way.

'Here, Friday, come,' and the dog bounds to him and jumps up at his chest and Richard staggers against the wall and all but falls. 'Down, boy, down,' hisses Richard and the dog lies immediately flat on the tarmac and looks up with a sort of Famous Five eagerness. Smiling, Richard leads the dog back inside. 'Home,' he says as he closes the heavy kitchen door behind them, and he goes to the fridge for a steak for the dog. 'Home.'

Chapter 6

It seemed to Annie that Terminal 3 had been designed to make leaving the country easier. The mean low ceilings. The overcrowding. The incessant overloud public address system. To work here would be a species of hell. Compare it with the airports of the tiger nations, the places that looked ahead rather than back – Singapore, Hong Kong, Dubai. Hugely spacious halls, the ceilings as high as the ceilings of medieval cathedrals.

'Shit, I hate Heathrow,' said Paul, placing coffees on the too small cafeteria table which Annie had wiped with a paper serviette after shifting the mass of detritus left by previous customers. When Paul sat it seemed that the winsome little chair might buckle and splinter. Everything felt shoddy, gimcrack, tawdry.

Paul had insisted on coming with her all the way across town on the Tube, on carrying her bag, even on queuing beside her to check in. 'It's Saturday,' he said, when she said for the tenth time she'd be fine. 'What am I supposed to do? And besides, we live together, don't we?'

She looked up into his face.

'Don't we?' he repeated.

Oh no. At that moment Annie knew a speech was coming, or something similar. The unresolved proposal had hung heavily between them.

Paul put down his coffee, kept both hands curled round it and looked into the cup as if something swam there. 'You know I don't go in for this sort of thing much, Annie, but I want to say a few things before you go. Is that all right?' And he raised his eyes like a hopeful child. Annie nodded but felt a tiny dread.

'First, I like you very much. You're good to be with and you're easy to be with.'

'Like a bloke, you mean,' said Annie, before she could think. Immediately she wanted to call the words back. They seemed so sharp. But Paul was unfazed.

'Well no, not really, for obvious reasons, but yeah, if you mean like a bloke because I'm comfortable in your company, then maybe, yeah and I don't see what's wrong with that. You don't puzzle me and I'm not always worrying about what you're feeling. I've got a pretty good idea I know what you're feeling most of the time and if I haven't you don't burden me with it. So I like living with you. And you don't keep pressing me to talk about feelings I don't have. I may not be the most sensitive bastard in the world but I'm not going to start pretending I have feelings I don't have. I mean, what's the point? I hate lying and you don't make me.'

Annie made to interrupt but he held up his hand.

'Please, I've sort of half prepared this in my head. So I like you a lot. But I've never said I love you because I don't know if I know what love is. I mean in the sixth form I was obsessed with this girl called Sandra Walls. She was Barbie doll pretty and I fantasised about her and sort of hung around her like a puppy dog and if she said jump I jumped and I thought that was love. She enjoyed making me jump, of course, but I don't think she liked me very much as me, so to speak, and the whole business didn't make me happy and it didn't lead to anything and I'm bloody glad now it didn't. Was that love? If so, well, fuck it. If not, well, I don't know what is.'

Annie looked down into her own coffee. She'd known plenty of Sandra Wallses and she felt a pang of something that was more sympathy than anything else, affectionate sympathy for gangling seventeen-year-old Paul, but she kept her eyes down and swirled the last of her rapidly cooling latte.

'But I do know one thing, Annie. I'd like to have kids. Lots of kids. Everyone's all down on big families, these days. I'm not. I came from a big family and my childhood was happy as hell and I'd like my kids to be happy. And I can't see the point of living a life without having kids. It's just a plain dead end and plain bloody selfish, and most people without kids seem to me to be plain bloody miserable. Because their own life becomes their everything and when that fails to live up to what they hoped, they've got nothing to fall back on, no bright-eyed little brats to cheer on as they go into battle against the world.'

'That's some speech, Paul.'

'I haven't finished. As I said, I don't think I love you according to what everybody tells me love is or ought to be, but I do like you a lot and I do fancy you and I think you'd be a brilliant mother and if someone broke in here now and tried to hurt you I'd kill them. I mean literally, I'd happily break their bloody neck or whatever, with no doubts that what I was doing was right. And we've only been living together for six months.'

'Eight,' said Annie. Then, 'Sorry.' And she laughed and looked into his face with its heavy eyebrows and he looked straight back at her without smiling and she sensed the urgency in him, the sincerity, and she looked back down at the table. 'You know how old people are sometimes asked the secret of their long marriage and they always say there are good times and there are bad times and the secret is perseverance or whatever, you've got to work at it, and everyone says, "Ah, isn't that lovely and old-fashioned. What a pity we aren't like that any more." Well, I reckon the old buggers are right, you do have to work at it and the best sort of marriage comes from two people having spent a long time together sharing a house and a bed and having so much to do bringing up half a dozen kids that there simply wasn't the time to wonder whether they'd hitched themselves to a soul mate. And then when the kids leave home one by one to go and do the same thing themselves the two old codgers are left together and discover that they're

41

fused at the hip. And maybe that's actually what love is and everyone more or less knows it but doesn't like to admit it because they prefer the Hollywood version. I don't know.'

Annie looked around. No other couples seemed to be talking this earnestly. Indeed most sat in silence, looking across the crowded concourse, their hand luggage packed around their feet like plumply obedient dogs.

'And one more thing. I'm in too far already so I might as well say it. I'm not too bad a bloke. No, I'll rephrase that. I'm a good bloke. I know blokes pretty well. I've spent a lot of time with blokes. And some of them are pretty nasty and a lot of them are bloody selfish or vain or they lie a lot, especially to women. Well, I may not be the most sensitive or emotional bugger on the planet, but I'm not nasty and I won't bloody deceive you, just as I'm not trying to deceive you now.

'So, Annie, yeah, go to New Zealand, go back home and I hope you find your dad and anything else you may be looking for. And I'll be here when you come back, and I'm yours if you want me. But if you do want me it's on the condition that we're going to get married and start having a whole tribe of kids. Which will probably mean you'll have to give up work, and I'll have to earn a heap more money and, but hell, it can't be that hard, can it? I mean raising a family's not exactly unheard of. No, don't say anything. I'm glad to have got that all out. Now I'll be off.'

They both stood. He opened his arms to draw her in and kissed her on the lips and then folded her, pressed her against his chest and it was like being clamped in a warm cupboard. He kissed the top of her head.

'You have a good flight,' he said. 'And email me when you get there, okay?'

By way of a reply she squeezed herself tighter against his chest and stayed there a while, her cheek against his ribs, and then she pulled away and they stood facing each other and he stroked the sleeve of her coat and was half bashful schoolboy again and she felt a surge of affection and he said, 'Be seeing you, Annie,' and smiled and turned away. She stood where she was in the cafe and watched him till he reached the automatic glass doors and he turned and waved and she waved back, though she wasn't sure that he'd have made her out. Then she turned and breathed deeply and went to join the absurdly long queue for security, at the far end of which she'd be obliged to remove her shoes.

* * *

Some time during the night Annie went to the toilet, then leant a while on the bulbous emergency door, peering out of the window over what was probably central southern Russia. Each settlement 40,000 feet below was visible only as a cluster of lights, joined to other clusters by roads that showed as the frailest of gossamer threads. Annie felt a sense of the world's vastness, of all the millions down there leading lives as remote from hers as the lives of plants or antelope, people she would never meet or hear of, in landscapes quite unlike her own, yet all of them doing the same things, growing up, finding mates, starting families, raising kids. And though the plane was travelling at however many hundred miles an hour it seemed only to crawl across this landmass, this lump of territory that someone down there called home and thought was all in all.

And when the best part of a day later, a day spent in the limbo land of long-haul air travel, Annie saw the mountains of the South Island rising out of the ocean, she had only a sense of how impossibly remote, how pin-prickishly small amid all that water was the place that she called home. Slivers of rock thrust up by the meeting of two crustal plates, slivers we think of as static and permanent only because we measure time against our own brief lives. These little islands owed their very existence to the same forces that had just afflicted Christchurch, that had ended two hundred human lives and disrupted perhaps half a million more and all in geophysical terms without doing very much at all. It made the whole of life there seem as contingent, as arbitrary and as opportunistic and as meaningless, as it obviously was. But at the same time it had to be lived. 'When you get down,' and Annie could hear Mrs Fernyhough's quavery voice, 'the house is a maelstrom of loves and hates, where you, having got down, belong.'

Annie knew she belonged, could feel it from 40,000 feet, could feel herself being drawn, pulled by a sort of emotional gravity as the plane passed over the green ribbon of the West Coast that looked barely touched by the human beast, over the impossible white beauty of the Southern Alps, the snow of their peaks and flanks ironed by the air, then down over the foothills, the rivers of the plain gathering strength as the tributaries nosed from the countless valleys and merged in their push towards the sea, the whole thing laid out like a geography lesson. And then the great alluvial plain of Canterbury, the human presence everywhere in the quilt of paddocks, the dots of sheep, the squares of ripe wheat or barley, the toy farmhouses governing all this farmed fertility.

The plane swung out over the ocean and came in across the heart of the city. Everyone craned to see destruction. From her aisle seat Annie caught only glimpses of seemingly undamaged roof. And then the wheels hit tarmac and the brakes gripped and suddenly the plane was a beast of the land again and Annie was home.

The air bridge had been lined with photos of bush and was loud with recorded birdsong. Though Annie had rarely set foot in bush and had never heard such a chorus of birdsong, her heart still rose to the sound and the sense that here in the South Pacific this wasn't Europe. It was unique, different, small but brave. And unlike Heathrow it hadn't forgotten how to smile. Maybe it was a gimmick, but the grin and the 'Welcome home' from the man in passport control did something to Annie's heart.

She emerged into the arrivals hall through sliding glass doors that she had seen on the internet earlier that week as search and rescue teams arrived from around the world and were met with applause that had brought a lump to Annie's throat 12,000 miles away. And there was Jess, squealing and bouncing with welcoming delight, with that overflowing vitality that had always been her trademark, her signature, her self. It was this irrepressibility that had attracted Annie in school, and the friendship, unlikely though it was, had endured. Big, forthright Jess, and she was bigger still now, whom Annie thought of as a force of nature. And now she burst around the barrier and hugged Annie with an intensity that brought smiles, Annie noticed, to the faces of the others waiting to meet the newly arrived. Had anyone ever hugged Annie with quite such absence of reserve, such commitment? Her mother? No. Paul? Rarely. Her father? Oh, it had been so long ago. She wasn't sure that she remembered right.

'So we've got another disaster tourist, have we?' said Jess, releasing Annie from the hug but keeping a proprietary hand on either flank of her and studying her with unfaked interest. 'What would you like to see first? Smoking ruins? The morgue? Two ex-cathedrals? Liquefaction? Collapsed cliffs?'

'Bed,' said Annie, 'or rather a bottle of wine, then bed.'

'Spoken like a star. Hand over that bag and follow me, my darling.'

'Jess,' said Annie as Jess steered the Ford Fiesta towards the car exit, 'you are sure it's all right for me to come and stay. I mean, you will say if...'

'Not another word, sweetheart,' said Jess, laying a hand on Annie's forearm. 'Your arrival is a blessed relief from the guilt of having a spare room and no one in it. You can stay as long as you like. It'll be a laugh.' And so saying she wound down her window to feed a ticket into the parking machine, found she was too far away to reach and had to get out of the car. The driver behind blasted his horn. Jess laughed, fed the ticket into the machine then turned and blew the driver a theatrical kiss.

'You want to be careful,' said Annie as Jess got back in.

Jess snorted. 'Relax, darling. If you take the initiative, blokes simply have no idea what to do. Now, tell me about this hunk of a Pom you've left behind.'

'Paul? He asked me to marry him.'

'And?'

'And nothing.'

'You said no?'

'I said nothing. Sort of couldn't say yes and couldn't say no.'

'That'll have gone down well, I bet.'

'He's remarkably tolerant. But then at the airport he suddenly launched into this speech about being an ordinary bloke who just wanted dozens of kids and me pretty much chained to pram and stove for twenty years while he went out and forged an exciting career. It was such patronising, old-fashioned chauvinism that I almost said yes on the spot.'

'But you didn't.'

'No.'

Jess turned to look at her.

'Oh, and he said that he didn't love me, but that by having a dozen kids and twenty years of raising them we'd find we loved each other by the end, or something.'

'And if you don't?'

Annie shrugged. 'The possibility didn't seem to arise. Though I suppose by then it's too late to matter much.'

'So what are you going to do about him?'

'I said I'd tell him when I got back. He's in a bit of a rush to start breeding.'

'So should you be if you're going to.'

'How's *your* love life?' asked Annie. 'Is that Irish guy still on the scene? Or has some wise doctor finally beaten down the door to your heart and is even now preparing to whisk you off to Fendalton to frighten the expensive wives?'

'Neither of the above,' said Jess. 'But work's good for a change. Bizarre injuries, terror, power cuts, aftershocks… It's full on, the sort of thing you went into nursing for. Or at least I did.'

'By the way,' said Annie looking out the window at the neat houses lining the road, 'where is it? The quake. I don't see it.'

'No, sweet pea, you won't, not out here. In these parts it was just a bloody good shake, a bit of crockery down perhaps, the odd crack in the plaster. A couple of miles that way, however,' and she jerked her thumb in the direction of the city centre, 'well, you've seen the pictures. And as for where we were brought up, well, the word everyone's using is munted. It's about right. Avonside's munted. Still, we'll cope. Never say die and all that. Though quite what the hell you've come back for I haven't a bloody clue.'

'Yes, well, here I am, anyway.'

Later, sitting outside with a bottle of shiraz, Annie felt the exhaustion of the journey stealing over her, but the late-evening warmth was a blessing, and the rich Aussie wine, and with the weatherboard house behind her and the view framed by the wrought-iron corners of the verandah, Annie felt comfortingly where she belonged.

'Cheers, Jess,' she said, 'and thank you.'

'Thank me once more and I'll turf you out,' said Jess. They chinked glasses. The last of the sun was streaming shadows across the lawn.

'Jess, if you wanted to find someone, how would you start?'

'I see,' said Jess. She looked across at Annie with eyebrows raised. 'Well now, have you tried finding a phone number? Old-fashioned, but you never know.'

'And failing that?'

'Google?'

'What about medical records?'

'Medical records are private.'

'Oh, I wouldn't want to read them. I'd just want to know if a record existed in Christchurch, or anywhere else.'

'Still private. And no, I'm not going to put my...'

'Of course not, Jess, of course not.'

They sat a while saying nothing. As Jess had said, you wouldn't have known, here in this Hornby garden, that there had been a quake. The evening air swam with insects. 'How am I supposed to go looking,' said Jess, 'if I haven't got a name?'

'I love you, Jess,' said Annie.

Chapter 7

She ran her finger along the names. Stopped dead when she found his. Fifth from the right in the back row. She raised her gaze and counted and there he was aged seventeen. Annie gasped, felt her heart lurch. She could see the man in the boy. That grin, as if forged on his face by some inner warmth, the crinkle of the upper lip, those eyes. She would have recognised him without the name beneath. And what hair he had. What hair they all had. The back row looked like a Beatles convention. Great fingers-thick luxuriance, the abundance of youth as it chose to present itself in the seventh form in 1969. And it had been a windy day. High above his head a magpie had been captured forever on the point of turning in the air, looking tattered and unaerodynamic. She traced his features through the glass with her fingertip, caressed his cheek.

The prefects sat at either end of the row of staff, but he was up the back with the unanointed. His head was framed in the blue of a summer she'd never seen, a decade before her birth.

She made a note of the names of the boys to either side of him, then went back a year, testing herself by running her finger along the second-to-back row and found him easily. Less hair in 1968 because less senior presumably, less brave, but with the same grin and that crinkled lip. The boy to his right was different but on his left stood unmistakably the same character, with an explosion of blond frizz and a face the shape of a shield. V.P. Mahoney.

The school had been Jess's idea. It had survived without great damage, would reopen within days. But for the first time in its existence it would be accommodating girls, the sister school having been all but written off. They would retain, however, a virtuous Catholic separation. The boys would have the place in the mornings, the girls the afternoons.

Everyone had so much to do to prepare for this that the secretary had simply given Annie the freedom of the place. The school photos lined a single daunting corridor of history, all screwed to the wall in dark wood frames and quite undamaged. Every photo was different yet effectively identical: a seated row of priests and masters, small boys cross-legged in shorts at their feet, and then behind them four rows of boys, rising towards the sky as they grew older. You could trace almost all of them as Annie was tracing her father from little boy to young man until pop, off they went into the world. And you could trace the priests and teachers too, as year by year they moved towards the centre of the picture and the headmaster's throne, shedding hair as they went, gaining furrows in cheek and forehead, getting corpulent, hunched, shorter, until, after up to forty photos, pop, they too, rather more ominously, disappeared. And in every one of those forty photographs they were surrounded by an unchanging sea of youth. And if you looked along the row you could watch a pine tree growing to a different time scale, the only living thing to feature in every photograph, going in a century of snapshots from slender sapling to massive, unmissable entity, its lower boughs protruding ever deeper from the right.

Of the four most junior teachers in 1968, the outliers on the staff row, little more than seventh formers themselves, two stayed into the twenty-first century, both of them in clerical garb. Annie made a note of their names. The last had retired, bent, bald, fat and presumably single, in 2009. That corridor held the whole of his adult life.

She needed the names below to pick out her father in his first-year photograph, sitting quite close to the headmaster's brogues, and in the second year when he was near the end looking abnormally earnest. It was as though he came into being as himself only in the fifth form.

'Can I help you?'

A priest or father or whatever – he was wearing a clerical collar – had stopped behind her.

'Thank you, I'm fine. Though I don't suppose by any chance... no, silly me. Of course not.'

'Your father?'

'Yes.' She pointed him out in the seventh form and the priest took off his glasses and leant in. 'What hair they had then,' he said. 'He looks such a whole-hearted young man. I hope he… I mean I hope it isn't the quake that brought you here.'

'No, well, yes and no. I'm hoping to find someone who knows where he is.'

The priest looked at her for a moment, then said that it shouldn't be too hard. The old boy network was remarkable. When had she last seen him?

'Twenty years ago.'

'I see. I'm sorry. If I can help in any way,' and in her notebook he wrote his name and a phone number. Just that, no Father or Monsignor or whatever it was. 'A lot of people seem to be trying to reconnect at the moment. Perhaps in the end we'll be grateful for all this in some way.'

Her way out took her to where the front quad backed onto the playing field. Here was the pine, now casting a massive afternoon shadow across a cricket pitch. By moving around Annie found more or less the spot where the panoramic camera had been placed every year and from there she estimated where her father would have stood on a chair in his final year photograph and she stood there herself and tried to imagine and failed.

* * *

The central city was cordoned off. The cordon almost every feature that people associated with the name Christchurch – the Victorian Gothic of the cathedral, the provincial chambers, the Arts Centre, Christ's College, the various squares, the brutalist sixties town hall, the multiply-bridged, grass-banked, winding tameness of the Avon, all of it masked from view behind barricades and soldiers, accessible only to the privileged or the powerful. Through the temporary fencing Annie had caught remote views of tower blocks with shattered windows, a hotel on a lean, fallen facades. Already there were mutterings of discontent from those whose livelihoods remained within the cordon. The authorities, it was said, were becoming arrogant, high-handed. The state of emergency, the media attention, the hard hats and hi-vis vests had made them feel like men and women of action, the inner coterie, the makers of the big decisions, and they handed down those decisions to the mob with the disdain of royal decrees.

The north of the city around the school seemed little damaged, but the bus that took Annie east went from there into a different world, a world she'd seen on television but not grasped the scale of. Roads buckled. Houses broken. And limitless liquefaction, a heavy grey silt that had been squeezed from the land by the shaking. It dried on the edges to a gritty talcum powder that flew with slightest breeze and lodged in nose hairs and eyes and throat and in the whorls of the ear. But mostly it stayed wet and heavy, turning suburbs that had always struggled into sodden moonscapes. From the bus window Annie saw householders shovelling the stuff listlessly into barrows. She could sense the water-laden weight of every shovelful. They emptied the barrows onto heaps that had grown into ramparts, lining the road like snow drifts that wouldn't melt.

Eventually the bus turned back towards the centre of town. How its suspension coped with Pages Road Annie wasn't sure. She got off on Stanmore and went north on foot towards the Avon. It was clear that weatherboard buildings had fared better than those built of block or brick. Brick, in particular, was hopeless, undone by its own rigidity. The mortar cracked, the bond was lost and down came whole murderous frontages. On the corner of Worcester Street a flat above a shop lay open to the world, pictures on the walls and a pair of green armchairs still aligned to a fat, old-fashioned television. Two rooms along stood a single bed, its brightly patterned duvet ruched and crumpled from the last careless waking now more than a week ago. It and other ruins were all fenced in by yet more free-standing fencing. How much of this had she already seen? Where had it been beforehand? Did every city have miles of it in store awaiting disasters? And a vast cache of traffic cones? There had to be thousands of cones on the streets of the city, a forest of witches' hats that had erupted almost overnight like some sudden orange fungus. Who organised all this? Who planned it? Or had the authorities merely reacted as everyone else had reacted to this sudden surprise? Because people did react. Immediately and instinctively they had dealt first with what was around them, then the circle had widened to family and basic needs, and then they had started to look wider still, at their streets and their suburbs, and they had begun the business of cleaning up. And some had acted with enormous kindness. University students, most of whom lived in the relatively unscathed north and west, had formed a volunteer army of young strong limbs, touring the south and east with shovels and wheelbarrows in search of liquefaction to be shifted, drains to be cleared, gardens to be disinterred, any jobs that needed strength and youth and hope to put things right.

For a moment Annie didn't recognise the aftershock for what it was. Then she half heard, half felt the rumble underfoot. With no walls to magnify the sound and movement, and nothing overhead to fall or break, it did not feel threatening. There was give and bend in the natural world. But a woman on the other side of Stanmore stopped and pulled her little daughter to her and looked around like a deer on the plain that has sensed a predator. The woman's eyes met Annie's across the road and she smiled but the smile was stretched like wire.

The bridge over the Avon, and Annie leant against the iron parapet. Before her lay the view she'd seen on television in Turnpike Lane, the hundred or so yards of the world where much of her childhood had happened. There was nowhere she would ever know more intimately. River Road.

The river seemed wider and shallower, though she doubted that could be so. Ducks and Canada geese floated on the rippled surface. The big willows still stood, trailing twigs in the water like finger bones, but the grass bank had slumped in places and in others it had simply split, like torn skin. The road was humped and twisted, the footpath too, which now supported a cluster of three portable toilets in orange and white. There was old Bateman's place, a stucco villa on a raised concrete pad that had all but split in two. Just beyond it, the house she'd grown up in. There was no one about. As she stepped down off the bridge ducks grumbled and slid into the water, and the Canada geese glided pointedly to the other bank.

She stood across the road from her childhood home. The two storeys of weatherboard had been recently painted but in roughly the same shade of cream. There was the bedroom window from which she'd looked down on the ducks one winter morning twenty-something years ago. The front garden was neater than it used to be, the front door now blue. She couldn't remember what colour it had been. She was surprised by how little emotion the place aroused. She would have liked to see the back garden, long and narrow, with a wall of espaliered fruit trees, but the only way in was down the side of the house and she didn't like to unhitch the fencing.

Annie sensed movement in a kitchen window of the neighbouring house. An old woman was filling a kettle at the sink. Annie thought, yes, she was sure, and she shouted and waved but the woman's stooped back had turned away to plug in the kettle. Across the road and through the little iron gate – still the same one with the latch she remembered, though much rusted now. Then she tapped on the kitchen window. The woman turned, her eyes widened by alarm.

'Mrs Yeats, it's me, Annie, from next door. Remember me, Annie?'

The old woman was staring.

'Annie,' mouthed Annie again, exaggerating the syllables, 'next door. Can I come in?'

The alarm in the old woman's face subsided a little. A few moments later the door opened on a security chain.

'Yes,' she said through the gap, 'what is it? What do you want?'

'Mrs Yeats, it's me, Annie, from next door, Raewyn's daughter, you remember, all those years ago.'

The old face looked worn with time and care, but the fear had waned.

'Annie, you say,' and she fumbled with the chain. 'Come in, Annie,' and the door opened. How tiny she had become, tiny and bent and frail.

There was a putrid smell in the hall and the living room was a wreck. Ornaments, books, pictures lay scattered. The television had fallen on its face. By the main window the floor sloped where the concrete beneath had split and subsided. Between floor and skirting board lawn was visible.

Only one chair looked to have been used. Surely there had been a Mr Yeats, a quietly cheerful man forever in the garden. Annie swept ceiling plaster from the sofa.

'Can I get you a cup of tea, dear?' said Mrs Yeats. Her hair was pitifully thin, the scalp shining through. 'What did you say your name was again?'

'Let me make it, Mrs Yeats,' and Annie and she was on her feet before the old woman could protest. 'And I'm Annie. We lived next door, years ago.'

'Yes, dear,' said Mrs Yeats.

On the kitchen bench stood a box of Bell's tea bags, a sliced loaf and a butter dish. In the fridge a litre of milk, still within its use-by date, and half an onion that looked to have been peeled and saved before the quake. The pantry shelves had leapt on their brackets and the meagre provisions been thrown to the floor. It seemed from the smell that a bottle of vinegar had broken and a split bag of flour had caked everything in a ghostly volcanic ash.

'So how are you coping?' said Annie as she poured the tea.

'Oh, all right, dear. We've got the water and power back on now so everything's fine. No need to worry about me. There's others worse off.'

'Has anyone been to see you?'

'Like who, dear?'

Had there been children, grandchildren? Annie couldn't remember and didn't like to ask. Mrs Yeats seemed to divine her thoughts. 'But don't you worry about me. I don't need much at my age. I'll get along just fine.'

It took Annie an hour or so to bring some order to the kitchen, despite Mrs Yeats' protestations. She shifted the pantry heap with brush and cloth, straightened the shelves on their brackets and placed on them the few cans and packets she managed to save. She cleaned the floor of the pantry and then of the kitchen as a whole with a mop and Handy Andy. How we all cling, thought Annie, to the brands we're brought up with, the familiar furniture of our lives.

The source of the foul smell proved to be the toilet off the hall. Annie gagged as she opened the door, took one glance and closed it again. Promising that she would get someone to see to it, she took Mrs Yeats out to the Portaloos on the street and showed her how to use them.

'I wondered whose they were,' said Mrs Yeats. 'I didn't like to, you know.'

How many more Mrs Yeats were there in the city, Annie wondered, as the bus to Hornby battled the broken roads, old people who had been discarded? Only in the wealthy Western world could such a thing happen. For the first time in the history of the species the old had become encumbrances. We neglected them, segregated them even in walled villages of their own kind with minders to look after them, benign concentration camps, leaving to the young the actual world beyond the walls.

* * *

'Is the sewer working?'

'No,' said Annie.

'Then if you tell me the address we can see about getting a Portaloo delivered.'

Annie explained that Portaloos had already been delivered. Rather she was concerned for Mrs Yeats' general wellbeing, living on her own at that age in a damaged house and in an almost deserted street.

In which case, the woman replied sympathetically but firmly, it was not the council's business. Perhaps Annie could try the local medical centre.

Annie did. But because she was not a relative they would not tell her whether Mrs Yeats was on their books and nor did they make house calls for the purpose of assessment. Had Annie tried the Red Cross?

Annie hadn't and for the moment she didn't. But within a few calls she found a commercial cleaner, a Mr Butts, who was willing to accompany Annie to River Road to address the fouled toilet and generally render the place more habitable.

Chapter 8

'Mr Mahoney?'

'Vince,' he said, smiling and holding out his hand. Despite herself Annie had been half expecting a seventeen-year-old, a youth with an explosion of snowy hair. The man in front of her was sixty years old. He had the scrawniness of one who has kept himself fit but whom the years have still bitten. He was as bald as a cue ball.

She'd first rung a retired teacher who hadn't remembered her father and had seemed to resent the intrusion. In the background she'd heard the sound of a television quiz show. Then she got a wrong number brought about by a coincidence of names and initials. But her third call had found a former pupil who unhesitatingly recalled her father. 'Rich,' he said, 'we knew him as Rich.'

Rich had been good at art and running, but he and Rich had never been close. 'His great mate,' said the man, 'was a boy with blond hair – Mahoney, that was it, Vince Mahoney.'

And Annie could hear the smile in the man's voice, more than a smile, an ache at the memory of boyhood and energy and hope. 'Yep, Vince is the boy you want to talk to. He and Rich were pretty well inseparable.' Annie had loved that use of boy. Vince, like all of them, would be sixty-ish.

And when she'd rung him he too had sounded delighted to have been blown out of the flatness of late middle age and into the gold-bathed memories of youth. 'Rich's daughter, eh?' he'd exclaimed. 'Well I never.' The note of surprise was unmistakable.

Vince Mahoney had proved eager to meet, indeed had invited her to his home on Hackthorne Road. 'Just watch out for the road cones,' he'd said.

He'd not been wrong. The cones along Cashmere Road around Princess Margaret Hospital were a forest of dwarf orange, reducing early-evening traffic to little more than walking pace. Liquefaction had spurted from the Heathcote's banks but Annie saw none of the wholesale inundation there'd been in the east.

On Hackthorne Road the damage to buildings seemed arbitrary. One stone-built 1920s house, which any real estate agent would have dubbed a residence, was an obvious write-off, its front porch sagging down the hill, its walls rent and ruined, its roof line skewed. But two doors up stood Vince's weatherboard villa, trim, recently painted and apparently undamaged.

'I know, I know,' he said when Annie commented. 'I've been embarrassingly lucky. I lost a bit of crockery and the books fell off the shelves and that was about it. I've made a donation to the mayoral fund as a sort of half thank you, half apology and half guilt offering. If you can have three halves, that is,' and he grinned and looked straight at her. 'I'm so pleased to meet you, Annie.'

The books were back on the shelves now and everything was impeccably in order, with a sense that that was how it always had been.

'It'll be nice to talk of something other than the quake,' he said. 'Here's something for you to look at while I fetch the drinks.' And he handed her a picture frame with what looked like a scrap of golden paper pinned behind the glass, and a cellophane booklet of perhaps a dozen photographs. Most were black and white, the rest in colour that had faded to tints. All were of her father. Had Vince put it together that day specially for her?

Here he was by a stream in flared jeans, on the apex of a tin roof, sitting back against the brick chimney and clutching a beer, pillion on a motor scooter, smiling with that inner radiance, his arm draped over the shoulders of Vince on what looked to be South Brighton beach, both of them wearing old-fashioned swimming togs, like cut-off shorts. And Annie felt an ache in her chest that wasn't far from pain.

She had no photos of her father. Not one. Mum had got rid of them, burned them, down the end of the garden at River Road. She'd hauled out everything associated with her father and flung it on the fire, smoke and little smuts of ash rising over the fruit trees and Annie had just stood and watched from her bedroom window, holding the curtain to the side of her face. The curtain was pink with a paisley pattern.

'I can get copies made, if you like.' Vince was standing before her holding out a glass of wine.

'Oh, would you? Oh, yes, please.'

'What do you make of the thumbnail sketch?'

'The what?'

Vince gestured at the picture frame. Behind the glass was what turned out to be, on closer inspection, the front of a Benson & Hedges cigarette packet, and in the space below the brand insignia Annie could make out a few lines or indentations in the gold surface.

She shrugged.

'It's a cat. We were in the pub, the Zetland, because they didn't ask too many questions, and someone wondered why a thumbnail sketch was called a thumbnail sketch so Rich drew that with his thumbnail. I kept it in my wallet for years.'

Annie looked at him.

'They were the best days of my life, Annie. Everything since has been dull in comparison.'

All Annie knew was what Vince had told her on the phone. How they'd been friends at school but then Vince had gone south to varsity while her father had gone up to Auckland and that had been that, all over.

'Believe me, Annie, you don't want to know what a blameless career in stainless steel looks like. I had a marriage of sorts, two nice kids, one boy, one girl, of course, brought up in Sydney and Singapore and anywhere else that stainless steel took me, before going back to Auckland and an amicable divorce that neither of us regrets.'

'And the kids?'

Vince shrugged. 'I wasn't much of a dad, Annie. I tried, and I'd have died for either of them, and I was a good provider, but it was their mother that raised them really. One's in Auckland, the other Brisbane. They've both got kids. I visit. But I'm not much of a granddad either, as it happens. No one minds when I leave. No, really, I'm not kidding.'

'And your ex?'

'Remarried. Happily. Fifteen years we did together and apart from the kids it's left nothing with me. Not as much as one night in the Zetland in, what, 1968, or thereabouts. But hey, no complaints.'

Vince had taken early retirement. He did 'a bit of consulting', sat on a couple of boards, but didn't really need to work. 'I'm sixty, Annie. When I was a kid, sixty was the end. You put your slippers on as soon as you could after that and became an officially old person and waited to die. But I feel fine. I've kept myself fit, I go running, I even play squash. I just don't know why. What's the point? I mean there's a good chance I've got thirty years in front of me and at the moment I don't want them. I've led my life, for better or worse, had my kids, made my money and now there's nothing for me to do. I'll level with you, Annie. I welcomed the quake. It was something happening. And I'm only sorry in a way that it didn't do more damage to my life, didn't force me out of the path of least resistance. But at least it put me in touch with you.' And he smiled, rather boyishly.

'Do you want to help me find my dad?' said Annie.

'Try and stop me,' he said.

* * *

The known facts were listed down the left-hand side of the sheet of A3. They weren't many. Year of birth, mother's Christian name (Meg) but not father's, name and dates of secondary schooling (but not primary). The rest was all speculation or a possible plan of campaign, apart from an oil smear from a piece of battered cod and a sickle-shaped stain from the foot of a wine glass.

'Do you think we'll find him?' asked Annie. 'We know so little.'

'I don't know.'

'That wasn't what I asked,' said Annie. They had drunk a bottle and a half of Rook's Lane shiraz. 'Do you think we'll find him?'

'Yes,' said Vince. 'I do. It's hard to hide these days. And besides, in business I've always found that if you believe you're going to succeed, you tend to succeed. If you don't believe, you won't. And more to the point, thank you, Annie.'

'For what?'

'I'm looking forward to tomorrow.' And he opened his arms to offer her a hug. He smelt of fish and chips and eau de Cologne and shiraz.

'I slept with your dad once,' he said.

68

Chapter 9

'Chernobyl,' says Richard, laying the crumb trail on the window sill. 'I saw it on the telly. It's the new Eden. Bears and birds and flowers and everything flourishing but no people. The cleansed earth. What do you think, Friday? The city heals itself. You'll have to fight for your living. No more sponging off the master species. No more sucking up to *Homo sapiens*. You'll have to go out and be a dog again. Join a pack, maybe. Hunt. How does that sound?'

And it clearly sounds good to the dog because his tail sweeps the floor, and Richard tosses him a chunk of mini-bar biscuit, which he leaps and captures in midair.

'Now, you know the drill, Friday.' Richard gestures downwards with his palm and the dog lies slowly, folding itself to the floor, then lowering its head onto its paws but not quite relaxing, retaining a little of the weight of the head with the muscles of the neck, ready to stand, ready to respond.

'Stay.'

Windows on this side of the building have popped in the aftershocks, burst from their frames by the twisting and the strain, going off like gunshots, followed some seconds later by a distant tinkle of shards reaching the street, shards to slice open a skull. Richard settles himself at an empty window frame, his backside propped on an easy chair, his left hand laid upwards on the sill like a crab's claw, reddish-blue and hardened, a little mound of crumbs in the palm. The right hand waits, charged with more crumbs to toss and tempt with.

It is early days in Eden. The air is sweet and warm and the world is quiet but the only birds to come are the urban invaders, the birds that came with the people who built the city. The starlings are gangsters in flashy suits, strutting like hit men on the far edge of the sill, their sword-beaks jabbing at each other in perpetual squabble. But they are cowards, greater cowards than the house sparrows, who for all their being just dowdy balls of fluff and feather, hop past the gangster brutes and are rewarded for their courage with fat-laden crumbs, crumbs to fire a sparrow's tiny high-revving heart. But they remain shy of the claw. They hop to within inches of it, then pause, and Richard holds his breath and wills himself not to cough, but they sense somehow that the hand is animate, that it constitutes a threat. None has yet pecked from it.

In twenty minutes the starlings have cleaned up the more distant scatter, the sparrows the near stuff. Twice Richard has tossed out replenishments with his good hand and the birds have withdrawn, hopped back with instantaneous, precisely synchronised alarm. Richard becomes immersed in the birds, the chance-driven miracles, miniature feathered dinosaurs with hollowed bones, Darwin's brilliant, pointless children.

A city pigeon lands heavily on the sill, disturbing the warring starlings. Greyish brown, it has one good pink foot and one that's clenched to a sort of upturned fist, so the bird lurches as it crosses the sill towards the crumbs. It pauses only once to cock its head and eye Richard's hand as if for final confirmation, then unhesitatingly it takes the last two drunken steps and stoops to peck. And through the hard, scarred and puckered skin Richard feels the insistent little hammer of the beak, and the muscles of his face turn up the corners of his lips and lift his grey and whiskered cheeks and crease the flesh around his eyes and the dog who you'd have said was sleeping senses something changing and flicks up its eyes to see the man is smiling and it thumps its tail and the birds take off. As one.

Richard sighs as the tension of concentration slides from him and throws the last of his crumbs through the window frame. 'Good boy, come here,' though the dog has anticipated the call and has his head already against Richard's thigh and is being patted in the luxuriant fur of its neck.

'A cigarette, Friday, a glass of wine, and then tea time, I think.' He jams a Rothmans into the V of his claw, lights it and draws on it cautiously, wary of the paroxysms of coughing that twice have left him curled on the floor too weak to move for minutes. Once Friday pawed at his shoulder as he lay weak and incapable, pawed with such vigour that he tore a hole in the shiny parchment of Richard's skin and drew blood that soaked into the thick pile of his dressing gown.

The wine seeps goodness into him. He can feel easing of something in tissues far down in his body and his mind. It is not the first drink of the day but it is the first to tip him over the base level of need into the zone of pleasure. The knack is to stay there as long as possible, for the dog as much as for himself.

'Fetch the lead,' says Richard and the dog lollops across the room and drags the dressing gown belt from the handle of the door. 'Good boy.' Richard stubs out the cigarette on the window sill, takes the belt from the dog and with a little gasp heaves himself onto his feet. And down the corridor they go, man and dog.

Crossing the foyer troubles Richard. The plate-glass frontage gives onto the street. He is sure that a cordon has been set around the inner city, but he has seen police and soldiers patrolling within it and men and women in hard hats and bright vests. There would need to be only one of these on Cashel as he and Friday crossed the foyer and that would be that. They'd be found. They'd be chivvied from the place like vermin. So he keeps the dog on the lead and to the extent that he is capable of scuttling he scuttles across the foyer, and through the bistro restaurant and into the dark kitchen beyond. Where, for the first time, Richard is aware of a background hint of a smell, a suspicion of sweet rot.

Unleashed, the dog goes straight to the stainless steel double doors of the wardrobe-like fridge. Richard opens them, inhales and closes them immediately. 'Shit.'

The dog sits. Richard notices and three seconds later he laughs, laughs loud and the dog's tail wags and, still laughing, Richard pats the dog's head but his laugh becomes a cough and he bends, still coughing, and lays his head against the cool of the stainless steel workbench. 'Jesus,' he mutters as the cough finally subsides and a wave of weakness runs through his arms and back and legs, so strong a wave that he almost falls to the ground. 'Jesus.'

He stays there until the dog's head pushes against his thigh and he reaches down to stroke it.

'Oh Friday,' he says, 'you'll be the death of me,' and he smiles to himself, but is careful not to succumb again to laughter. While he waits for a little strength to return, he runs the dog's ear between finger and thumb as if assessing its silkiness.

He scours through drawers till he finds a long carving fork and he clamps a tea towel over his mouth and nose and opens the fridge and with the fork he flicks out one, two, three, four steaks. Even as he prongs them he can sense that they have become slimy and the sound of them slapping onto the floor makes his gorge rise. But the dog is undismayed, ingesting them with greedy gulps, its back arched with the urgency of the effort.

Richard goes to the back door with a cigarette, sucking at the cauterising, throat-catching, smell-masking bitterness of smoke. Late afternoon and beneath a scatter of birdsong he can hear, he thinks, the distant sound of traffic. The dog licks the last traces of flesh from the floor, then looks up at Richard, searching for a hint of further food or play, gathers nothing, is unconcerned and goes rootling around the yard in search of smells of interloper dogs or cats or anything that breathes. The evening is thick with summer insects. Swallows dance and weave between and around and over the deserted buildings, silhouetted like distant fighter planes, carving the air to commit a thousand insect murders.

Dust and soil and crud have collected in a corner of the yard to one side of the door. And already it is tinged with green, with the all but unstoppable will to life. Richard props the door open with a stool and searches for dinner. There's the cupboard of eggs, and the bags of onions. The spuds have begun to sprout. The pans and plates he's used for previous meals still lie on the benches. Such mess he's made in so few days.

He pulls a fresh frying pan from the wall hook and fills it with an inch of olive oil and sets it on the gas. He snaps the fleshy sproutings off two potatoes and cuts them into chip-sized pieces. As he works he becomes aware of the smell of rotting meat and he ties a tea towel round his mouth and nose like an old-style bank robber, but he soon finds himself defying the cloth, breathing in as deep as he can in a bid still to detect the putrefaction, as if the senses resist deception, are aware that their job is to read the world for him. He dumps the tea towel and lights another cigarette.

From the lobby bar he fetches a bottle of Johnnie Walker, pours a slug, takes a swig and feels the earthy burn of it, the old fake fire. The oil is close to boiling. He drops the chipped potatoes in. The oil soars and bubbles, threatening to overflow the rim. Richard goes outside and smokes until the chips are done, then drains the pan over a vast commercial sieve and showers the chips with salt, and drenches them with white wine vinegar because he can't find malt and tips them onto a platter and goes back outside. Dusk is coming. A few late swallows still wheel in silhouette against a pink and orange sky. He blows on a chip and bites cautiously into it. And he's a boy on Brighton beach.

Chapter 10

'A more distinctive surname would have helped,' said Jess. 'Do you know how many Joneses there are in the South Island?'

'Sorry,' said Annie, though she'd always rather liked the ordinariness of it. She'd been surprised to find Jess still up, sitting at the kitchen table, a cat splayed on her lap.

'Was his middle name Hugh?'

Annie shrugged.

'Born 1952, which would make him fifty-nine or sixty. Would that be about right?'

Annie nodded.

'No GP record but a hospital admission, June 1992, after what seems to have been a traffic accident. He was a bit of a mess. Here, see for yourself.'

Annie scanned the notes made in Jess's expansive handwriting, the dots over the i's appearing as circles.

Suspected kidney damage, a broken rib, heavy bruising in the groin area and emergency surgery had been needed to save his left hand. Annie felt weak with sympathy, even at this distance.

'Your dad, if it is your dad, discharged himself after one week against medical advice,' said Jess. 'Does that sound like him?'

Annie wondered a moment. Had that been how he was? 'I don't know,' she said. 'I was a kid. He was my dad. I mean dads are different when you're a kid, aren't they?'

And hers had been the dependable presence of loving kindness. But scarcely human. As a girl she couldn't have imagined him being afraid, or unwise or hesitant or doubtful or worried or any of the things most people are most of the time. Or injured in any way. Did all kids see their dads like that? Even the weak ones, the distant ones, the cruel ones? She didn't know.

'Was there anything else on file?'

'Just an address, and you didn't get it from me,' said Jess, handing over another scrap of paper. 'You didn't get anything from me. How did you go with your sleuthing?'

'I found his best mate from school, who hasn't seen him since they left. He claims to have slept with my dad.'

'I wouldn't worry too much about that,' said Jess. 'Young guys do it all the time. Hormones.'

'But he really loved my dad, I think. And he's nostalgic for when he was young, free, happy or whatever. He's made his pile, had his divorce and is wondering what the point of it all was. So he's delighted I've brought him something to do. Nice guy.'

'Sounds like he's got you halfway into bed already. Talking of which, I've got an early start in the morning.' Jess lifted the cat off her lap, kissed it and placed it in a padded wicker basket by the log-burner. 'Night night, Sherlock,' she said to Annie. 'I won't wake you in the morning. Finish the bottle.' Annie listened to Jess's slippered feet trudge heavily down the floorboards of the hall. The toilet flushed. A tap ran. Then silence.

It was midday in London and her body clock was still as much there as in Christchurch. She turned again to the sparse file of notes. The address Jess had given her was central, on Park Terrace. A flat by the look of it. She'd go there tomorrow.

Nineteen ninety-two. She'd have been in her last year at intermediate. They'd often played netball at Hagley Park. From the courts you could see the hospital. Could it have been that one Saturday morning while she and her friends squealed with excitement under the empty winter trees, and their breath misted their air and they pulled on those stiff cotton bibs and their thighs below their skirts were pink with the cold, her father had been lying in a hospital bed almost within earshot?

She pictured him sitting up in bed, drawing a picture perhaps for a nurse. But the face she'd given him, she knew, was not the face of the forty-year-old he would have been, nor even the face she'd known him by, the details of which had become vague. It was the face of the boy in the school photo. Though she did remember precisely the way he held a pencil, the deft economy with which he drew, the picture taking shape in just a few lines. He held the pencil in his left hand.

At the kitchen table Annie opened Jess's laptop. The Hugh might make a difference. 'Richard Hugh Jones, Christchurch' she typed and in less than a second the hundred thousand-strong list of hits had taken shape on her screen, already ranked in decreasing order of accuracy. To Annie it was still a form of magic, impossibly brilliant and yet also sinister, threatening. How was it possible to escape it?

But her father seemed to have done so. She found nothing new, nothing she hadn't seen and dismissed before. Where was he? For some reason she felt more strongly now that he was out there. But if Google couldn't find him, what chance did she have?

The cat erupted from the basket and was out through its door before Annie felt the shake. Then it was as if the house had been gripped from below by some impossible force. It threatened everything. Annie knew she should go to a doorway at least but she found herself pinned, gripping the table edge, wide eyed, paralysed by forces that dwarfed her and the house and the city. The fear was existential. The quake lasted perhaps a dozen seconds, a rolling subterranean thunder, a growl of the gods. Annie wasn't sure that she breathed during it.

'Welcome to Christchurch,' Jess shouted down the hall. 'You all right, sweet pea?'

'Shit,' said Annie. 'Was that pretty big?'

'Four point five or so. We're all seismometers now. Night night.'

Chapter 11

The pigeon is on the sill already, waiting. As Richard and the dog approach it edges back towards the open air, lurching on its club foot. But it does not take off. From a yard away Richard tosses crumbs. The bird goes straight to them, pecking without concern. Richard can hear the noise of its beak tap-tapping on whatever shiny synthetic stuff the sill is made of. Boffins somewhere trained a pigeon to sit inside a missile and steer it by pecking on a video screen. If the missile was ever fired, the pigeon died.

At a word from Richard, the dog settles on the floor. Moving slowly, Richard seats himself at the window and slides his claw towards the bird. Its head cocks to eye the crumbs in the palm and it lurches forward and pecks and Richard feels the blunt stab of the beak against his damaged flesh. Slowly he raises the right hand and the bird looks up but does not withdraw. Richard lays a trail of crumbs up the inside of his left forearm, like a powder fuse. The pigeon doesn't hesitate, stepping onto the palm so that Richard feels its weight for the first time. That weight is less than the bird's apparent plumpness would suggest. A million feathers clothe the pigeon's neck, overlapping with impossible precision, adjusting without effort to every movement, insulating, independently intricate, collectively astonishing, much more than a miracle, on the neck of a dowdy, crippled, urban pigeon.

As the pigeon pecks its way up his forearm, rocking and balancing on the pallid skin, Richard slowly lifts the hand from the sill. The pigeon shifts for balance but is not alarmed.

Starlings and sparrows have come to the sill. With his right hand Richard scatters more crumbs close to the claw, too close for the starlings to dare. The pigeon leaves his arm and pecks at the crumbs, two sparrows hopping about it, just beyond range of its beak. Together they clean the sill in a minute. When Richard makes to stand, the sparrows and starlings erupt into the air at the first hint of movement. The pigeon, more cumbersome, but also more at ease, limps to the edge of the sill before dropping onto the air and a long swoop that Richard follows with his eyes before, with a few strong beats, it rows to the broken parapet of the Edwardian building across the road.

'Good boy,' says Richard to the dog, to the world and tosses a piece of biscuit down the corridor for the dog to chase.

The smell in the kitchen has worsened. Richard wants to gag, but he defies his nausea to feed the dog. Holding his breath, he opens the fridge and there's a sudden scampering and a blur of furry bodies, slithering over the door sill, dropping to the floor and diving under tables, ovens, anywhere. The dog pounces and a rat screams momentarily as the dog throws it into the air and pounces again as it lands and shakes it once, twice, snapping its back and letting it fall. The rat wheezes and briefly scrapes at the air with its paws and then is still and silent.

The dog is already looking around for more, standing taller, head held alert and alive, fired by instinct, pure ancestral dog, happy in killing and keen to kill again. The rats have fled, but the smell of them lingers, melding with the smell of putrefaction. Richard feels a surge of dread, of Eden sullied, and he takes the Johnnie Walker outside.

He sits on a bar stool no doubt put there by kitchen hands who smoked, as the dog continues scouring the kitchen for rats. Will the rats rise through the building? How will he feed the dog? How long can a dog cope on a mini-bar diet, on Pringles, peanuts and Cookie Time biscuits? And what about himself? He pulls at the Scotch, and watches from the door as the dog, brimming with hope, sniffs at the skirtings, at the cracks and crannies down which the rats slithered. It is preoccupied, engrossed, oblivious.

* * *

Mr Butts the cleaner was waiting in a van. And taggers had visited. Across the pastel weatherboards of Mrs Yeats' house was a screaming signature in purple, black and fluorescent orange. 'Rodik94' it said, in violent swastika-like lettering as jagged as the rents in the riverbank. Annie felt a surge of resentment, of anger. And a tinge of fear.

'I'd string them up, I would,' said Mr Butts getting out of his van and indicating the tagging. He was a strongly built man in white overalls, with the sort of buck teeth that orthodontics no longer allowed to flourish. 'The little bastards,' he said. His forthright indignation was a tonic.

They knocked on the front door but got no response. Annie peered in through the kitchen window. The bench looked as clean as when she'd finished with it the other day, but there was no sign of Mrs Yeats.

They unlatched the gate just as Rodik94 must have done to get at the side wall. The nerve, the intrusiveness of it.

The back garden would have upset Mr Yeats. The lawn stood tall and brown and had gone to seed, the little orchard a couple of seasons unpruned, littered with the remains of rotting fruit. Had there really been no children? Annie thought she remembered talk of a son, gone overseas – to Canada, was it? Did he not keep an eye out for his widowed and feeble mother? It wasn't hard, surely, even from that distance.

Weeds had pushed up through the cracks in the patio. Two standard roses in tubs were in need of deadheading. Had Annie ever known Mrs Yeats' Christian name? She thought not. She'd been Mrs Yeats, no, 'Nice Mrs Yeats', throughout Annie's childhood.

Annie tapped on the glass of the French doors with a single knuckle and kept tapping even as she was taking in the sight of

Mrs Yeats' thin old legs lying inert on the floor with one knee drawn up as if frozen in the act of running on her side. Her torso was hidden by the sofa. Annie knocked harder, tried the handles.

'Bloody hell,' said Mr Butts, who also tried the handles and shook the windows, then turned his back to the doors and shoved his elbow through a pane, reached through the shards, turned a key and they were in.

Mr Butts knelt beside Mrs Yeats and leant in over her and for one absurd moment Annie thought he was about to deliver the kiss of life with those extraordinary teeth of his, but Mrs Yeats was breathing, and had suffered no obvious injury. By the time the ambulance arrived, they had her sitting against the side of the sofa, propped up with cushions.

She looked dazedly around at Annie, at Mr Butts, at the paramedic.

'Where's Sid?' she said.

'Mrs Yeats, it's me, Annie. You've had a little fall, but you're going to be fine.'

Mrs Yeats looked at Annie in bewilderment. 'Where's Sid?' she said. 'He'll be wanting his tea.'

'Sid's in the garden,' said Annie. 'He'll be along shortly.'

When the ambulance had gone with Mrs Yeats on board Annie didn't know what to do about the house. Mr Butts did. He cleaned up the glass, tacked a square of hardboard over the broken pane, donned mask and paper suit and cleaned out the downstairs toilet with remarkable speed and thoroughness, locked the place from the inside and emerged from the front door with a key that Annie promised to deliver to Mrs Yeats in hospital.

And when Annie tried to pay him for his time he wouldn't hear of it, backing away with his hands raised as she tried to put the notes in his pocket.

'Poor old dear,' he said. 'I've got half a mind to come back with a blaster and get rid of that for her,' and he cast a look of contempt at the 'Rodik94' and shook his head.

'Bless you,' said Annie, and she kissed him on the cheek and his round face broke into a snaggle-tooth smile. Then he got into his van and drove away. Diagonally across the van's back doors were the words 'Cleaner Butts!'

The sun glittered bright on the river. Canada geese had gathered on the bank near the huge old willow with the split trunk. Their crap littered the grass. She did not remember the geese from her childhood. Perhaps they had arrived only in the recent weeks, the pioneers of a reversion to nature. If left alone, the geese and ducks and weeds and grass would see off even the taggers, would reclaim the place for their own form of warfare.

More accustomed now to the broken city, and somehow emboldened by the drama with Mrs Yeats, Annie lifted apart two sections of the fencing around her childhood home.

The shaded path down the side of the house was the same mossed concrete she remembered, ending in a gate whose catch she could have operated blindfold. Less had happened to the back garden. Lawn, fruit trees on the long brick wall, and at the bottom end where the bonfire had burned stood vegetable patch, tomatoes and sweet corn fat and ready to harvest amid yellowing leaves.

An ugly conservatory had been pinned onto the back of the house. Annie tried the doors. Locked. She didn't much mind. She made a shading tube of her hand and peered through the glass. There was nothing to see. What had been her childhood home was someone else's now. There were no such things as ghosts.

* * *

Richard wedges the door open with the bar stool, and heads for Manchester Street. He is wearing fluffy slippers, a pair of trackpants that say 'BARKERS' down one leg in large letters, and a hotel dressing gown, tied with a sash. The lane is perhaps thirty yards long, flanked on one side by some windowless commercial building and on the other by a fence of corrugated iron painted off-white. At the end of the lane Richard peers tentatively around the corner.

To the south he can see almost to Moorhouse Avenue. Cars line the road, left since the quake, now grey with rubble dust. In places the facades of buildings have shot tongues of brick or masonry halfway across the road. Red traffic cones denote a way for vehicles to negotiate the chaos, but no vehicles are moving. Nothing is moving.

Across the road the small convenience store looks not too badly damaged, though plaster and masonry have fallen from the second floor. A Chinese guy ran it, Richard remembers. Bald as a vulture, his cheeks dotted with skin cancers, he was forever sweeping the floor and the pavement with his plastic broom. That broom was his trademark, his stage prop, his identity. He would sometimes level it at Richard like a gun, and sight down the handle and pretend to pull the trigger. 'Lazy man, drink man,' he'd say to Richard, 'lazy man, drink man,' but he would be smiling and if Richard had money he would sell him tobacco readily enough. How would he be coping away from his empire?

Richard struggles through the chunks of plaster and rubble. His slipper soles are little more than sheets of fluffy cardboard, slowing his progress, and here in the street he is hopelessly exposed. He wishes he had brought the Johnnie Walker.

The shop's front door is locked, even though the window to its left is shattered, great chunks of it missing, and others hanging from the frame like the blades of guillotines. Richard smiles to think of the man locking it amid the chaos.

Richard steps through the broken window. Glass crunches underfoot. The floor is littered with cans and packets and bottles and there is the smell of rats or mice here too. Someone has been here before him. The doors that hide the temptation of tobacco from the underage and the recently quit hang open and the racks have been stripped.

'Dog food,' says Richard to himself, 'dog food.'

A noise behind him, a crunch of glass. Richard's heart leaps like a cat in a cage. And a gust of fear goes through him even as he turns and sees the dog.

He clutches at the shelving for support, his breath coming fast. 'Friday,' he gasps, 'for fuck's sake.' And the dog could not have been more pleased. It fusses around him, its bare paws seemingly untroubled by the broken glass. Richard reaches down with his good hand and mauls the dog's neck and back.

There's a small bag of Tux and a ten-kilo sack. He wants the sack but can barely lift it, let alone carry it all the way back. He calls the dog and makes it stand and with a grunt he heaves the sack up into his arms like some swaddled baby and lays it lengthwise along the dog's spine, keeping a grip on the plastic handle to share the load. The dog writhes in protest.

'No, Friday, no. Steady, boy, steady.'

With a hand on the sack to keep it stable, Richard urges the dog back out over the litter of broken glass, and onto the pavement and still there is no one there. As they cross the road the sack slips from the dog's back before Richard can stop it.

'Friday,' says Richard, 'come on, boy.' But though the dog stays near it will not let him replace the sack. They are exposed in mid-road.

Richard hooks his claw through the handle and hauls, dragging the sack over the tarmac, the noise upsetting, scary. Worn by the friction, the sack starts to fray at the base and biscuits spill onto the road. With an effort Richard flips the sack over, lifts it into his arms and carries it like a bride the last few yards to the safety of the alley, then leans panting against the fence of corrugated iron, too weak to go further. He fears a coughing fit.

The dog has already found the spilled biscuits.

'Here, Friday, here.' But the dog ignores him.

Richard drags the sack a few yards, stops to pant and lean, does another few yards. In time he reaches the kitchen door, lugs the sack over the threshold and sits a while to recover. Then he goes back down the alley for the dog.

'Oi.' The voice is loud and male. The dog looks up and stays looking up at a point further down Manchester Street.

Richard turns and heads for the hotel in a gasping, lurching trot.

'Oi,' calls the voice again. 'Here, boy.'

Just before the hotel the dog passes Richard and dives in through the kitchen door, a Tux in its mouth. Richard shoves aside the bar stool and closes the door as quietly as he can. Despite the scurry of rats' feet and the stench of putrefaction, Richard sags against the work surface, his breath coming fast and shallow, the blood pounding in his ears.

He thinks he hears boots outside in the alley but if he does they turn and go away again quite soon. And everything returns to quiet in the hotel. And he has most of a sack of dog biscuits.

Chapter 12

The old red brick building on the corner of Bealey Avenue and Park Terrace was cordoned off with more Fahey fencing. What had it been? Private hospital? Old folks' home? Annie somehow associated it with unwellness and money. But its flanks were ripped open with great sheer lines through the brickwork, running higgledy-piggledy down three or more storeys like black veins, so that you felt that you could push the whole thing over with a stick. The contrast with the other side of the road was stark, almost comic. There the huge willows still swept down to drag on the surface of the Avon as if nothing had happened. Ducks swam, and on the far side of the river, a pair of joggers trotted side by side through the stand of pines. 'Keep calm and carry on' had already become the half-ironic motto of the whole traumatic business, but jogging? Couldn't that energy be put to slightly better use? Annie had read in the paper that morning so many stories of suffering from the east of the city and a growing discontent with the authorities.

But then again, she wasn't exactly shovelling up liquefaction herself.

The apartment block stood. Glass shrouded, and expensively overlooking the park, it had an eighties feel to it. An orange sticker on the door announced that it had undergone an engineering check and was provisionally deemed safe to occupy. No names alongside the bell pushes, just apartment numbers. Annie pressed 4A.

'Yes?' Even in that single syllable Annie heard the unmistakable voice of Canterbury money, of high country stations and horses and moleskins and collars turned up on Aertex shirts.

Annie had given no thought to what she would say.

'I'm sorry to trouble you,' she began, discovering that her mission was hard to summarise plausibly. 'My name's Annie Jones. I'm looking for my father.'

'Your father?'

'Yes, you see...'

'I can assure you, Miss Jones, that your father is not here. There is no one here except me.'

'But he used to live here, I think, Flat 4A, twenty years ago. If I could just come up and ask you a few questions. I promise not to take up too much of your time. It's just that...'

To Annie's surprise the buzzer rang and she was able to push open the heavy door.

When Annie emerged from the lift an elderly man was waiting at the door of 4A. He was leaning on sticks. Despite the authoritative voice he was shrunken and bent almost at a right angle at the waist. 'I'm sorry,' were his first words. 'I fear I may have been rude to you. It was unchristian of me. But we are all a little stressed at the moment so I hope you will forgive me. My name is David. Won't you come in?'

And so saying he turned with some difficulty on his sticks and led Annie into the apartment. The pace they went at allowed Annie an abundance of time to take in the smell of furniture polish and the line of empty picture hooks and the rips in the wall linings in corners and above the door frames. She tried to imagine her father living here, walking this corridor. It did not somehow seem his sort of place.

'Were you here for the quake?' she asked as David sat at the table, grimacing a little as he did so. He wore a neatly tied tie, but there was half an inch of air between his collar and the folded leather of his neck. White hairs bristled from his nostrils.

'Yes,' he said, 'I was. It was a little dramatic. This place sways rather alarmingly. But the authorities in their wisdom assure us it is safe and it is quite amazing what one can get used to. And besides, people have been so kind. Even the young ones of whom it is easy to despair. You should have seen the mess in here, but now, look at it.' And he gestured to the kitchen, which was indeed clean and neat, though a partly opened cupboard revealed the shortage of crockery.

'Is there anything you need?' asked Annie but David insisted that he had plenty of people keeping an eye on him. 'My family, for better or for worse, is impossible to escape. It is sewn into the very fabric of this city. I can't walk down a street in Christchurch without meeting a relative. So no, thank you, you are kind, but I want for nothing. Now, what was all this about your father? He has gone missing in the quake? And why do you imagine he might be here?'

Annie told him. He listened intelligently.

'It's none of my business of course,' he said when she had done, 'but why are you looking for him now? Why not five years ago, ten? What's special about now? Was it the quake or...'

'I don't know. I've asked myself the same question. It may be because I'm thinking of getting engaged, but it feels more complicated than that.'

The old man looked at her thoughtfully.

'I hope you find your father, Miss Jones,' he said, 'but I fear that I can do little to help you. There has to be some error in the hospital records. This flat, you see, has been in our family since the day it was built and as far as I am aware it has been used exclusively by family members from the very first. Indeed, within the family it has become known jocularly as the Railway Station. In that everyone who uses it is on his or her way somewhere else. Sometimes it is the young about to board a train to God knows where, and sometimes it is the old such as myself on their last ride to the inevitable terminus. I can make enquiries for you, of course, but I very much doubt that your father ever set foot in it. And I for one have no memory of any family connection with a Richard Jones, though our family is extensive, to say the least, and as various as all families are.'

Annie conceded that it seemed unlikely that her father had ever lived here. How could he have afforded it, to start with?

'Perhaps,' said David, 'if you left me an email address I could let you know if I uncover anything.'

'You're on email?' said Annie. 'Oh, I am sorry. That was rude of me. I shouldn't have been surprised.'

'Now we have each been rude to the other,' said David, and Annie laughed.

* * *

Everyone in the ward at Princess Margaret Hospital was old. No one was talking. All those who were awake watched Annie as she made her way to the far end. Mrs Yeats was sitting upright in bed, and she too was watching Annie. She looked shrunken and fragile, an impression only emphasised by the bruise that had drained to cover a quarter of her face, presumably from when she fell.

'Hello, Mrs Yeats.'

Annie's words seemed only to alarm the old woman. And as Annie moved closer Mrs Yeats nervously clutched at the blanket edge, furled it up over her chest. She avoided looking Annie in the eye.

'It's me, Annie.' She spoke quietly, aware that hers was the only voice in the whole long ward. 'Annie. I came to see you, remember? We had tea.'

The wrinkled profile continued to stare across the ward, the fingers playing with the blanket's hem.

'Mrs Yeats? I've brought your house key.'

'Where's Sid?' And the old woman turned with awful, frightened eyes to look straight at Annie with a sort of desperation. 'Where's Sid?'

Annie tried to take Mrs Yeats' hand but it shrank back under the blanket. Annie, afraid that the old woman was going to cry or try to get up, got up herself. 'Don't worry, Mrs Yeats,' she said, 'everything's going to be fine.'

Half a dozen old women watched her walk back down the middle of the ward. The nurse took charge of the door key. 'Though I don't think she'll have much use for it,' she said. 'Do you know if there are any relatives?'

Annie mentioned the possibility of a son in Canada. The nurse shook her head.

'Don't worry,' she said, 'we'll find her somewhere.'

Chapter 13

'He was beautiful, your father.'

'I know, I've seen the photos.'

'They don't show the half of it. In the sixth and seventh form he was just stunning. You couldn't take your eyes off him. Up till then he'd been nothing special to look at, but something happened to make him physically different and you could see people reacting to his beauty. They were just drawn to him, charmed by him. But some guys hated it. It drove them crazy. As if it was somehow wrong for a bloke to be that bloody beautiful.'

The remains of the noodles Vince had cooked lay on the table behind them. They'd sunk into easy chairs in the front room, looking out over Christchurch as dusk thickened. Vince was doing as he'd promised. 'I'll cook you a dinner and tell you everything,' he'd said. 'If that's not too boring.' It wasn't. Indeed there was something good, something soothing, about sitting in the half light with nothing asked of her but to listen. It was like being read to.

'We were in the Square one night, and we were talking to these two girls and just laughing and that, and this pair of first fifteen guys we both vaguely knew ask us what we're playing at. "Come on," I say to Rich, "let's go," but Rich just smiles at them and says "It's okay, it's cool," and turns back to the girl we were talking to and then one of the guys thumps him.

'He wasn't a big guy, your dad, and he went down but he was more or less okay, just a bit groggy, and the girls had a go at the other guys and kept them off while I got Rich away, but that's what was going on. Those blokes sensed his beauty and hated it. Don't ask me why. It's the saddest thing.

'Rich and I had been mates for years. We knew instinctively what the other guy was thinking or what he might do. But in that last year at school the whole intensity went up a notch. For me at least, though for him too, I think – I hope. Do girls have friendships like that? Do women? I don't think my wife did.'

'Yes and no,' said Annie. 'But go on.'

'That last year we were inseparable. Everything was vivid. It was as if whatever we were doing mattered, was of epic scale. I remember so much that happened then, remember it in colour over forty years later. Whereas I couldn't tell you anything that happened last week.

'It was that gap between the end of childhood and the start of everything else. We spent most of it surfing. Rich lived in Brighton. His mum was lovely. Dad wasn't around. Dead or divorced, I didn't know and never asked.

'We had these old long boards and if you got it right you rode like a king. This was the sixties, remember, all freedom and the Beach Boys and it felt like the dawn of the world. It was always going to come to an end, but that was part of the wonder of it. Come February he was going north to art school. And I was going the other way, to Otago.

'And there was this one particular afternoon and we were in the water and Rich caught a wave and stood and he was silhouetted against the sky, and I can see him now, so lean and handsome and I felt this sort of crushing in my chest. It was so sudden and so strong.'

Vince paused. He had been looking out across the city as he spoke, but now he looked across at Annie.

'I've never told anyone this,' he said.

'You know you don't have to,' said Annie.

'Oh, but I want to. I used to be ashamed of it, or at least scared of someone finding out. But that wore off and since then I've sort of hugged it to myself as a secret, something private and vivid and good. But telling Rich's daughter feels like the right thing to do.'

Annie looked at him. He seemed happy, this sixty-year-old man reliving memories from before she was born, happy.

'We ate fish and chips on the dunes that evening and our shadows stretched thirty, forty yards across the sand and dunked our heads in the sea. And then we went up to the Ozone – the landlord there would serve anyone – and we bought a bottle of port, Sailors' Port it was, I can still see the label, and we were heading back to the dunes through this line of macrocarpas, when I heard Rich call. When I turned he wasn't there and he called again and I looked up and there he was in the tree, grinning. He reached down to haul me up and I can see and feel now how we gripped each other's wrists. His wrist was thin but he had long, strong fingers and veins on his forearms. We climbed high into the tree, higher than I would have dared to go alone.

'From up there we looked out over the dunes and the sea to one side and Brighton on the other and the headlights of cars moving along Marine Parade. And we sat each in the crook of a branch with our backs against the trunk and we passed the port between us and drank from the bottle and I don't remember that we said much. It was just magical up there, overlooking the world, and that brilliant sense of no one knowing we were up there.

'Rich lit a cigarette and when he struck the match his face lit from below like some Halloween lantern, only beautiful, and he saw me looking and he smiled and blew out a cloud of smoke. Pall Mall was the brand he smoked. For as long as I smoked, I smoked Pall Mall. I'm boring you.'

'No,' said Annie, 'you're not boring me. The opposite in fact.'

'We finished the bottle and swung down out of the tree like gibbons, letting go of one branch without knowing where the next one lay below. It must have been midnight or so, I don't know, but Brighton was silent and the moon was so bright it cast shadows. It felt like we owned the world. And through the dunes you could feel the thump of the waves.

'We crept into the house to avoid waking Rich's mother. I'd stayed there a hundred times, sleeping on a mattress pulled out from under his bed. But that night when the door of the bedroom shut behind us, Rich spread his arms and smiled. Even then a part of me wanted to back out, a part of me was shouting no and he must have felt it in the muscles of my back and he just held me and eventually I relaxed and I ran my hands over his back and without saying anything we got undressed and into bed.'

He looked up. Annie held his gaze but said nothing, not wanting to break the spell.

'When eventually Rich fell asleep he was lying across my arm, and I could feel the rise and fall of his breathing, and in the half dark I stared at the features of his face, the smooth skin of his shoulder and chest. The curtain was thin and the window beyond was bright with moonlight and I didn't want to sleep and though I lost feeling in my arm I kept it there as long as I could without waking him. I can remember it all with such clarity. It was as though I knew this moment would matter to me more than any other. Though in the end, of course, I fell asleep.

'When I woke in the morning, we were wrapped around each other. I can remember precisely the feeling of how nice it was to wake up pressed against someone else. The feeling lasted about two seconds. Then the guilt came. I was seized with guilt. There's the world for you. Guilt.

'I knew, there and then, just knew we'd be found out. Rich was still sleeping. I wanted to kiss him but I didn't dare. I didn't regret what we'd done. But I dreaded being found out. And I was sure we would be. I peeled his arm from my chest and slid out of bed. Our clothes were scattered together on the floor. I dressed as quietly as I could.

'Rich's mum was already banging around. I liked her but I didn't want to face her then. I listened at the door till she went to the bathroom. I turned for one more look at Rich. His eyes were open. He was smiling. "See you, Vince," he said. "Take it easy."

'I was wound up so tight I felt I was going to snap and he looked so relaxed I half wanted to throw myself back into bed or burst into tears or scream or something but I didn't.

'"Yeah," I said or something like that, and I just turned and left and let myself out the front door. And it seemed to me extraordinary that Brighton was still there and unchanged. I somehow felt the world ought to have been altered by what we'd done. It should have been a different place.

'I got a bus back into town. I remember blushing on the bus because I was sure people knew. And I've never told anyone. Except you. His daughter. You've got to laugh. Now, at any rate. You've got to laugh now.'

Vince paused. 'That was the last time I saw Rich.'

'What, ever?'

Vince nodded. 'I thought I'd wait for him to ring. He didn't. There were no mobile phones back then, of course. There were only a couple of days before I headed south to varsity and I had lots of stuff to do. Then I got on a train and went south. And he presumably went north. And that was that. I got immersed in a new life and I got a girlfriend and it was all new and different. When I came home for the first holiday I rang Rich's place and his mum told me he'd got a flat up north and I wrote down the phone number. But I never rang it. There seemed no point at the time. I always sort of assumed we'd catch up again one day.'

'That's sad,' said Annie.

Their glasses were empty. Night had settled over the city. No lights had come on in the centre of town.

'Oh, I don't know,' said Vince. 'I don't know.'

Chapter 14

The corridor ends in a heavy security door. 'Exit via Car Park', it says, and there is a picture of a stick man running from a fire. Richard turns the handle and puts his shoulder against the door. The door opens a little and the dog squeezes through but the closing mechanism is too much for Richard and the door clangs shut. Within seconds Richard hears the dog's claws on the door, mildly at first, then with increasing vigour.

'It's all right, boy,' says Richard through the thick door. 'It's all right.' But the claws keep scratching. The noise chafes at Richard's head. Halfway down the corridor a rubber plant stands in a brass pot. Richard tips the pot on its side and rolls it. Gravel spills from the surface but the soil seems to be held in place by the fibrous roots. He puts his shoulder to the door and the dog shoots instantly through the gap as, with a grunt of exertion, Richard heaves the pot over the transom to prop the door open.

Richard supports himself on the door jamb, panting as the dog leaps about him in delight. He pats the dog, calms it. 'I wouldn't leave you,' he says.

Together they step out onto the roof of the world, the top storey of five, open to the skies, a raw concrete deck and a scatter of cars. From the parapet Richard has a view up High Street. At the far end a group of men and women in suits and skirts topped with hi-vis jackets and hard hats are moving towards the Square. They go slowly, like tourists in Rome, gawping at ruins. Then they disappear behind the BNZ. Beyond it Richard can see the top of the stump that was the cathedral spire.

A bright blue Audi convertible, low-slung and costly, has been left with the roof down, its plush interior now grey with plaster dust and dotted with birdshit. Leaves and blown litter have lodged in the foot-wells. Richard tries the handle on the driver's door. Instantly the alarm sounds, ringing over the city. Richard dives back to the door, the dog with him, and they head deep into the hotel to hide. The alarm stops. Why, Richard doesn't know. Silence seeps back in. Richard's ears are pricked for footfalls, for voices. Nothing.

* * *

'What sort of person is your mum,' said Vince, 'if you don't mind my asking?'

Annie shrugged. 'It's hard to say with parents, isn't it?'

'Is it? When you're young, maybe, but I think I've got a pretty good idea now what sort of people my parents were.'

Annie smiled. She took a swig of wine. 'She lives in Blenheim now, with a man I've met a couple of times and who seems a reasonable bloke. She bullies him. I keep in touch and all that, but to be frank it's a chore. I'd rather not. And I don't blame Dad for what he did. These days, anyway.'

'What happened?'

'Guess. I don't know how Mum found out he was having an affair but when she did all hell broke loose. I heard her screaming at him late that night when I'd gone to bed. I couldn't make out much of what they were saying – or shouting – but it ended suddenly with the front door being slammed shut and then there was silence. That was all.'

As she spoke Annie felt again exactly how it had been as she lay and listened and waited and heard her mother's footsteps coming up to bed. And in the morning Dad hadn't been there but her mother had said nothing and Annie had gone to school as usual.

When she'd come home that afternoon her mother had been through the house for everything associated with him. There had been framed drawings of his lining the stairs and hall. They'd all gone.

Her mother had hugged her and said that her father had betrayed them and it was just the two of them from then on and he wouldn't be coming back and Annie had cried and gone upstairs to her room and expected her mother to follow but she didn't and Annie had lain face down on the bed crying. Later she'd stood by the window watching her mother carrying stuff out to the bonfire, carrying it out with utter determination till it was almost dark, his clothes, his shoes, his books even. She burned his books. 'To be fair,' continued Annie, 'she did try to be a good mum after that, for a while at least. It didn't come naturally to her, I realise now, but she did try. And she was forever buying me stuff. I think she must have struck a pretty good deal with Dad somehow, but at the time I just got on with things. And at nine you're pretty resilient. I missed Dad but I got over it.'

'What did Rich do for a living?'

'I've thought about that. I don't know exactly. Something to do with design, I'd guess. He took me to his office a few times. I remember big windows and angled boards that you stood at to draw on, but that's all.'

'Could we ask your mother?'

'No,' said Annie. 'She doesn't know I'm in the country. And I'd rather she didn't. And besides, if she thought it would help find Dad she wouldn't tell us. I guarantee it. She's never forgiven him and she's not going to now. But it shouldn't be too hard to track down where he worked, should it? It's not as though it's last century or something.'

'Actually,' said Vince, 'it is. But I've got a few contacts.'

* * *

On the north side of the car park roof a shed-like construction houses the pedestrian stairs. In front of it there's a small porch where Richard establishes camp. It offers shade from sun and shelter from rain. More importantly, it makes them invisible from above. Helicopter traffic has shrunk since the first few days but several still drone in each day to hang like vast wasps over the ruins.

Richard drags out a chair and footstool and arranges them under the porch. Then a bedside cabinet that he fills with bottles, glasses, snacks and dog biscuits. On the other side of the chair he sets cushions for the dog but when he stops to sit and drink a beer, the dog curls on the concrete, its shoulder warm against his ankle, head and paw draped possessively over his foot.

Half snoozing, Richard is suddenly aware of a blather of wings. The pigeon is lurching towards his chair. Three yards away it stops to cock its head, its eye a black ball bearing. Saying calming things to the dog, Richard reaches slowly into the pocket of his dressing gown, finds crumbs and baits his claw. He makes the kissing sound he uses with the bird. It flutters up to land on the forearm, and Richard can feel it seeking a point of balance on its clenched and crippled left foot even as it pecks at the biscuit.

He adds more crumbs. Slowly, he sits forward. The bird sways and flutters its wings for balance but stays on his arm. He stands. For a moment he thinks the bird will fly but it stays with him, and he does a little tour of the car park roof with the bird perched on his arm, like some sort of debased urban falconer. He smiles at the image.

He sprinkles crumbs on the parapet, the pigeon hops off, he returns to his chair and the dog settles back at his side. He breaks the seal on a baby bottle of cabernet sauvignon, as purple as venous blood.

'Cheers,' he says to the bird on the ledge and the dog at his feet and the world out there. 'Cheers.' Neither bird nor dog pays any attention.

* * *

'Listen to this,' said Annie, sitting with her laptop at the table, as Jess fussed in the kitchen.

'"Dear Miss Jones,

'"I am aware that the convention is to begin emails with hi, but I simply cannot bring myself to address anyone in a manner that seems to me best suited to a Californian beach. Nor do I yet feel sufficiently well acquainted with you to address you by your delightful Christian name, and I refuse to use the ugly neologism Ms.

'"All of which, I suspect, is sufficient to identify me as the ancient you met in the apartment on Park Terrace. My day was entirely made by your visit. It is not often that an old man gets to spend an hour with a beautiful and intelligent young woman (except, that is, when the beautiful and intelligent young woman is a relative in search of money, which, I'm afraid to say, she too often is).

"'I digress, of course, because it is expected of an old person, and because I have time on my hands. But you do not have time on your hands, I would imagine, so let me, in that unfathomable phrase, cut to the chase.

"'I promised to find out for you whether it is possible that your father had the lease of this apartment in 1992. It is not. As I may have mentioned the family name for the apartment is the Railway Station, in that it is a place of arrivals and departures. In other words it is occupied by members of the family who are making their way either onto the world's stage or off it. I shall be the third family member to die here (assuming that the good Lord is sufficiently merciful to spare me the horrors of a rest home), following in the disciplined footsteps of my Aunt Julia and rather less disciplined ones of Cousin Charles. And several younger scions have made use of the apartment while they found their feet. Among these is my great-nephew Ben, who had the lease in his early twenties from 1989 to 1993, which rather precludes your father's being here at the same time.

"'I am sorry to have to disappoint you, Miss Jones, particularly because I had hoped that your researches would lead to a further visit, but I cannot now see any reason that that might happen.

"'I wish you success in your search for your father and of course if there is any way in which I can be of use, please do not hesitate to ask."

'What do you make of that?'

'He sounds like a bit of a poppet.'

'He is.'

'If he's telling the truth, that is.'

'Why wouldn't he be?'

'You realise you're dealing with Christchurch aristocracy here, don't you? You won't find a public committee or a property development or an election campaign without some member of that family being in it or on it or behind it in some way. They have power. And power and the truth don't always go hand in hand.'

'You're a cynic, Jess. The old boy couldn't have been sweeter. I've got half a mind to pay him a surprise visit in a short skirt.'

'He sounds as though he could cope. You know who the Ben in question is, don't you?'

Annie didn't.

'Oh, he's pretty prominent. In the family tradition he did a spell on the city council in his twenties – people always elect a name they recognise and besides he was rather pretty back then. I remember there was a fuss about young girls souveniring his campaign posters. Then, once he'd ticked off public service, he went into property development – as you do. Basically, he took over the family portfolio and doubled it, according to the media. The family trust must be one of the biggest landlords in the central city.'

Throughout this, Annie had been pecking at the keyboard. 'Is that him?' she asked, swivelling the screen so Jess could see it.

'Yes,' said Jess, 'that's the one. You can see why the posters went missing. Mind you, that was at least fifteen years ago now.'

'How do you suggest I find him? He's a long shot but at the moment he's the only shot I've got. Maybe I'll just ask the old boy where he lives.'

'Ever heard of Google, darling?' said Jess. 'There's officially no such thing as a secret any more.'

Chapter 15

Glandovey Road was bent but far from broken. Some lawns and berms had sprouted molehills of liquefaction, but there were no road-lining slag heaps of the stuff, none of the smothering ruin of the east side of town. It didn't seem fair. Indeed it wasn't fair, but then, reflected Annie, the notion of fairness didn't apply in plate tectonics. Nor for that matter in the sheer fact of there being an east side and a Glandovey Road.

The house was surrounded by lawn and the lawn by tall cream walls and a metal gate. Annie pressed an intercom button in one of the pillars. But even as she did so a golden retriever came lolloping round the corner of the house. It stopped when it saw Annie at the gate, its tail plumed and horizontal.

'What is it, Bossy?' said a female voice, and round the same corner came a woman in her thirties, wearing ironed jeans and a white T-shirt. 'Oh, hello.'

'Hello,' said Annie and the moment she spoke the retriever relaxed and came gambolling to the gate so that Annie could reach between the bars and stroke its head and chin. 'I'm sorry to trouble you, but I was just wondering whether I could have a word with Ben.'

'Ben's at work. Could I ask what it's about?'

Annie began to explain through the grille but as the gist of the story emerged Ben's wife said, 'I think this requires coffee, don't you?' She opened the gate, introduced herself as Steph, told Bossy to calm down, and led Annie into the vast kitchen done up in a style that, if pressed, Annie would have described as rustic French with gadgets. Steph turned dials and knobs on the Gaggia coffee machine as if in the cab of a steam train, and laid Tim Tams on a blue-ringed plate while Annie explained her mission and the series of events that had taken her to Park Terrace and Great-Uncle David.

'What did you make of him?'

'You can't beat old-world charm, can you?' said Annie and Steph nodded as if she had expected precisely those words, that sentiment.

'But you still came here to find Ben,' she said.

'He's the only lead I've got at the moment,' she said. 'If he comes to nothing I may well have to give up. For all I know Dad could be anywhere in the world. Or dead.'

'Oh no,' exclaimed Steph, shaking her head in vigorous sympathy so that its layered blondeness shimmered like an ad. 'I'm sure he's not dead.'

'Yours?' said Annie, indicating framed photos of kids on a shelf. 'May I?' Two girls and a boy, the girls childishly chubby, the boy thin-limbed with a pair of wire-rimmed glasses and a strangely bunched face, as if too many features had been crammed into too small an area. But all three kids wore the uninhibited grins of their age, posing briefly on the lawn with Bossy the dog. And here were the three of them again climbing on what had to be Ben, the girls cantilevered out on either side of his waist, the boy high on his shoulders, proud as a king. Ben was trying to smile for the camera despite the strain of supporting the three of them. A slight man in his thirties, fading already from his election poster days, his hair receding at either temple to leave a tongue of thatch above the centre of the forehead.

'Proud dad,' said Annie, and noted how Steph seemed to bask in the words, to savour them.

The kitchen window gave a view of some tributary of the Avon, its banks impeccably shaven, well-governed exotic trees dotted along it. There were a few cracks in the plaster high up on the kitchen walls but the house seemed by and large undamaged.

'We're lucky,' said Steph, as if reading Annie's mind. 'When you see the TV news in the evening it doesn't seem quite fair. But what are you supposed to do? Move to Aranui?'

Steph took Annie's contact details and promised to let Ben know she'd called.

* * *

It took an hour and a half and two changes of bus to reach South Brighton. From her seat at the window Annie watched the landscape change from workable suburban affluence to something post-apocalyptic. Forced into detours by downed bridges, ruptured drains and shattered roads, the bus took her down the back ways of Avondale, Bexley, Parklands. The streets lined with bulldozed heaps of grey and sodden silt reminded Annie of photos of the trenches on the Somme. Crudely painted notices begged drivers to slow down, or urged rubber-neckers to go elsewhere. Already, after only a couple of weeks, you could tell which houses had been abandoned since the quake.

Annie alighted by the pier. On the seaward side of Marine Parade the dunes stretched down to beach and sea as they had always done, soft-edged, irregular and quite undamaged by any shaking. But across the road, in a pattern that was becoming familiar, the rigidity of the houses had taken a thumping. Here bricks had rained like lethal confetti. There a jerry-built top storey had simply been flung half off the building underneath. Annie followed duckboards through the dunes and onto the beach where the waves boomed and women were walking dogs and a few wet-suited surfers bobbed beyond the breakers. One paddled in with a wave, like some fiercely crawling insect on the water's skin, then caught a swell and rose to a crouch, to a three-quarter stand, his body lithely black, his shins and forearms white, as he rode the shifting world diagonally across the afternoon, a ten- or fifteen-second ride of triumph and defiance before the tumble into a cold salt sea.

How many Sundays her father had brought her here to visit Grandma. She remembered buying ice creams from the van by the surf club; occasional plagues of copper blue jellyfishes that washed up and died on the beach by the million and whose air sac burst with a pop when you stamped on them; her father chatting with a woman while Annie threw a stick into the shallows for the woman's collie and every time the collie fetched the stick it took it back up the beach to drop it at the woman's feet rather than at Annie's. At a familiar stand of old man pines Annie passed back through the dunes on the duckboards that the sands had swallowed and there was Jellicoe Street, looking much as it always had but for a swarm of young people with shovels, buckets and barrows. The famous Student Army. Further down the street a loader was filling a truck with vast scoops of silt.

Annie picked her way through waiting piles of silt and dozens of cheerful shovellers to the house that Vince had so often slept at but that for her would always be her grandmother's house. In the front room there had been cake and chocolate and fizzy drink, and a lightness of mood. But when Annie was seven the afternoon teas had shrunk and Grandma stopped getting up to hug her and she wore a scarf around her head because her hair had grown thin and Dad said she was very sick. And one day when Annie put her arms around her in her chair and caught a whiff of her breath and it was foul and she said 'Ugh' and let her go and turned away.

When she looked back her father had put an arm around his mother and laid his head against hers and Annie saw that she was quietly gulping.

'There, there,' her father said, 'there, there,' just as he might have said to Annie when she had stubbed a toe. And Annie had watched as the old woman sank into her son's embrace and in time had turned and smiled at Annie and asked her how she was doing at school. Though when they left she hadn't reached out to Annie for a kiss.

Mum didn't go to the funeral and didn't want Annie to go, but Dad had collected her from school at lunchtime and they drove to Lyttelton. It was the first church Annie had been in and it was made of stone and there were only half a dozen people there and Annie knew none of them, though they all seemed to know Dad. And afterwards they had gone up to the cemetery above the port and the grave had already been dug and Annie remembered watching a huge ship being nudged into its berth by tugs as men in black coats lowered the shiny expensive-looking coffin into the hole and the priest read from his black leather book. It was windy. Whirls of dust blew from the earth heaped beside the grave. And the priest threw a handful of that earth and Annie heard the clatter as it landed and watched it scatter across the lid. The mourners all threw little clods of earth as they left and her dad did too but Annie didn't want to and clung to his leg.

The house that had been light green was now a freshly painted buff. But it was still little more than the original weatherboard cottage, a single storey divided into four rooms, and with a lean-to kitchen on the back. The basic house of New Zealand and her father had been raised there and in that room there at the back by the pear tree he had slept with a boy who would never forget.

'You looking for a job?'

A freckle-faced girl was proffering a shovel.

'We can share the barrow,' she said.

'Why not?' and Annie set to work digging a foot of sodden silt from what had once been her grandmother's front lawn.

'Is anyone living here?'

The girl thought not. Silt had not been shifted from the front door and there were few footmarks round the back. 'Lots of people around here just moved straight out, went to stay with relatives and that.'

More students joined them, their cheerfulness infectious and the speed with which they cleared the gunk remarkable. Twenty shovels heaved it onto wheelbarrows that piled it on the street to be scooped onto a waiting truck and away. Half an hour and the garden was cleared. The body of shovellers moved on. Annie didn't follow them. Resting the shovel against a shed where she was sure they'd find it, she toured the outside of the house peering in at windows. Soiled plates in the sink, a nest of used coffee mugs. The rooms had been brightened and modernised, but Annie recognised the shape of the room where she had made her grandmother cry, and the room that

had been her father's bedroom and that had witnessed such…
but every house had its history.

'Annie.'

Vince was standing by a pile of silt on the road front. The sun
gleamed on the skin of his scalp and he was clearly trying but
failing to suppress a grin. He looked like a neat bald schoolboy.

'You could do everyone a favour by turning your cell phone
on once in a while. It would save old buggers like me having to
hunt you down to tell you the good news.'

'What good news?'

'I'll tell you over a drink. My car's down there.' And he
started towards Marine Parade.

'There's no one in the house,' said Annie. 'Don't you want
to…' But he was away. Vince pressed a key fob and lights
blinked on a low-slung bottle-green BMW convertible. He
handed Annie into the passenger seat with mock gallantry.

Annie looked at him and smiled. 'This would turn a few
girls' heads.'

Vince snorted.

'Oh, come on,' said Annie, 'you're a catch and a half. Not
broke, not drunk, not saddled with a beer gut, not stupid and
not still married. There must be hundreds of women ready to
fling themselves at you if you so much as nod in their direction.'

'There are,' said Vince, as they pulled out onto Marine
Parade, accelerating with a high-engineered growl, then
slowing immediately to negotiate a missing patch of tarmac.
'But the shame of it is I've grown into just the sort of bloke I

despise, the one that fancies women half his age. Dirty old men we used to call them when we were kids, dirty old men.'

'I'm half your age,' said Annie.

Vince seemed not to hear her. 'I dress nicely and talk politely but beneath the skin of the gentleman beats the heart of a lecher.'

Annie laughed.

'No, I'm serious. Though I don't think I'm unusual. Most blokes are waging a constant battle to seem decent. One drink too many, one clumsy step and the ice cracks beneath us. It's what every bloke's movie is about, every bloke's book, every bloke's car, every bloke even. But I don't think women have ever really believed it. Or else they think they can change us.'

He looked across at Annie. 'Sorry,' he said.

'It's okay,' she said. 'What's the good news?'

'I'll tell you when we've got a drink in front of us. You've earned it after all that shovelling.'

They drove past the surf club and a stand of wind-crabbed pines, past the squat stone war memorial and the butt end of the pier that surprisingly and rather endearingly swelled to become the swish new library.

On the other side of the road, the car park of the tired little shopping mall rolled like frozen sea. Vince slowed often to negotiate drain covers popped up by the pressure of the liquefied land, or fissures in the road surface, like cracks in a crevasse, their presence advertised by a cluster of livid orange cones.

'I was driving this thing when the quake happened,' said Vince. 'On Moorhouse Ave, near the car yards. I didn't know what was going on at first – I had music on and I didn't hear a thing, and the shock absorbers took the violence out of it. The road ahead swelled and rolled and I felt this sort of swaying and my first thought was that I was having a stroke. It was only when cars started stopping right where they were, without pulling over, that I realised what was going on. But what I'll never forget is the tyres. There was this great blue barn of a building, stacked with racks of tyres going way up above head height. Down they came, of course, the tyres – big buggers, truck tyres, tractor tyres. Some of them must have weighed half a ton or so. And they all bounced. But they didn't bounce regularly. They bounced off to one side and the big ones were easily big enough to kill. It was like being inside some video game. It was weird. But it was also funny. I saw this woman who looked like she'd just been doing the accounts or something come out of the office to be confronted by these bouncing tyres, dozens of them, and she just stopped in her tracks, literally open-mouthed, unable to move, just staring. Then suddenly she turned and ran back into the office. And I laughed. I remember laughing. It was like a cartoon. Only lasted a moment, of course, but that's the image that comes first to me when anyone mentions the quake.'

Everyone had a quake story, Annie realised. Half a million people were somewhere when the quake struck. She felt half envious, half guilty for not having been there.

'Shit,' exclaimed Vince, 'look,' and he was stamping on the brakes.

Behind more temporary fencing, a yellow machine with something resembling a giant crab's pincer attached to its hydraulic arm was hacking and tearing at a rambling old weatherboard building. As they watched it tore off a chunk of one side, snapping timbers, and turning the chunk over to show the ancient wallpaper and the skirting boards, and bits of electrical wire hanging like veins.

'The Ozone,' said Vince.

For a moment the name meant nothing to Annie, and then she remembered and she turned to look at Vince.

'Come on,' he said and they got out of the car and stood like kids at the fencing. The demolition was violently pornographic. The intimate details of private rooms, of indoors, were ripped open, exposed to the gaze of the world. Innards met sunlight for the first time in a hundred years. And it was all so peremptory. The claw reached in and gripped and twisted and the building yielded. Nails and timber gave way with little more than a graunch. In ten minutes half the third floor disappeared, four or more bedrooms, the beds and wardrobes with them, ripped out, broken apart and dumped at random angles on the heap of spoil. Neither Vince nor Annie spoke.

The driver shut his machine down and climbed from the cab. A slim, surprisingly young man, clean shaven, crew-cut. He smiled at Annie and Vince, no doubt used to the theatrical appeal of his profession. He started up a truck with another hydraulic arm on the back, this one ending in a claw. It lifted scoops from the pile and swung them onto the truck bed, where they fell with a terminal clatter, wood on metal.

On the far side of Marine Parade, a track led into the dunes. Rising beside it the shaggy dark green pyramids of a stand of macrocarpas.

* * *

In Salt on the Pier, Annie watched a hefty black-backed seagull ride the air in silence not far beyond the window, its low flat arch of wings adjusting to the wind with magisterial precision. It lay on the moving air as comfortably, more comfortably, than Annie sat now on her bent wood chair. It seemed to expend no energy, shifting its skull from side to side to oversee the chance of food from beach or fisherman.

All around her women talked, leaning in towards each other over coffee or wine or salad, dealing urgently with matters that mattered, while just above them, just beyond the glass, this sleek and faultless creature floated on the air in self-sufficient silence.

'It's not the Ozone, but still.' Vince placed a misted glass of pinot gris in front of her. 'Cheers.'

He opened his laptop, and a few seconds later turned the screen towards her to show the website of an outfit called Hamilton Design. He pointed at the introductory blurb.

'Formerly known as Hamilton and Jones,' read Annie and she looked at Vince, who nodded.

'According to the registrar of companies,' said Vince, 'Richard Hugh Jones sold his half share of the business to his co-founder, Karl Pierre Hamilton, in 1994. Premises in Lichfield Street a block down from Ballantynes. Does that sound right?'

Annie shrugged. 'I just remember tall windows and a view of the sky. Is the company still there?'

Vince shook his head. 'The building, if it's standing, is inside the cordon. But Karl Pierre Hamilton shouldn't be hard to find.' He clicked on Contact Us, and up came an email address and a cell phone number.

'And you haven't…'

'Of course not,' said Vince. 'All yours. You going to ring him now?'

'Tomorrow, I think,' said Annie. She wanted to think about what she might say.

Vince looked disappointed.

'But you've done brilliantly,' she said, 'thank you.' And she leant across from her chair and hugged him.

Chapter 16

The dog takes itself over to the far side of the car park roof and peers through the concrete parapet.

'What is it, Friday?'

The dog's tail wags as Richard joins him at the wall. There's a noise of distant voices, men's voices, coming from beyond Colombo Street, beyond the fallen mess of Cashel Mall. Then they come into view, a dozen or more figures, tiny from up there on the roof of the world, scampering half-heartedly through the tongues of fallen masonry. They move and shout as though they want to be caught. Richard wants them to be caught, too. He wants the authorities to remove them, to re-establish the peace.

As if in response, half a dozen figures in New Zealand army green appear at the intersection with Colombo, cradling firearms. The men stop. The soldiers advance. Two policemen arrive. A brief discussion and the little group turns and goes back the way it came, escorted by the police, and the soldiers calmly watch them go, and Richard feels relief and his hand on the dog's shoulder relaxes. A pain stabs through him, stabs like a heated blade through the side of his gut. He screams and bends double. The pain stabs again, searing.

Gasping, bent, he staggers, then crawls across the car park to the hotel door. The dog paws at him as he goes, alarmed by the strangeness. Out of the sunshine into the gloom of the corridor and, half blinded, Richard scrabbles at the door of the first room, but another burst of pain flings him to the floor of the corridor, writhing, clutching at his gut.

* * *

'Do you mind if we watch the news?' said Jess, heaping carbonara onto plates. 'There's supposed to be something about the hospital.'

But the main item was a band of thirty or so tradesmen and small business owners making a raid on the central city. They wanted access to their commercial lives and had been lobbying the emergency authorities for days, but those authorities had neither blinked nor even smiled. They had soldiers at their command and they had extraordinary powers and they saw no need for flexibility or concession.

Knowing the power of publicity, the aggrieved had alerted the television companies and so there on screen was footage of them scaling the fence on Cambridge Terrace, running across the Bridge of Remembrance and then dodging the rubble in Cashel Mall, slowing as they tired. They didn't get far but then they hadn't expected to. A couple of cops followed them in a leisurely manner. A posse of soldiers blocked their way as they approached Colombo Street. No guns or even voices were raised. The encounter was affable and the insurgents let themselves be ushered back outside the cordon. But the point had been made.

The dour ex-soldier who'd been flown in from up north to secure the central city announced, while clearly hating to do so, that limited and escorted access to the central city would be granted to those who needed it over the coming days, though a perimeter cordon would be maintained so as to allow the authorities to maintain appropriate control, etc., etc.

'Good on them,' said Jess. 'Honestly, you can just see that guy seething at the thought of conceding anything. You just know the bastards would love to institute martial law, shoot on sight, string 'em up, soon have the country licked into shape. God, why are men such power-hungry bastards?'

'Are they?' said Annie.

'The ones in power are.'

The on-screen discussion moved to the tallest building in the city. Film of it clearly showed it was leaning at an angle of five degrees or so.

'It could fall any time,' said the ex-soldier. 'Or not. It's simply too dangerous to let people work in its vicinity. We are in the process of deciding how to deal with it.'

A ridiculously young reporter asked whether they'd considered blowing it up. You could hear in his voice the sense of his own importance at the job he had.

'No decision has been reached at this moment in time,' said the ex-soldier and the reply was like a door slammed in the kid's face.

* * *

The flies rouse him. He can sense them crawling on shin and thigh. He stirs and the flies lift as a single unit, fizzing. He sees the dog, lying close, curled nose to tail. He is too weak to do anything and his eyes close again and the flies clamp back down. Evening sunshine spears through the door and reaches to his face and beyond. The dog has sensed his stirring and gets to its feet. The flies circle the dog, who snaps at them, teeth clacking as they miss. The dog bends and licks Richard's face. His eyes open. 'Good boy,' he tries to say. His voice is a husk, a wisp. 'Good boy, Friday.'

Feebly he reaches out with his bad left hand to touch the dog's paw, its leg, its head. The pain seems to have gone but he cannot ignore the smell and the stickiness and the flies that fizz and settle with every movement.

He is lying on his front, like a corpse flung from a window. He runs his hand slowly from the dog to his own thigh, and his hand recoils.

The noise he makes is half groan, half wail, a desperate noise. The dog looks down at him with curiosity, as he rolls onto his side, reaches for the door handle above, driven by an imperative of instinct and of horror, hauls himself to his knees, to his feet, the flies a cloud around him, the dog snapping at them, and he pushes the door open, almost falling through it but staying on his feet by force of will, stumbling to the bathroom.

He knows the taps have long run dry but turns one on anyway. Not a trickle, not even a gasp of old air, and he props himself against the wall by the toilet and with his good right hand he unscrews the housing around the flush button on the cistern. He has to pause to rest, his head against the cool plaster. A minute and he's back at work. The housing comes loose and he wrenches the ceramic lid from the cistern. It clatters to the tiles and snaps in three big pieces and the dog leaps back in alarm. He shucks his bathrobe without looking down at it, flings it in the bath, dunks a towel in the trapped water of the cistern, soaks it deep and runs it loosely, horribly, down the inside of his thighs. One pass and it joins the robe in the bath. Another towel, and another and another.

He turns and lurches naked from the room to the room next door and again he unscrews the cistern lid and sponges at his thighs and knees. He is aware that the foulness is blood as much as shit, a sorry torrent from a failing gut, from inner organs pushed towards their point of seizure. The blood does not alarm him so much as the sense of the future. What further revulsion, what disabling indignity, awaits? Weak as water he goes to one more room, one more cistern, to clean the last scraps and stains, to make things good as far as it is possible to make them good. The dog pads along with him.

He dons a new bathrobe, white as a gull's breast, new fluffy slippers. The stench still fills the corridor, the flies still humming there, in the lance of evening sunshine, a dancing, gorging chorus sparkling black. From a maid's trolley he fetches bleach and a fierce-looking aerosol and tips the bleach over the carpet, all of it, the whole searing bottle. The flies rise in protest. He fires at them wildly with the aerosol, seeking to drive them out the door to the rooftop car park and the world beyond.

In the room on the far side of the stairwell, Richard gives the dog a bowl of Kiwi Spring water and half a dozen Tux, drinks a little water himself, then screws the top from a Johnnie Walker, sniffs at it with unaccustomed caution and sips. He traces its descent past the back of his tongue and down the gullet to drip into the gut. He sees the whisky as a kill-or-cure device, a cauterising force. Nothing happens. No protest from below, no convulsion of the gut, no startling jab of pain. He lies back on the bed and sighs and swigs the Scotch, then pats the bed beside him. Unhesitatingly the dog leaps up and fusses about him, balancing poorly on the deep sprung mattress, then circling, scratching at the duvet, flattening grass, perhaps, or hollowing the soil to form a nest, an action going back so far beyond hotels and human landscapes that Richard finds it soothing. 'Good boy,' he murmurs as the dog settles, its spine a semi-circle, its snout folded into its rump, a self-containment from the world, and he lays a hand upon the rough fur of the dog's neck and the dog sighs like a man and thumps the duvet once with its tail, then closes its eyes. 'Friday,' whispers Richard, 'Friday.'

Chapter 17

'Steph,' said Annie into the phone, 'it's me, Annie. I came round the other day, you remember?'

Steph remembered, but not very warmly, it seemed. Or was Annie just being sensitive? It had been her way for as long as she could remember to be overly sensitive to any hint of hostility, of dislike. It was a weakness, she knew, one that led her to concede too often, to placate so as to avoid conflict. But she was as she was. 'I'm sorry to trouble you again, Steph, but it's just I won't be here an awful lot longer and I was wondering whether you'd had a chance to...'

'Yes, I have, and Ben has never heard of your father. So that's that, I'm afraid. I'm sorry.'

'Oh,' said Annie, startled by the abruptness, 'are you sure?'

'Am I sure?'

'Sorry,' said Annie, 'I didn't mean it like that. I meant... oh, it doesn't matter. But I don't suppose Ben's home from work yet, is he?'

'I don't see…'

'I was just wondering whether there was a time when I could ring him, I mean in the evening or something. I'd be really grateful.'

'I've told you, Annie, my husband has never heard of your father. And now, if you'll excuse me, I've got things to do.'

'Of course, I'm sorry.'

'That,' called Jess coming into the kitchen, 'didn't sound like the most productive call.'

'Ah well,' said Annie, replacing the phone on the wall of Jess's kitchen. 'That's that, I suppose. She said Ben had never heard of Dad.'

Jess looked at her. 'But you don't believe her.'

Annie said nothing.

'You don't, do you?'

'I don't know,' said Annie. 'She just sounded as though she didn't want me to meet her husband.'

'Who could blame her for that?' said Jess. 'You're not exactly ugly. But why don't you just go and ask him yourself?'

'You mean… Oh, now you're being ridiculous.'

'Do you want to talk to him or not?'

* * *

'Is this legal?'

'Being parked on the side of a public street?' said Jess. 'Yes, oddly enough, it is. Nice pad.'

As they'd driven past the gates Annie had caught a glimpse of the two chubby girls and the rickety little boy playing on a caged trampoline. Now sitting in Jess's car with the windows down they could hear the kids' excitement, the squeals of 'Watch me', the sudden disagreements that flared momentarily, then died back down.

Annie had longed for brothers and sisters, brothers especially. The difference it would have made. That intimacy, that sense of shared adventure. Surely the way to bring up children, as Paul had said.

People always saw Annie as competent, reliable, steady. If they'd only known that she was that way because of fear, not of anything specific, but of life itself, of getting involved, of making mistakes. Surely brothers would have cured that. Look at Paul. He had brothers and he feared nothing. Or Jess. How many brothers did she have? Three, was it? And what was there, in this world or the next, that Jess was afraid of?

Two boys on bikes came down Glandovey Road in the blue and black of Boys' High, chatting as they rode. Each wore a cycle helmet with the strap undone. Neither had a hand on the handlebars. Annie almost dissolved with envy of their nonchalance, and of the sisters they no doubt disregarded.

'What are your brothers up to these days, Jess? Are they still around?'

'Barry's in town. We see each other at Christmas, which is often enough. The other two are in Aussie, or at least they were the last I heard. Doug's got a couple of kids already, though the little darlings have yet to meet their Auntie Jess. What a treat in store. By the way, do we know what sort of car lover boy here drives? Or is the great property developer coming home on a bike?'

Annie shrugged.

'And is that him?'

A cream BMW slowed as it passed them. Annie felt her gut contracting with dread. But to her relief the car turned into a drive on the other side of the road.

'Oh Jess, I don't think I can do this.'

'Course you can, girl. When he pulls up at the gates you just go quietly up and say you're the woman who's looking for her dad and could he spare you five minutes to answer a few questions. What's the worst that could happen? He ignores you? He tells you to fuck off? He calls the cops? No worries. You've done nothing wrong. And besides he won't do any of those things. He'll say fine, come in, or call me at the office or whatever.'

Glandovey Road was a suburban idyll. The overall image was of green. The houses set well back from the road, curtained by mature trees casting deep late-summer shade. Glimpses of dappled lawn and half-timbered facades and vast low three-car garages, full of Japanese four-wheel-drives and European saloons.

Someone was practising the violin, a repeated scrap of Mozart – was it? – coming from an open third-floor window. A yellow rose had climbed to and around that window over who knew how many summers. Annie thought back to Turnpike Lane, to the long cold nights and the snot-grey skies and the endless swishing traffic, its lights refracted in a cold wet urban world. Ten days or so and she'd be back among it. And down here, this side of the planet there'd be all this light, this green.

She felt an elbow, looked up. A fat black four-wheel-drive was turning in towards the gates, which were already opening.

'Go, girl, go,' and Annie stepped out. She was maybe twenty feet from the car. She felt like an assassin. The driver's window was down. She could see Ben's face in profile. He looked so affable that courage came to her and she was on the point of calling out when the kids burst through the gate, climbed onto the running boards and clung and squealed and Annie crossed the road and walked by unnoticed as Ben nosed his vehicle, festooned with children, down the gravel drive towards the family home.

'Don't say a word,' she said, as she got back into the car. 'We're going home for a drink.'

But instead of starting the car Jess let out an uninhibited laugh, twisted in the driver's seat, opened her arms and gave Annie a hug that, for all the awkwardness of handbrake and steering wheel and jutting seat belt bits, was welcome. 'You great chicken,' said Jess. 'Way too nice.' As they drove back to Hornby Annie wondered whether she really did want to find her father. She knew now that the man she'd set out from London to find was a man of forty. A man of sixty was a different proposition. And the more she gleaned the more she worried that it might be unwise to go further. Why might he not have remarried, had children, daughters, half-brothers and sisters to Annie, who could be approaching adulthood now? Whenever Annie pictured her father rubbing another daughter against his bristles, drawing pictures for her, telling her stories in bed, well, she coped, she was the sort of woman who coped, but she wasn't sure that she wanted to know about it. What was the point? And if he'd wanted to, couldn't he have come looking for her? Indeed, why hadn't he? None of which she said to Jess.

* * *

'Nothing gets past the old boy,' said Annie as Jess set a hefty glass of pinot gris on the kitchen table. 'Listen.'

"'Dear Miss Jones,

"'I suppose I should hardly be surprised that you did not accept my word that Ben knew nothing of your father. In your shoes I suspect I would have done the same. I will admit nevertheless to being a little disappointed.

"'But in consequence I was wondering whether you would indulge an old man by accepting an invitation to luncheon here in Park Terrace on Friday, an invitation which I shall also extend to my great-nephew. This will afford you the opportunity to ask him face to face the very questions that I have already asked him on your behalf, and me the opportunity to enjoy once again the company of a delightful young woman. Such opportunities, as I may have mentioned before, come rarely at my age, and almost invariably with strings attached.

"'If you can fit this into your busy schedule, I shall pop open a bottle of eminently respectable Méthode Champenoise about noon on Friday.'"

'Ben must have told him you were on the case,' said Jess. 'Or his wife did. Anyway, I presume you'll go.'

Annie wasn't sure. There seemed little point. If there was anything to hide, the old boy would hardly have invited her to lunch, let alone with Ben. And besides she felt a familiar twinge of guilt for having gone behind David's back.

'I wouldn't worry about it if I were you,' said Jess. 'Given that family's business interests, he'll have seen and done a lot worse.'

It took Annie three attempts to write the reply. In the end she removed the apology, thanked the old man for the invitation and promised to be there.

'Whatever you do,' said Jess, 'don't take wine.'

Writing to Karl Hamilton of Hamilton Design proved no easier. There was a head-and-shoulders shot of him on the company website, relaxed, smiling, in an open-necked shirt, a large, soft-looking man. In the end she settled on similar factual simplicity.

Jess leant over her to read the screen. 'Fine. He'll answer.'

Annie hovered the cursor over 'Send'.

'Go on,' said Jess. 'You think too much.'

Annie remembered standing by a letter box on Stanmore Road and feeling similarly hesitant, in her hand a Valentine's card addressed to Graham Moseley. In her memory she saw his dark eyes, his smile, his hips.

She pressed 'Send'.

Graham Moseley had never responded. He'd probably received a dozen Valentines. Yet the thought of him had consumed her night and day for a month or more. Ah well. Love. Where was he now?

They ate in the garden, under the wrought-iron verandah. Jess brought out what she called pasta bake: chunks of fish, a grapeshot of frozen peas, slivers of apparent carrot, a glutinous white sauce that blistered the tongue, the whole thing tasting only of cheese.

The evening air was warm as a bath and dense with insects. An unseen neighbour was clipping a hedge with shears you could hear were rusty. When Annie finally put her plate aside she was assailed with the scent of jasmine.

A bottlebrush was awash with flowers, each like a punk's mohawk. Beneath the bush a blackbird chick, all but fully fledged, yet still dependent. The male fluttered in, hopped a couple of steps on the damp sparse lawn under the bush, cocked its head, stabbed at the soil, pulled up an amorphous wriggle of ooze and immediately the fledgling opened its beak to be fed.

'Finished?' asked Jess, standing up. The blackbirds were gone before her backside left the cushion.

'Leave all this,' said Annie, 'I'll clear up.'

'Sure? I need an early night. I'll be gone before you get up.'

Annie sat on in the evening warmth. A swallow darted four, five times over the patch of lawn, swerving with astonishing deftness. A skein of geese passed high overhead, a silent chevron of birds rippling across a sky that was almost white.

By an outdoor light in a corner of the verandah a spider wove a web. In little more than an hour it built a trap a thousand times the size of its own humped body. Once a series of three small aftershocks rattled the house in quick succession, shivering the ironwork. The web just gave with the world and stayed strong and the spider didn't pause in its work.

Evening sank towards night. Bees ceased to hum and fumble. The day's insects died or shrank into the slits and splits and cracks and underhangs of the house. A mosquito whined at Annie's ear. Moths batted her face. And down at her feet she heard a chink of cutlery. A hedgehog was snuffling at the congealed remnants of the pasta bake, nudging knife and fork out of the way. In the jungle of suburban Hornby Annie could hear the little beast snuffling and snorting. In the gloom she could make out its shape but no detail. She rose softly from her chair. The beast half-coiled on the instant. Annie turned on the outside light. The coil became complete, a ball of brown spikes, perfectly folded, the joins invisible, impenetrable.

Annie's movements had affected the little garden world more than the aftershocks. Slowly its life resumed. Moths besieged the light, clambering over each other in a bid to burn. Most somehow blundered past the web, fluffing its edges, blind to the narrowness of their escape, thousands of them, millions, in one small garden.

The hedgehog unfurled and scuttled off with monomaniac intensity of purpose. Scorched moths fell from the bulb and writhed on their backs, broken, spinning desperately on the polished wooden deck. Annie gathered up the crockery, came back to turn off the light, said goodnight to the world and went to bed, feeling easier of heart.

Chapter 18

Dawn finds him on his back. As he wakes, a tongue of sun, oblique through the window, lies slantwise up his body, and without moving he studies what it illuminates, as if it were a court exhibit. The distant toenails, thickened and yellow-grey, like aged dried resin. Each foot a fan of bones and tendons, so close to skeletal, yet topped with a feeble tuft of hair, a faint, ridiculous primate legacy. His shins gleam like cracked old Sellotape.

The bathrobe maps the contours of his midsection until the rift of the lapels reveals the sternum, sallow, sown with scrubby hair, like bleached badlands. He surveys it all with indifference, surprised by its tenacity, this all-but-gone thing. He looks on it as one might an insect on its back faintly stirring its legs by reflex, but without hope or purpose, awaiting only the moment of expiry or the quick thoughtless jab of the bird's beak. This husk, this bone bag.

Friday, curled on the counterpane, has woken with his waking, and without unfurling is watching him be. He reaches out and lays a hand on the dog's flank, feels the ribs through the fur and skin, the healthy warmth, hears the dog's tail beat against the bedclothes once, twice.

'Friday, Friday,' he says and the dog slithers off the bed and stretches, a long, loosening concave arching of the skeleton from back legs to hips to spine to shoulders and neck.

'Oh Friday,' he says and smiles despite himself. With a sigh he swings his legs off the bed and stands but he is feeble and he sits back down, his hands on his thighs. He is acutely conscious of his breathing, and dizzied by what feels like a stream of little bubbles in the head.

'Patience, dog,' he whispers, because to speak any louder would take energy. 'Patience.' But the needs of the dog oblige him and he heaves himself to his feet, keeping a hand on the bedside table. He slides bone-fan feet into fluffy slippers, and shuffles towards the door, not raising those feet, one hand out to steady himself at all times, against the wardrobe door, the wall, the back of a chair.

Sunshine does not reach into the corridor. He misses the warmth on his flesh, and he struggles to open the fire door on either side of the stairwell. On the second of these doors, the dogs stands on its hind legs and scrabbles with its front paws and its extra weight helps and the door opens on what he thinks of with a shudder as the corridor of catastrophe.

Flies still. Despite the bleach. Not in such appalling abundance, but attendant, hateful. He shuffles past the scene of collapse, drawn to the bright-lit frame of the doorway, grateful that the rubber plant is still blocking open the heavy door. And they are out on the rooftop again, and his flesh, like a lizard's, drinks at the warmth of the sun.

The dog wanders down the ramp to piss, sniffing at the walls and concrete as it goes to check for evidence of interlopers in the night, and finding something of interest on the way, to sniff at protractedly and then to cock a leg above, to overscent.

Richard grips the back of the chair, wheezing a little. It comes to him that this is where and how he will betray the dog. He will shift the planter and the heavy door will fall shut with him on one side and the dog on the other. And then, he tells himself, he will withdraw deep inside the building, will put walls and doors between himself and dog. Every dog is a pragmatist. If scratching and whining do not work, in the end the dog will stop scratching and whining and will go elsewhere. The key will be to go beyond earshot.

It will not be long. He has Tux for perhaps another week. But he could not mount another raid on the convenience store, even if he wanted to.

While waiting for the dog now, he sits at his little concrete shelter, his head in the shade, his legs in the sun. He pours Evian into Friday's bowl, and some into a glass. To which he adds, after thought, a miniature of vodka. It is the purest drink, wisest for a fragile morning. He is aware of drained strength.

A flutter, a beating, a brief clamour of wings and the pigeon lands unsummoned on the rooftop by his chair, lurches to the dog's bowl and dunks its beak. Richard watches as it drinks, not raising its head to tilt the water down its throat as other birds do, but sucking at it with its beak immersed for several seconds. He admires the petrol sheen of the bird's neck, the layered loveliness of its wing feathers. He crumbles a little biscuit on the arm of the chair. The bird cocks up a round black eye, assessing, seemingly unworried, then crouches and launches easily upwards to peck at the crumbs.

Friday, his reconnaissance done, comes loping towards them. 'Sit,' says Richard when the dog is still a few yards away and it pauses in puzzlement. 'Sit,' he repeats and with infinite slowness the dog lowers its haunches, its eyes scanning Richard for some explanation of this strange behaviour. Richard offers none till the dog's rump touches concrete, then he smiles. 'Good boy,' he says and lobs a chunk of biscuit.

He pops a chunk into his own mouth at the same time, and lets his saliva soften it before he takes it on with what remain of his teeth. When he swallows he is surprised by the almost immediate sense of gained strength. The blind urge to get better, to re-establish wellbeing, hard-wired into the flesh, uninfluenced by the will. He raises his glass, and the bird, without alarm, hops down and conducts a rocking club-footed tour of the area around the chair, and Friday, now familiar with the idea, lets it be and drinks instead, sloppily, noisily, wastefully, from his bowl of mineral spring water that people once brought all the way from France.

* * *

Jess had gone to work. Annie peeped into her room. A double bed, the sheets royal blue, the duvet flung in a heap. It screamed not just of living alone, but of expecting to continue living alone.

Annie took her coffee onto the verandah. The web by the light was tattered and sagging, its edges ragged and two large holes torn into it. Annie touched its stickiness, shook her finger, and the spider stirred, half unfurling itself from a corner of the woodwork then pausing, reassessing, shrinking back into its crack in the world.

The phone rang. 'Have you heard from Hamilton yet?' asked Vince.

She was mildly surprised that she hadn't. And besides, she didn't see how anyone could ignore the simple personal appeal of her quest. A daughter seeks her father.

'He's in hospital,' said Vince.

Vince was clearly a far more diligent and effective sleuth than she. Karl Hamilton, it seemed, had been at lunch in Cashel Mall when the quake struck. They'd had to dig him out. A crushed pelvis and sundry other injuries. He would be in hospital for a while yet.

'How on earth do you find this stuff out?'

'I'm learning as I go,' said Vince, but with more than a hint of smugness. 'A late participant in the information revolution. Anyway, do you want to go and see him?'

Did she? She was no longer sure.

'Annie?'

145

'Sorry, yes, just thinking. Is he visitable? I mean, can we just breeze in?'

'According to his wife, yes. He's bored stiff.'

'His wife?'

'Yes, I rang her. Lives in Mount Pleasant. But don't worry, I just said I was an old business contact. Apparently he's strung up in traction and there's only so much daytime television a man can cope with. Will you go? Because I will if you don't.'

* * *

On the floor above the car park roof Richard is in search of bottled water for the dog. He finds it in a conference centre along with data projectors and spiral notebooks and hotel-branded ballpoints and cupboards packed with paraphernalia: boxes of gilt candelabra; a disco mirror ball; a set of fashion mannequins with curved plastic bodies; Christmas decorations and a Santa Claus outfit; half a dozen banjos; a dozen parasols still in their original plastic wrappers.

Beyond the conference centre, double doors open onto a grand hall or auditorium, abandoned in the process of being set for a banquet, with round tables spread about the floor, and thick, stiff tablecloths spread over them, now wearing a dandruff of plaster. Friday scours the corners, the skirtings, perhaps the first dog ever to walk this floor. Richard sits at a table, tired from the ascent of two flights of stairs. The dog finds nothing of interest.

'Shall we throw a party?' says Richard.

The dog's ears prick at the tone of voice and its eyes brighten.

'You can be guest of honour, Friday. It's a sad dog that doesn't love a party.'

And Richard laughs and coughs and hunches over the table, spluttering, and a sudden stab in the gut makes him fear for his bowels. But they hold, and in time he sits up again and reaches into the pocket of his robe and chooses at random from the miniatures jostling within it and fishes out a Gordon's. His fingers tremble as he raises it to his lips and sips it neat.

'The Last Supper, Friday. What do you reckon?'

And with the gusto of his kind Friday gives every sign of approving.

Chapter 19

Prince William was coming. He had been dispatched on a condolence tour of bits of the former empire that had been thumped by calamity. Christchurch was his last stop. He would be taken on a tour of the central city, a place still forbidden to those who lived or worked there, and he would be guest of honour at a memorial service in North Hagley Park. They were building the stage for it now.

On her way to the hospital Annie was typically early. Though it was now officially autumn, the sun retained the intensity it rarely seemed to achieve in Turnpike Lane, biting at her forearms with carcinogenic seduction. Annie loved it. Who was the character in a Mansfield story, stuck in a London winter, whose whole being unfurled and reached towards the memory of sunshine, the idea of warmth?

Three trucks stood by Victoria Lake, scaffolding poles on their flatbeds, wiry men tossing them onto the grass with a clang. Was that a wolf whistle? She looked around. A skinny guy in jeans and singlet on the back of the truck was smirking at her.

She couldn't remember when she'd last heard such a whistle, and as for one aimed at her, well, she'd never been the type. She'd always supposed it was something to do with her height, the curly hair that she kept cropped short, her long, quick stride. In her experience, the women men whistled at, or used to, were doll-like creatures who flaunted breast and hair and hips but who were also small enough to be dominated or protected. But what was the guy on the truck expecting? Why bother? Did he imagine it was a compliment? Or was there some sort of irony to it?

But the man did not seem troubled by any thoughts of this nature, indeed by thoughts of any nature. He had apparently forgotten Annie already – that was more true to form – and was now blithely and usefully lobbing clamps onto a pile, each landing with a satisfyingly metallic clunk.

With time to kill Annie took a seat by the little artificial lake to watch the stage being built, the stage that in a few days' time would be trodden by a future king.

That king was engaged to be married. His Kate, who would not be accompanying him on this tour, had done what a million girls had fantasised about, especially when William was at university and briefly boy-band beautiful. (Though how rapidly that beauty had faded. His hair had thinned, his cheeks had lost their roses and month by month you could just see him becoming his own heavy-jawed uncle. It had been almost cruel to watch.)

Kate nevertheless remained in the role of Cinderella, that most enduring piece of mental furniture for girls. At home in London now, preparing for their wedding and imprisoned by a phalanx of telephoto lenses in the street below like a machine-gun battery trained on her night and day for the rest of her life, Kate was about to embark on the good ship *Happily Ever After.* Just as William's mother had.

Annie had been in the sixth form when Diana died. On Avonside Drive, half a world away from Paris, girls clung to each other and wept. Jess had openly scoffed at their red-eyed misery in a way that Annie admired but would not have dared. But the mournful had drawn succour from each other, feasting off each other's emotion and generating something close to a firestorm of grief, or at least of the symptoms of grief. But for what? What precisely were they mourning? Annie hadn't known then and didn't now.

All she did know was that it was part of the same odd emotional dependence that made William's visit the opportunity for a memorial service. Though many had said that it was too soon, that the feelings remained raw, that there were still scraps of flesh unretrieved in the burnt rubble of one building.

'May I?'

An old man in trackpants was gesturing at the bench.

'Of course,' said Annie and she hitched her tote bag needlessly a little closer to demonstrate her acceptance. The man lowered himself towards the bench but with six inches still to go gravity proved stronger than the muscles of his thighs and his backside finished its brief descent in a sudden rush, a plummet. He gave a little gasp. Annie felt the planks of the bench flex and rebound, like some sort of indecent and intimate connection.

The man was breathing heavily, leaning forward with his fists on his knees. Annie waited. She looked away to where the workmen were still lobbing clamps from truck to grass, but the start of a conversation clearly hung in the air between her and the old man, awaiting only his recovery from the exertion of sitting.

'Buried a friend last week,' he said, and rather than turning his head to look at Annie he swivelled the whole of his body, as if his neck were a single bone.

'Oh,' said Annie, 'I'm sorry,' and she began to plan her departure.

'You've got to wonder where he is.'

'Indeed,' said Annie.

'I mean we were told as kids that heaven was up there,' and he pointed briefly and with some difficulty skyward, seemingly restricted in his movements as if not just his neck but most of his skeleton was somehow fused. 'But I've been up there, and there was no one there, well at least up as far as 95,000 feet.'

He started to breathe heavily and fast and Annie was alarmed until she realised he was laughing. Again he swivelled his frame to look at her, to see how well his wit was going down. Despite herself, Annie tried to look as if it was going down nicely. It did not feel convincing to her, but it seemed to satisfy him.

'US Navy fighter jet,' he said. 'Nineteen seventy-eight. Ninety-five thousand feet and nobody up there. Not a soul,' and the man resumed his heavy-breath chuckle.

'I see,' said Annie.

'And if you started to dig, right here,' and he scrabbled briefly on his knees with his fingers as if playing a snatch of Chopin, 'and you kept on digging right through the centre of the earth, if that was possible, which it isn't, of course, as we know' – he paused to breathe a bit, to recover – 'do you know where you'd pop up on the other side, do you know where our antipodes is?'

'Portugal,' said Annie and instantly regretted it.

The man did not reply. He was clearly accustomed to conversations that were effectively monologues, that required from his audience only expressions of assent. Annie had shot him down. She could feel him striving to reinflate the balloon of his self-confidence.

Why could she not have let him bore her for a bit more and then slip away? Why did she have to wound? She was as bad as he, really, well no, not quite… 'I'm sorry,' she said, 'I must be going.' She stood.

'I'm seventy-seven today,' the man said. He said it as if playing a picture card. And he looked up her in rigid appeal, his eyes reverting to liquid, his mouth pulled slightly open, his teeth ruinous.

Oh God, thought Annie. 'Many happy returns,' she said and she reached out and patted the old man on the shoulder, as one might pat a child. His shirt felt damp and clammy. 'I'd love to stay and chat but I really must be off.'

From the look on his face it was impossible to tell whether she'd repaired the damage she'd done, whether he'd forgotten her sharpness. She hoped so. The best you could do in this world, she supposed, was to avoid causing unnecessary pain. Though why it was always she and others like her who did the avoiding… Well, she had no answer but to flash the old man a smile, turn and walk away. Was it really his birthday? She doubted it. But better, by far, to go along, to pretend.

Still with time on her hands, she followed the loop of the Avon through the park, looking across the weed beds and the gravel bottom sprinkled with beer bottles to the botanic gardens it enclosed. Sunlight shafting through foliage lit patches of water to an old green gold. She glimpsed an eel nosing under the far bank, a grey-faced heron poised immobile and intent. She stopped to watch, stood as still as the heron.

Seventy-seven. Did anyone get to seventy-seven well? He'd been to 95,000 feet in an American plane. You didn't invent detail like that. He must have been someone, as it were. And a husband? A father? Most men were, weren't they? His kids then, now forty, fifty years old, families of their own, did they know where Dad was on what may have been his birthday? Did they know he was accosting strangers with stories in a park? And if they did, did they care?

The heron bent towards the water with infinite slowness. Patience, that was the quality. The bird stabbed the water and came up with a fingerling held crosswise in its beak, wriggling but hopelessly pinned. With two flicks of practised deftness the heron aligned the fish with its gullet and swallowed it whole and wriggling, down the long and pretty throat to where it would writhe, briefly, in gastric juices, and then die.

Vince was waiting in the foyer of the public hospital. With him a tall grey-haired woman in dark linen trousers and a white shirt.

'Mrs Hamilton,' said Vince. 'Denise.'

'We've met before,' the woman said without smiling, or offering her hand, 'though you wouldn't remember. You were two. How's your poor mother?'

In the lift to the fifth floor, Denise stood facing the doors, as if willing them to open.

Annie flashed a look at Vince, who gave her the faintest of shrugs. It wouldn't have been hard for Vince to find Denise, but why was she here now? Annie sensed again a web of stuff, of complexity. But then, it had been twenty years. A lot happens in twenty years.

The fifth-floor corridor was the essence of deepest hospital, the linoleum uniquely cushioned, swabbed and squeaky, and the smell of disinfectant. A high-sided cot bore a load of scrawny age, white haired and shrunken, propelled by a porter in pastel pyjamas. Nurses with strong calf muscles, a white-coated doctor toting the stethoscope that Annie always suspected them of wearing as a badge of status. Why did nurses never have one?

Were they not allowed to use them? Their heraldic device was the fob watch inverted.

Somewhere in this warren of a building, Jess would be cheerfully bullying staff and patients for their own good, making things happen, scrubbing the world with her energy and forthright courage.

Denise led the way, striding past wards and windows and dispensaries, and sanctuaries for nurses only, and rooms where patients sat in dressing gowns and stared at televisions, and a waiting area where three couples in their sixties sat in outdoor clothes and it wasn't immediately clear which of each pair was sick.

They stopped outside a ward. 'Would you mind?' said Denise, gesturing to them to wait in the corridor, and she went in without waiting for a reply.

'She insisted,' whispered Vince. 'I could hardly say no.'

'It doesn't matter.' They turned to the window overlooking Hagley Park. In the distance she could make out the vast acreage of netball courts, where she'd spent so many winter Saturday mornings in what seemed now like another world. And as she'd played on one particular Saturday twenty years ago, had her father lain up here all broken and alone, unvisited perhaps?

'Darling,' said Denise in an overloud, oversolicitous voice, 'this is Annie, Raewyn's daughter, you remember? She's come all the way from England,' and she gestured to Annie to step forward, as if directing a play.

Karl looked like a patient in a cartoon. One leg was plastered and held off the bed by wires and ratchets, and round his hips was a sort of metal girdle, a shiny immobilising clamp. Threaded metal rods with wing-nuts on them appeared to pass directly through the clamp and into his flesh and presumably bone. It was hard to look at.

'Annie,' he said, and he smiled softly, and held out a hand to her, which she took as if to shake but he just laid it across her palm and kept it there, holding hands as little children are supposed to do, though Annie couldn't remember ever having done so.

'Let me look at you,' he said and Annie remembered him, remembered the size of him, the shape of his mouth. She remembered him standing against tall sash windows, windows full of sky, and other men sitting on stools at angled drawing boards. He'd been wearing green corduroy trousers, ribbed like a ploughed paddock, and an open-necked shirt. The neck of his pyjamas now framed a forest of hair, a simian mat of it, greyish and swirled like seaweed.

'It's your birthday soon,' said Karl. 'Am I right?'

Annie looked at him in a surprise that threatened to become pleasure.

'Rich always took the day off. He had it written into a contract. I thought it was a joke at first. I mean we were friends. We didn't have to put stuff like that into contracts. But he meant it, and he kept to it, even after, well...'

He turned his head a little towards his wife. She looked tart, pursed, tense.

Annie watched as he seemed to struggle with his thoughts. His face darkened and then seemed almost to crumple.

'I'm sorry, Annie. I did what I could. But nothing did any good.'

'You did everything anyone could do,' said Denise. Sitting on the other side of the bed, she had kept a proprietorial hand on her husband's forearm. She patted the forearm now, as one might comfort a child. 'No one could have done more.'

'It was all such a shame.'

'What was?' said Annie. 'What was such a shame?'

But the big man on the bed had closed his eyes and he was gulping.

'That's it,' said Denise, standing up and taking command. 'No, that's it, I knew this would happen. I must ask you to leave now. Now.' And she turned, eyes wide, and shooed Annie and Vince away from the bed. 'Go now, please, just go now,' and as the two of them retreated she pulled the curtain round the bed. From behind it there came a sort of long moan, a strange, keening sound, almost a wail. A nurse clip-clopped past them at speed and slid through the curtain.

Denise emerged. 'Go,' she said fiercely, 'I said go. The pair of you. You've seen the state he's in. You've seen what you've done. I want you to leave now.' She advanced on Annie and Vince flapping at them with her hands as if shooing geese, forcing them back into the corridor and then down it.

'I'm sorry if...' Annie began but Denise was having none of it, and they went, Vince leading the way through swing doors that gave onto a set of stairs. The doors closed behind them. Denise didn't follow.

'Jesus,' said Vince.

Chapter 20

'A tube of delight,' he says, sitting back and fitting the cigarette into a crook of his left hand. 'Not that you approve, eh Friday? But you fit the world better than we do. You're happy here, aren't you, you dumb brute?' And the dog responds to his tone by looking up into his face with eyes the colour of old furniture.

Richard sucks at the smoke with caution. Coughing threatens his bowels. Infirmity he can cope with. But his bowels appal him.

The dog is licking at Richard's calf, persistently, firmly. The flesh tingles. Richard leans forward, holds the dog's head away to one side, and studies the wound of sorts on side of the calf. Not a cut, just a split, like a lipless mouth. It isn't the first time he has noticed it. He doesn't know why it doesn't hurt. He presses the edge with his finger and a bead of thick fluid, maggot-coloured, forms in the heart of the lesion, swells as he presses until the dog licks it away, cleans the wound, the breach in his flesh. Richard is intrigued, not alarmed. Gently he tries easing the two edges apart. At the top of the lesion the skin is mica-like in texture and it tears suddenly with a little stab of pain and a rivulet of blood follows the path of least resistance down his calf until the dog cleans that away too with a single muscular slurp of the tongue.

'Good boy,' says Richard. 'And the women went to wash the corpse...' He giggles to himself, pulls a miniature from his pocket and unscrews the cap and raises it to his lips without looking and he knows immediately from the dirty petrol smell that it is Scotch and he savours the burn on tongue and throat and the sense of calm, the quenching of fires of unease.

He surveys the room. He has achieved little and it has taken hours. To move a single table takes an effort and then a rest, a drink, a regaining of breath and courage. But there is now at least the suggestion of a party, four tables brought together in the centre of the room and covered with starched white cloths, their folds still clearly visible. And Richard knows where he will find the cutlery and stemware, the decorations, the trimmings. But he has done enough for the day. It must be noon or so. He will take Friday to the car park roof and then if it is warm enough he'll sleep there beneath the little overhang, though if the wind is keen he'll go to a room.

'Here, boy,' he says as he raises the Scotch again to drain it, 'here, Friday,' and without looking down he feels the dog slide in beneath his left hand, soft fur against hard flesh. He strokes the dog and tips the little bottle and then he feels the dog stiffen, straightening its frame, suddenly alert. He senses the surge of a growl in the dog's throat. 'What is it, Friday? What is it, boy?' but even as he whispers he hears the drilling start.

* * *

'But why was he so upset?

'Search me,' said Vince. 'One minute he was holding Annie's hand and telling her when her birthday was and the next he was blubbing like a baby. And that's when she stepped in and shooed us out. Though she'd clearly been dying to do that from the start. Sausages are ready, by the way.'

'What was all that about "I did what I could"?' said Jess, laying out cutlery and crockery on the garden table.

'That's what he kept saying, and she kept saying it back at him. Which would seem to imply that it hadn't worked, whatever it was and whatever it was trying to achieve.'

'Or that he actually *hadn't* done everything he could and was feeling guilty about it,' said Jess, pouring wine into three glasses. 'So, where to from here? Annie?'

Annie didn't know. She had been touched by Karl's reaction to her visit, by the soft but insistent grip of his hand, by the way he remembered her birthday, by the sheer strength of the emotion that her father's memory had aroused, but she didn't feel she had any right to go back to the hospital and question him further. She didn't like upsetting people at the best of

161

times and he was clearly in a condition that didn't need more upsetting.

'If you don't like these, you don't like food,' said Vince, placing a plate of split and glistening sausages on the faux-rustic table. And Annie sensed in him once again a sort of prissiness, a neatness that was both appealing and slightly distancing. It was there in the way the sausages had been arranged on the plate, in the garnishing of parsley tufts from Jess's garden, in the cleanness and softness of his hands, the cut of his trousers. It had even been there, she thought, in those distant school photos. You could tell from the tie at the collar, from the better-ordered hair, that Vince would never quite be the one to let himself go, that he might ride pillion with anarchy for a while but in the end he'd dismount. Her father though, well, that hair of his.

'As I saw it,' said Vince, 'the old boy clearly felt that he actually could have done more to help Rich. And she clearly felt he'd done too much. In other words, he liked your dad, she didn't. Agree, Annie?'

Annie thought she did, on balance. But she wasn't sure it got them very far. Nothing much had got them very far. Detective work in real life wasn't like detective work on TV. The pieces of the puzzle didn't arrive neatly and sequentially and nor did they seem to lead to any solution. Indeed any additional piece of information seemed just as likely to complicate the mystery as to clarify it.

'Do you know anything for sure?' asked Jess. And over the course of a plate of Le Traiteur sausages, a bowl of mixed salad and two bottles of chardonnay they agreed that the only things they knew for sure were that Annie's father and Karl Hamilton had gone into business together the year before Annie was born, that Richard and Raewyn had got married six months before Annie was born, and, thanks to Vince's research, that the business had prospered throughout the 1980s, employing half a dozen draughtsmen until around 1990, when things started to unravel. Richard had an affair and either left home or was kicked out.

'Do we even know that for sure,' asked Vince, 'that he had an affair?'

'Mum was pretty emphatic about that, and she certainly played the part of a woman scorned.'

'And since then,' said Vince in conclusion, 'we know only that he suffered some sort of accident and underwent surgery, that he gave as his address a flat belonging to a prominent local family who claim never to have heard of him and that Karl bought him out of the business some time after that. Since then, nothing. For seventeen years.'

Silence. From over the fence on the warm, thick evening air came the uniquely cracked voice of Gene Pitney, 'Twenty-Four Hours from Tulsa', transparently faked emotion from long before Annie was born.

'Is he dead?' said Jess. 'Sorry, Annie, but it's got to be faced.'

'No,' said Vince. Annie shrugged. She'd entertained the thought, of course. Sixty didn't have to be old – Vince wasn't old. But Vince wasn't her father.

'Do you want to go on?'

'I think so,' said Annie. 'But I'm not sure what leads we have left. I'm going for lunch with the old boy on Park Terrace tomorrow and he's promised to drag Ben along. But if they had anything to tell me they'd have told me by now and if they were trying to hide something they would hardly have asked me to lunch. And I don't think we should really go and upset Karl again. Which leaves Denise. And she clearly didn't want to see us in the first place.'

'But why?' said Vince. 'There has to be a reason for feelings that strong. If you don't go and see her, Annie, I will. I've got the address.'

Annie smiled. 'I'll go,' she said.

'Have you thought, by the way, of putting a missing person ad in *The Press*, or even talking to a journalist? Someone out there must know something.'

'Yes, but Mum might see it. Or one of her friends who'd be only too pleased to tell her. And I really don't want her to know I'm here.'

'I thought you'd say that,' said Vince, smirking. 'Which is why I kept your name out of it. Is there any more of that chardonnay?'

* * *

The bus went only three-quarters of the way up Mount Pleasant. It was a remarkable journey. Larger and newer houses had crept up the hill, and the larger and newer the houses the greater the damage: panoramic windows split into vast shards; slab concrete walls thrown to Pisa-ish angles; plaster finishes torn like fabric; breeze-block walls with zigzags through them. On the corner of Oceanview Terrace a house was held up by three wooden buttresses each ending in a free-standing cube of concrete. But from right up there on the outer edge of the Lyttelton volcano you still looked out over the glitter of the Pacific, with nothing but water between you and Chile. And gulls rode the wind.

A vast macrocarpa hedge, trimmed rectangular, and an arch cut through it with a wrought-iron gate. The path led down to the hefty white house, a thing of tilt slabs and plate glass and a triple garage with a swimming pool on top of it. The pool looked to be empty but the house seemed not too badly damaged. Annie made herself not hesitate before ringing the bell. Denise came swiftly to the door. Trousers and shirt again, pearls, expensively cut hair and immaculate make-up.

When she saw Annie her face seized.

'You,' she said. 'I thought...'

'I know,' said Annie, 'and I'm sorry to trouble you. But I didn't want to upset your husband again and I would like to find my father and clearly you know something I don't, so here I am.'

The living room was as Annie would have expected. Modish spare furniture, plain white walls, a slate-coloured carpet, a magazine-like cleanliness and a floor-to-ceiling window that overlooked the ocean and had somehow survived the quake. Denise didn't offer a drink. Annie's spine didn't touch the back of her chair.

'It's none of my business,' said Denise, 'how your father behaved towards his own family, but I find it impossible to forgive what he did to us. Karl bent over backwards to help him and yet he still...'

'Please,' said Annie, 'can we begin at the beginning?'

There followed a series of questions from Annie and answers from Denise, who soon warmed to the task of putting her venom into words. She'd been suspicious of Richard from the outset when Karl had gone into business with him, but business was business and Karl said Richard had flair and anyway she was preoccupied with their children, three of them, all little and there wasn't much money around.

Annie had already noted the portraits on the piano, done in chalk and pastel, the kids' eyes unnaturally bright, the lashes lengthened, cheeks plumped, the easy lure of sentiment. Annie sensed, knew, that if she ever had kids she'd succumb to it too. Those kids on the piano would be Annie's age and more, would be parents themselves by now. Denise had been surprised but relieved when Richard had done the right thing by a noticeably pregnant Raewyn. Karl had been best man. Annie's birth had seemed to put Richard on the right track at last and for half a dozen years in the early eighties business had prospered. Karl had been able to take on staff and all seemed well.

'Then your father returned to his ways.'

'His ways?'

'The stories. It was all over town. It didn't seem to bother him that he had a wife and daughter. And it reflected on the business, of course.'

'What exactly...?'

'I'm sorry, Annie, but it's not my job to tell you things about your father that your mother hasn't. I'm not sure that I'd want to anyway. I know it's not fashionable but I happen to hold religious beliefs that say what your father did was a sin.'

Annie was on the point of interrupting but Denise swept on.

'Raewyn was dead right to kick him out. I begged Karl to do the same, to buy him out if necessary, anything, but Karl said personal life was personal and your father was the creative brains behind the business and so on. For me the firm was tainted after that. And I wasn't the only one. People didn't like it. Clients left in droves.'

A container ship bound for Lyttelton was steaming with infinite slowness across the sparkling horizon. And Annie noticed with a little frisson of shock that Shag Rock had all but gone. The old outcrop of rock that you could walk out to at low tide and clamber over, whose volcanic sharpness would rake your hands with a thousand tiny lacerations that stung in the salt water, had crumbled to almost nothing, levelled by the quake. Annie remembered the shape of it, remembered swimming further along the beach, remembered the dozens of happy dogs that romped there on weekend afternoons. Who else was in the picture? She could recall neither her father nor her mother. Only the dogs and the sharp scratchy rock and the blinding light on the sand.

The more Denise spoke the further Annie felt she was being taken from the remembered truth, the father who had shown her ducks, who had drawn for her, had held her to the window on a winter's morning.

'Of course,' Denise was saying, 'after his accident the writing was on the wall. He couldn't draw any more and that was the only thing he'd been good for. Karl tried to find things for him to do but nothing worked and he drank more and more and eventually Karl bought him out. Very generously, I might add, considering how he'd damaged the business's reputation. If it had been me, he'd...'

'Have you seen him since?'

'What do you think?'

'Thank you for your time,' said Annie. 'Please don't get up. I can find my way out.' And she did, astonished at her own abruptness.

Sin. The word rang in Annie's skull as she strode down Mount Pleasant Road. What had she meant? Did it matter what she meant?

That her father had had an affair? That he'd had serial affairs? That he'd had a gay affair? Whatever it was it had to be sex. Nothing upset a clenched woman like Denise as much as sex. Or rather the thought of sex. Or rather the thought of people enjoying sex.

Oh, how men screwed up over sex. With women it was the lure of love that felled them, the hope and the delusion of love, but with men, sex. Even her father, it seemed. Fathers were men. And men fell. Had she ever really known him?

When she reached the bus stop Annie kept walking. She wasn't due in Park Terrace till noon. She wanted to think and it was good to walk and the view from Mount Pleasant Road was startling, the sort of topographical panorama you never got from the city in a swamp. She looked now across the Heathcote valley to Ferrymead, where a swarm of primary-coloured concrete barns housed a supermarket and hardware stores and the surrounding salt marsh had become a car park.

Beyond lay the great blue sump of the estuary, draining plain and city, hooked in by the stretch of sandy spit that was South Brighton. There, thought Annie to herself as she counted the intersections down from the pier to Jellicoe Street, was the roof of the little wooden house where her father had grown up and which for Vince would always be the place where something happened that mattered more than almost all the things that had happened since. A little bit of love, beneath one tin roof out of thousands. And those thousands were dwarfed by the great sweep of Pegasus Bay, stretching far to the north until it reached the distant snows of the Kaikouras. To Annie's left the bulk of the city was little more than a smudge, its heart denoted by a scatter of taller buildings, but with nothing to tell you from here that it was no-go, was cordoned off, was most of it doomed to fall.

Somewhere in that city her sixty-year-old father might be living a life of sorts. But Annie was tiring of the search. And for the first time in a while she thought of Paul in London. Seen from this distance he looked good. Most people Annie met she found hard to define. They seemed such a mix of qualities, muddy and mingled, good and bad. Not so Paul. He was as clearly defined as characters in books and films. He was loyal and clumsy and honest. He could never be subtle or duplicitous or venomous or scheming. He'd do what he said he'd do. If he didn't like something he'd say either nothing or that he didn't like it. You knew where you stood with Paul.

And as for love, well now. The magazines were full of it, the movies were full of it, the arts both high and low were full of it – where would either opera or pop be without it? – but the world Annie lived in didn't seem full of it. It was a rare substance, it seemed, love, hard to define and far from durable.

Halfway down Mount Pleasant Road a roof of terracotta tiles had all but gone. The quake had simply flung them off, had scattered them like a wet dog shaking. It had left only a frame of wooden rafters to which a few last tiles clung. Annie could see through the frame of the roof to the sea below and the remnants of Shag Rock.

This part of the road was so steep that gravity all but hauled Annie into an involuntary jog. Up towards her came a hi-tech buggy, all plastic joints and buttons and moving parts, bearing a boy who looked old enough to walk. Behind him, head down so Annie could see only the crown of her hair, legs far out behind, a bag of shopping slung over the handle, the mother. The child, unaware of her fierce exertion, kicked his sandals against the footplate and squirmed as if bored. Annie wanted to slap him, or to help push. She did neither of these things. As the mother passed Annie heard the heaving of her breath.

Chapter 21

It comes from far below but after so many days of silence Richard senses it as though it were within his body, as if the building and he were the same thing. The drilling comes in bursts. He feels as much as hears the hardened metal biting into the concrete. Even here, so many floors above, it shakes the dusty air. He can see the motes jigging in a light shaft.

He has heard no preparations, no footfalls on the stairs or in the building. He has seen no vehicles or work gangs in the street. He keeps a calming hand on the dog's neck. When the burst of drilling stops the dog's neck muscles soften, the body shape changes. At the very instant it resumes, before Richard can register that it has resumed, those same muscles stiffen again. The dog thrusts its flesh forward to become tauter, taller, more massive under threat.

'It's all right, boy,' he says and he keeps his hand there, feeling for the time when the dog will relax. The drill is biting into the building. Perhaps a dozen years ago he watched the building going up, the giant foundation hole that the water had to be pumped from, the mass of steel, orange with brief rust before it was swallowed, encased by the concrete pours. The concrete trucks, whole fleets of them, like giant revolving eggs. It's into that concrete that they are drilling now, the concrete that's become the basis of his world.

He remembers hours spent watching from the benches in the mall, where the kids in low-slung trousers skateboarded and sometimes shouted out to him and he tried hard to say nothing back, but just to smile. They weren't bad kids, most of them, but they were kids, and he winces and dispatches the memory and reaches into his pocket.

The drilling is coming from a single corner of the building, the corner towards High Street. The dog whines, a noise it rarely makes, and Richard gets up without a plan and his thighs protest at the effort after the morning of work but he persists and the dog stays close as he crosses the banquet hall, leaning on furniture, against walls. On the landing he pulls open the smoke door to the stairs. The noise is magnified, bouncing off the raw concrete, the unsoftened surfaces. The noise gnaws at the skull. The dog hesitates. Its spine has curved towards fear, its tail quivers near its legs. Richard coaxes the dog through the door and together they climb.

He climbs to put distance between them and the threat. When a burst of drilling stops, Richard sags with fatigue, grasps the handrail, feels racked with infirmity. He looks up the well of the staircase. It is hard to tell how many floors remain. When the drill resumes they start upwards again, man and dog. Each step climbed is an act of flight, though the noise in the stairwell seems not to diminish. The space holds it, makes it ring.

Four floors, five, six, and it is clear now, when Richard looks up, that they are nearing the top. The drilling stops. Richard keeps going, hauling on the handrail. Five more minutes and they have climbed as far as they can climb. The stairs end in a door like any other, which opens onto a lightless corridor. Richard's slippers plough into deep carpet.

He gropes along the wall, finds a door frame, a handle, pushes open the door and is assailed by afternoon light that forces him to close his eyes and hold the jamb for a moment to recover from the sensory shock. He lets the light filter through his lids, the eyes adjusting slowly. Then he raises his good hand as a visor and opens them fully and here is a place of private luxury he had not thought existed.

Such glass. Floor to twice head height, and on the other side of it the city, the whole of it, spread out like a map. How it must have swayed up here in the quake. The place was vacated in haste. A low table lies on its side against the window, broken wine glasses nearby and some shrivelled dusty olives. Several Perrier waters, unopened, have been flung to the floor. With his slippered foot Richard nudges one of the bulbous little bottles, corrals it to where a pair of chaises longues are aligned to the huge windows. Wheezing from the exertion, he lowers himself onto the soft upholstery. When he unscrews the cap the water fizzes weakly. He sips at its peppery mineral warmth. The dog, intrigued by new territory, is fossicking round curtain feet and skirtings, has sniffed at blackened olives and found several shrivelled morsels to gulp down.

The view to the west and north is unimpeded. The alps like a young dog's teeth, the plains, the city in its entirety, the suburbs stretching to the sea, the winding silver ribbon of the Avon, the sea itself like wrinkled foil this late afternoon. And a sense of lordship, of dominion.

'I am the king, Friday,' says Richard and he chuckles. He swigs at the Perrier. But water is no drink for a king. The king rolls off the chaise longue onto all fours, then pushes with puny force on its frame to get himself to his feet. It does not take him much shuffling to find the bar. A glass-fronted fridge of champagne, a cupboard of standard spirits, most still intact, and another of lurid cocktail beauties, Curaçaos and peach brandies, several monk-brewed stickinesses.

Whimsically Richard mixes a Bénédictine and vermouth, pole-axer strength. He sighs at the imminence of relief, raises his glass to the dog, says 'Bottoms up', drains the glass, lets it shock his tongue and throat, and rests against the bar front as it seeps south. And he is seared with pain, a pain that doubles him over.

Hand on gut, groaning, crying, he fumbles along a wall and on a hunch he climbs a short stair, opens a door and he is in time. Sitting triggers a fierce and foul release, a draining ache of expulsion that makes him moan and bends him double, his body jack-knifed over his knees, his flesh suddenly sweat-drenched.

'Jesus wept,' he says. 'Jesus bloody wept,' as another burst, a racking, burning spasm, sucks all the strength from his body.

The spasm fades, the pain with it, like a wave receding. Calm comes, brief and sweaty, then the pain again like a knife thrust, a knife twist, that he's not sure he can bear and he writhes and screams and slumps. Again the pain withdraws, like a besieging army, gone away, he guesses only to recoup its forces, plan another attack. He sits still. He waits. His eyes are closed. He is scanning the horizon of his guts, surveying it in nervous dread of the first heralds of returning pain. If it comes again he thinks he will faint, will expire.

It comes again. He screams but it is brief and he does not expire. Relief. A minute. Perhaps two. He is scared to move, to hope even. But it seems to be over. He is sweating and he is cold. He is emptied. But already he is faintly yet undeniably reviving.

How persistent the body is. How independent of the mind. Its will to go on, to restart the stuttering engine, is beyond conscious control. It is wired in. It just is. Like the upturned fly that keeps buzzing its wings, trying to be again. And when even the wings fail it still feebly stirs the air with its feet, as if somehow there were yet a chance to recover. Flesh doesn't know the word hopeless. Flesh doesn't give up.

Still with his head down, his eyes closed, Richard becomes aware that the dog is at his side. He reaches out a weak hand and the dog comes to it, walks under it till the hand lies limp on the dog's shoulder. He draws strength from the contact, from the dog's mere being, from the heat of its flesh. 'I love you,' he says.

He opens his eyes, sees the dog's paws on the bright-lit tiles of the floor. Cautiously he raises his gaze towards the source of the light. The bathroom is glazed like the room below. The curved wall in front of him is a panorama of city, sea and mountain.

'Ha,' says Richard and he is surprised that the thought becomes noise, enough for the dog to turn its head towards him and its pure brown eyes. 'I love you,' he says again.

Chapter 22

When the lift doors opened a maid was waiting to greet her, a maid as in maid, black dress, white bib and frill, the works. 'Oh Jesus,' thought Annie, who was wearing cork-soled sandals, cheap calf-length cotton pants, a halter top.

'Shall I take your bag, madam?'

It was a tote bag from Santorini with a picture of a donkey on it. She'd bought it before taking a ride on a donkey. When she did she regretted both the ride and the bag. The beast was a slave. It lugged fat white tourists up and down the steep steps between port and town, driven by habit and the gruff men with whips and moustaches and roll-up cigarettes. The donkey had stunk and the ride had been physically as well as morally uncomfortable. Annie had dismounted halfway and walked the rest. The donkey had seemed not to notice. But you didn't waste a perfectly good bag. Annie handed it over.

'Annie, it is such a pleasure. I can feel my spirits lifting like a balloon. You look so very summery.'

He came in from the balcony overlooking the park, bent like a shelf bracket and leaning on his stick. Annie was awake to his flattery, the charm trowelled on so thickly it came close to being ironic, but she smiled nevertheless, was not displeased to see him. There was a value to the courtesies, the necessary lubricants of society, and a pleasure to be taken from his quickness of mind, however manipulative.

Behind the old man came Ben, silhouetted momentarily against the picture window, trim, almost boyish.

'My great-nephew. Have you met? I can't remember. Ben, Annie, Annie, Ben.'

The handshake took place from slightly too far apart. In profile in his car Ben had looked undistinguished, but now, front on, Annie could see how he had once been. A sensuous mouth, big eyes. She remembered the souvenired election posters.

'No, we haven't met. Though I have met Steph.'

'Really?' Ben looked momentarily alarmed.

'You were at work. Steph gave me coffee. Didn't she...'

'I can do better than coffee,' said David, and there was the maid again with a silver tray and flutes of bubbles. 'I trust you are not driving, Annie. And even if you are I shall insist on sending you home by cab. Nothing shall stand in the way of a proper luncheon to humour an old man.'

The spacious balcony had been set out with a table and chairs and sun umbrella. At each place setting a daunting array of forks, of wine glasses.

'Now,' said David, 'there is a reason for this little luncheon that I think we should get out of the way before we open the door to pleasure. As I have already told you, Ben, Annie is on a mission to find her father whom she has not seen for a long time. She has been led to believe that he lived here in this flat at the same time as you did. I have explained to her that this is impossible, but Annie is a young lady of admirable persistence who was unwilling to accept the word of a geriatric. So I have brought the two of you here together so that she could hear it from the horse's mouth, as it were, rather than from the mouth of the horse's great-uncle. Is that not right, Annie?'

Annie nodded and looked at Ben, but he was looking doggedly at the old man.

'I am truly sorry,' continued David, 'that we could not have been of more use to you in your search. But if there is anything that we *can* do, Annie, please don't hesitate to ask. The family has considerable resources and we are not without contacts in this city. Anyway, your very good health, my dear Annie.' He raised his champagne and the three of them chinked glasses.

'You go back to London next week, I believe. Perhaps you will be catching the same plane home as young Prince William. It is kind of him, is it not, to come all this way to condole with us when he is about to be married. But then that is the job of royalty, I suppose. I am thinking of renting out this balcony for the memorial service, or whatever the thing is called. It offers a perfect view. But I shall not be sitting out here myself to listen to the musical *pensées* of David Dobbyn and company. I am sure it is all very well intentioned but it does seem something of a mishmash, does it not? From Mr Dobbyn to a Buddhist blessing via Dame Malvina Major. But perhaps you have not seen the programme.'

'No,' said Annie, 'I haven't, I'm afraid.'

Ben had still said nothing.

'Every man and his dog,' said David, 'and his dog's favourite pop singer, and the pop singer's religious representative, and little Miss Westenra singing 'Amazing Grace' like the frightfully spiritual person that she no doubt is. But we all know who will be the star attraction. The crowd will flock to see William, with those equine teeth of his, and that unmistakably German jaw. Will he manage, what is the phrase they use these days, to bring closure? I fear he may have come a little early for that, perhaps, but who is to say what magic the royal touch cannot weave.' And he made such a theatrical job of failing to suppress a chuckle that Annie found herself warming to the old boy once again.

The maid brought out a platter of deep-fried prawns and other morsels on ceramic spoons.

'Please, Ben, Annie, do not stint yourselves. I am afraid I eat very little these days, the digestion not being what it was, but it gives me great pleasure to see a healthy appetite in the young. Just help yourselves. There is plenty of everything. Me, I shall merely sip at the glass that fortifies, if you'll forgive me. And please, Ben, Annie, do not allow me to prattle on. I spend so much time alone that I become loquacious in company, and when the company includes a beautiful young woman, well, I can barely contain myself.'

Annie looked Ben full in the face. He smiled in response but the smile seemed unlit from within.

'Tell me, Ben,' said Annie, 'what is it exactly that you do? Steph did tell me, I think, but I didn't really take it in.'

'Oh nothing much, this and that – the family business, you know.'

'No, I don't know.'

'Nor do you need to know,' exclaimed David. 'I am sorry, but I have not brought you here to talk shop. I was hoping that for once the conversation would soar on wings of inspiration, that it would transcend the humdrum and the everyday, and we would speak delightedly of, I don't know, of anything except the bloody family business. What do we think, for example, of our imminent controlled explosion, as if the phrase were not by definition an oxymoron?'

'I'm sorry?'

'Oh, perhaps you have not heard the news. We old men have so much time to read the paper we assume everyone else does. No, Annie, they have announced that they will bring down the hotel in town, the perilously leaning one, with a controlled explosion. It is apparently too dangerous to demolish by any other means. The decision has proved enormously popular. It seems that the earthquakes have done nothing to quench the human appetite for destruction. I believe the right to press the plunger is to be auctioned off, with the proceeds going to charity to ease the niggle of tastelessness. They will also be offering, if not ringside seats, at least seats at a convenient vantage point on, would you believe it, a temporary grandstand, as if for some sporting event. It's all a bit gruesome but apparently the precarious state of the building is preventing other work going on around it and it's all for a good cause and am I boring you?'

'No, no,' said Annie.

Ben was looking down at the table, apparently not listening.

The maid appeared with more and splendid food.

* * *

'I must be going,' said Ben. 'I'm sorry. Work. Thank you for the lunch, Uncle David. Can I give you a lift anywhere, Annie?'

'No, no, off you go, my boy. I'm afraid I'm going to keep Annie here a little while longer, not only to indulge an old man, but also for her professional skills. Meanwhile, dear boy, you must tend the family shop to ensure that I shall not be flung into a pauper's grave. Go on, be off with you and send my regards to your no-good father. Chop chop.

'Not the sharpest pencil in the box,' said David when they had heard the lift doors close on his great-nephew, 'but a nice enough young man and a surprisingly good father.'

'Surprisingly?'

'Oh,' said David, 'let us just say that there were times in his youth when one might not have predicted such a thing of him. But then we all have our periods, don't we? Especially in the turbulence of youth. Hormones have so very much to answer for. Stephanie has been good for him.'

'She didn't tell him I'd visited,' said Annie.

'Did she not? Well, I'm sure it's no concern of mine. Now Annie, I was serious when...'

'But you knew I'd been to see Steph. That's why you invited us here today.'

'Please, Annie, let us hear no more of this. I have kept you behind because as you can imagine at my age the doctors are forever foisting pills upon me. So many have now accrued that I am hoping you might cast a professional eye over them to reassure me with a second opinion, as it were.'

'I'm afraid I'm not a doctor.'

'Which is precisely why I have asked you, Annie. Doctors tend to see themselves as juju men and missionaries, savers of life, keepers of the great secret. They are, to be frank, smug. Whereas you, if you'll forgive the expression, it is meant as praise, are an ordinary woman, or to put it perhaps more felicitously, a woman of sturdy common sense. And if that sturdy common sense could just cast an eye over this battery of pills that seem to have become my lot in life, I would be forever grateful without holding you in any way responsible for any consequences, however catastrophic.'

The pills proved unremarkable, just the array, indeed, that Annie would have expected for an elderly man in reasonable nick but for some prostatic hyperplasia, elevated blood pressure and a little hardening of the arteries.

'You're in good medical hands,' she said.

'To hear that from your lips is the most enormous relief,' said David. 'I cannot begin to thank you.'

Though to be frank, Annie thought, he showed no signs at all of feeling relieved.

'Forgive me if I do not come down with you in the lift,' said David. 'I doubt we shall meet again. It truly has been a pleasure for me, even if for you Park Terrace has proved a dead end. And if I could offer you a skerrick of advice, as an old man who has had the chance to see a little of the world, I think you have done as much as anyone could ask in looking for your father. You owe him nothing. And you have a life of your own to live.

'But enough. I have, as you may have noticed, an appalling habit of playing Polonius. You must be itching to escape. The cab is on our family account. Please make what use of it you wish this lovely afternoon.'

The doors of the lift opened and Annie awkwardly half embraced the bent old man, laying a kiss of sorts near the bridge of his nose, and stepped into the lift.

'For the carnival is over. Bye-bye, Annie, bye-bye,' and as the metal doors came together he was waving with one old hand and with the other holding the walking stick that supported his slight and ancient frame. It was only as the lift was descending that Annie decided where she was going next.

* * *

'Is he expecting you?' said the guardian of the reception desk without warmth.

'No,' said Annie, 'but I think he'll see me.'

The woman made the sort of face that suggested she knew a bit more about such things than Annie did.

'I'll tell him you're here. What did you say the name was?'

'I didn't. Just say Annie.'

'Annie?'

'Annie.'

The first name clearly piqued the secretary's interest more than she wanted to let on. In a manner that struck Annie as last century and then some, she tottered in her heels to what was presumably Ben's office door, knocked on it with a single knuckle while putting an ear to the panel, then opened the door only wide enough for her to shimmy through, as though there were a bird flying loose in the office that could not be allowed to escape.

Ben emerged within seconds. When Annie saw his face it was as if the last tumbler had rolled in a complicated lock, and nothing now could stop the mechanism cascading till the door of the vault swung heavily open.

'Annie,' said Ben in an urgent, low voice. He named a bar on Lincoln Road. 'I'll see you there as soon as I can get away. I promise.'

And Annie went.

Chapter 23

He's made three place settings. Three knives at each, three forks, three spoons, set with sparkling precision on the gull-white cloth. Four glasses at each: a tumbler for water, a champagne flute, a tulip glass for the white wine, a balloon for the red. And he has composed an identical grove of mini-bar bottles at each place setting: wines, spirits, mixers, spring water. It has taken him all morning to fetch the bottles from the rooms. He has laid a Christmas cracker beside each setting, and cocktail umbrellas, and he has placed mini-bar food in courses: an hors d'oeuvres of Pringles, entrée of salted peanuts and main of a chocolate chip cookie. For dessert a thin bar of Suchard chocolate.

In the centre of the U formed by the three tables he has placed a bowl of water and a duvet folded to form a plump bed that the dog has already occupied. It lies and watches Richard work, its front paws crossed, its head laid to one side of them, its body a long stretch of spine that curls to allow the back legs to fold together on one side. When Richard pauses to recover from some small exertion, the dog's eyelids lower within seconds. When Richard moves again, whether in one minute or in five, the lids rise immediately.

The mannequins in the cupboard are low down and wedged in. Richard does not trust himself to bend so far, fearing nausea or worse. He drags a chair across, sits and pulls on a mannequin's arm, but he can get little purchase from his seated position. He undoes his dressing gown and pulls the sash from its loops. Still on his chair, he bends and loops the sash under the armpit of a mannequin and ties the end in a reef knot. 'Left over right and under,' he says, 'right over left and under' and he has a flashing memory of his grandmother tying… what? Parcels for Christmas, was it? And there had been a dog, a small white terrierish dog in the corner of the room, and he tries to add to the picture but is already losing the flashing vividness of the image, the felt reality, and he gives up, lets it go.

He pulls on the sash. The mannequin shifts a fraction, then stays wedged. He pulls again. Nothing.

'Here, Friday, here.' The dog rises slowly, stretches its front legs and neck in a slow luxurious bow, then the hips and rear legs, its spine inverted like the keel of a row boat. It pads across to Richard, its tail lazily swinging. He strokes the dog's head and neck, then offers the end of the sash. The dog looks at the sash, looks at Richard. 'Here, Friday, take it,' and he swings the sash, dangles it, in a bid to excite and entice. Half-heartedly the dog takes the end between its jaws. To get the dog to pull on it Richard pulls a little himself. The dog lets go.

Richard tries again. This time the dog won't even take the sash. It looks unnerved, worried. He calms the dog with stroking and soft words then slips the free end of the sash under the collar. 'Left over right and under, right over left and under,' he says again, though this time no image comes.

The dog squirms, ill at ease. Richard stands and goes towards the centre of the room, then calls the dog to him: 'Come, Friday, come.' The dog starts to move, feels the tension on his collar and twists a little to see what is holding it back, turns to nibble at the sash.

'No, Friday, no,' and the dog turns to look at him again, and he calls it to him and the dog obliges and hauls and the sash stretches. 'Come on, Friday, you can do it,' but the stretch of the sash goes only so far and then snaps the dog's head round and back and Friday whimpers.

'It's all right, boy,' and he steps forward and the dog jumps all over him in bewilderment and fear. Richard staggers but does not fall. 'It's all right,' he says again and he calms the dog slowly. When he tries to undo the knot on the collar the dog twists to see what's happening there behind his head, in the most vulnerable of places for a dog, and it nibbles at Richard's fingers. Richard says soothing things but the knot has pulled too tight for his fingers to undo and he has to unbuckle the dog's collar. Freed, the dog prances nervously around, shaking itself, puppyishly appeasing.

'Enough for one day,' says Richard. 'Enough.' And as the dog begins to settle he rootles in his pocket for a drink.

Chapter 24

Despite having drunk several glasses over lunch, Annie ordered wine. The bar was afternoon empty but for a young couple so engrossed with their cell phones that they seemed not to register the presence of each other, let alone the rest of the world. In a corner a battered old man playing a pokie machine. River Queen, the machine was called, and it bore a picture of a half-naked Amazon of sorts posing on the prow of what looked to be a Viking long boat. Her hair streamed, her breasts were metallic cones and her lips were plump as sofa cushions. But she was not generous to the battered man, whose breasts slumped unconically and whose lips were grey and whose sweater had holes around its limp base and who was mechanically feeding money into River Queen's slots. His face betrayed no emotion as she gave him nothing back.

Annie sipped her sauvignon. Part of her wanted to laugh. Here she was having crossed the world to sit in a shabby bar waiting for a man in middle age to tell how he'd had an affair with her father. And she wondered now whether she'd known for a while.

When Ben arrived the couple did not look up from their phones and the old man did not look up from River Queen.

'Annie,' said Ben. He sat on a stool across from her at the leaner. He looked a different man from the man she'd met over lunch. 'Look, Annie, I...'

'I know,' said Annie. 'It's okay.' And she smiled.

Ben looked at her and she watched his lower lip pucker like a child's, and he gulped as if trying to keep something down, and then his face crumpled. Now the battered old man did look away from River Queen. He swung his head slowly around and locked his gaze on Ben. But having stared fully and frankly for several seconds without any change of expression, he turned back to the bleeping, flashing machine.

Annie stepped off her stool, put her hand on Ben's shoulder and kept it there a while. Then she went to the bar.

'He all right?' said the barman.

'Fine,' said Annie. 'Just fine. Women trouble, you know.'

'Tell me about it,' said the barman.

'I'm sorry,' said Ben taking the drink. 'Embarrassing.' And he blew his nose hugely like a child.

Everything Ben told her, it was as if she had already known it. He spoke of her father as she remembered him.

'We'd been seeing each other for a while. Rich hated the deception of it. I begged him not to tell Raewyn. I could see it wouldn't turn out well. In the end she found out from someone else. And she just went for him. Called him everything under the sun. Filthy fag. Shirt-lifter. The works. How was her daughter supposed to cope with having a pervert for a father? All of that and then some.'

'Seriously?

'Do I look like I'm joking?' said Ben. 'She told him to get out and stay out, never to come anywhere near you. So he did. He thought it was simplest. For you.

'He used to spy on you. You didn't know, did you? Sometimes he'd watch you coming out of school, playing with friends. He'd report you were looking happy or had a new dress or had grown.'

Ben paused. 'Do you want me to stop?'

'No, no,' she said, and her voice came out steadier than she had feared it might, 'go on, please. Tell me.'

'I was young, remember, twenty-three, and my family had got its tentacles everywhere in this city, as you've seen. At Christ's College the honours board in the house I belonged to was covered with the family name. But mine was never going up there. I was no good at rugby and nothing special academically. There was this one teacher, with a pot gut and a little bastard of a moustache, he reckoned he'd taught fifteen members of the family and he was very keen to inform me at every opportunity that I ranked number fifteen.

'No one quite managed to pick that I was more gay than straight – it sort of wasn't really thought possible. Jeez, that place was a time warp – but I don't exactly look back on it as the best years of my life. And then I went off to varsity with no great ambitions. That's the trouble with a family like mine, you know you can't escape it and sometimes it's easier just to let it direct your life for you. I made a few little forays into the local gay scene, but it was hard because this is a small city where everyone knows you. But then I met Rich. And it was like opening a door into a different world.'

Ben was speaking now with the urgency and relief of confession. He held Annie's gaze. His eyes were greenish, his mouth wide and mobile. He had to be forty-something, but there was an innocence about him it would be hard not to warm to.

'In the world I came from,' he went on, bending forward over the leaner, 'all the big stuff was considered dealt with. Life meant doing well in business, making money. After that came raising kids, not disgracing the family, doing a bit of civic or charity stuff. No one ever said as much, of course but it was there behind everything that was said, lurking unspoken. It was in the water, for Christ's sake. You've seen what David's like. Brilliant in his way and dripping charm, but ruthless. It would never cross his mind to buck the system because we *are* the system. And it's been good to us. But with Rich, no, everything was different. Everything was up for questioning. Everything was to be doubted. And kindness mattered. "Be kind to people," he'd say, "be kind to people."

'I saw a TV programme recently about some Indian sect who sweep the floor before they sit down so they don't kill any insects. And I thought of Rich. A lover, not a fighter, as they say, and I'd never met a lover before. "It's what you go on for, isn't it?" he'd say. "Without love, why would you bother?" And he was right. I mean now, if it wasn't for my kids, well...'

Annie became aware that she had been holding her glass cupped between her palms. The wine was warm. She pushed it away.

'Can I get you another?'

She shook her head. She felt intensely alert.

'But he was down on himself. "What do you want with a broken down old man?" he'd say. He was, what, thirty-eight, thirty-nine, younger than I am now. He drank a bit but he was in good shape. If I told him I admired him, trusted him, fancied him or whatever, he wouldn't have it – he'd dismiss it or change the subject. Though it was a bit the same the other way round. I couldn't see what he saw in me. He was so far beyond me, so much cleverer, so much kinder, so much braver and so much more himself, I just couldn't see why he bothered with me.'

'I can,' said Annie.

'You're sweet,' said Ben.

His story was twenty years old but he'd never had the chance to tell it. It poured from him. Living with Rich hadn't been easy. Once the family found out, they'd leant on him. Uncle David was the patriarch even then. He'd worked on Ben subtly, pretending to sympathise, but sowing seeds in his head, tempting and manipulating. Underneath that mannered formality and old-world charm beat a heart of pure self-interest.

'Money became a worry. Rich gave almost everything to Raewyn and you. But then the business started to flounder. Karl used to come round for serious meetings sometimes. Have you met him? Lovely man, but he got depressed. Rich and he were partners but basically Karl was the businessman and Rich did the drawings. But this was the early nineties. Computers were just starting. Rich was a pen and pencil guy. And the company fell out of favour in town. Though I wouldn't be surprised if Uncle David had something to do with it.

'If I hadn't had the flat for next to nothing we'd have struggled. It didn't seem to bother Rich much, but it got to me. I suppose I was used to not having to think about money. It was sort of always there, not flashed around of course, but like a big cushion always behind you, the family stash. Rich said time spent worrying over money was time wasted, and he was probably right, but I was young and I wasn't strong and I worried. And then, well, you know about his accident.'

'Was it an accident?'

Ben sighed, paused. 'God, I hope so, Annie, I bloody hope so, but I just don't know. A jogger found him on the side of the road, down the far end of Salisbury Street, near the Barbadoes cemetery. His left hand and wrist had been crushed, run over by a car probably, bones broken. A raft of internal injuries, some of them serious, and his face had been smacked so hard the jaw was broken. He'd lost a couple of teeth and others were loosened. The cops said it was a hit and run. But I don't see how it could have been and no one's ever been done for it. Do you want me to stop?'

Annie shook her head, not quite trusting her voice.

'I didn't know where he was. When he didn't come home I thought he'd just got drunk. It was only when Karl rang the next day that I worried. Karl got onto the cops and tracked him down in hospital. We went to see him together.

'They'd had to operate to save his hand, and the docs were worried about his insides, his liver and kidneys and that. But they had to wait for the swelling to go down.

'I went in every day for a week. With his jaw as it was he couldn't speak so I'd just tell him things. Sometimes I just read to him. *Robinson Crusoe*, would you believe? There was an old copy in the nurses' room. Rich seemed to love it. If the other patients were asleep I'd hold his hand under the blanket, his good hand. The other one looked done for, despite the operation. He was a wreck, Annie, a real bloody wreck.'

Annie had been looking down into the grey Formica of the leaner, hearing only the words, unaware of anything else. She glanced up now.

The bar had begun to fill. The working day was coming to an end and professionals, young and not so young, were dropping in, people in suits and shoes. The cell phone couple and the gambler had gone. River Queen was bleeping desperately for attention.

'Ben,' exclaimed a loud, wiry-haired lawyer type, glass of red in hand. 'Oh, sorry, am I interrupting something?' He ran his eyes swiftly over Annie, and gave Ben a hint of a smirk of approval.

'Roger, mate,' said Ben, 'good to see you. We must catch up. I'll call you tomorrow, okay?'

'Do you want to go somewhere else?' said Annie. 'You wouldn't want Uncle David to know about this.'

'Oh Annie,' said Ben, 'he'll know already. Or within the hour at any rate. You've no idea what this city is like. But don't worry. I'm in credit these days. And besides, that's pretty well it. I was reading to Rich one afternoon and he put his good hand over the book and I stopped and he gestured for a pen. I found one and he got me to hold the book open while he wrote on it. Of course he was left handed, so with his right he wrote like a four-year-old. "Bye," he wrote in great big clumsy letters. I laughed. He was tired and I'd stayed too long. I kissed him on the forehead and left. And the next day he'd gone, discharged himself.'

'Why?'

'I've often asked myself. I don't know. Pride, maybe, hating to be confined, looked after. But I knew he wasn't coming back to me. Now he really was broken down. He didn't want to inflict that on me. And I think he suspected that he'd got me into trouble with the family. That's what the "Bye" meant. And then of course things started to happen in my life. Great-Uncle David was all reason and kindness and full of suggestions. And I did a bit of work and finished my degree. And Steph virtually flung herself at me and she was good, funny company and everyone loved her and she came emphatically from the Christ's College/St Margaret's side of the tracks, and everyone liked us as a couple and, oh, it was easy, Annie, and I'm not a strong guy. And I love my kids. I bloody love my kids.'

He smiled. 'I seem to have gone on a bit. Sorry.'

'Ben, do you know where Rich is?'

'No.'

'Do you think he's alive?'

Ben paused, then shook his head.

* * *

On Lincoln Road the rush-hour traffic was nose to tail, frustrated by a forest of road cones steering it around drain covers thrust up by the quake. Annie was surprised by how unsurprised she had been by Ben's story. It was as if she had known it from the moment she saw him in the car outside his house. Every subsequent detail had confirmed it, from Steph's frostiness to old David's bombast, and Annie had merely been waiting for the truth to push its snout out, sniff the air and then emerge to show its form.

The truth of Ben's words had been incontestable. He spoke of kindness, brightness, selflessness. Though she doubted she was much closer to finding her father, if indeed he was alive, Annie felt pleased she'd come. She had discovered a part of his life that she hadn't known before, something to put under her pillow back in wintry London.

How tired she felt. It was warm early evening and she must have drunk close to a bottle of wine since midday. Now as she took a minute or more to negotiate the intersection with Moorhouse Avenue, a lone pedestrian in vehicle-land, where all was exhaust fumes and gritty air and car yards with plastic bunting and the airborne anger of engines, she felt drawn to the coolness of the softly dappled world under the trees of South Hagley. Crossing the footbridge over the stream that was little more than a trickle now in late summer, she lay gratefully down in the shade of a small oak. She lay on her back, crossed her feet at the ankles, closed her eyes and breathed slowly. In the membrane of her eyelids she saw the veins of tiny blood, sensed the pink thinness of skin, its translucent frailty, made of heat and light like the leaves of the oak, sensed the whole random mud-stirred arbitrariness of it in the sun through the leaves and the warmth of the ground and the pulse of the blood in her flesh. Tiredness stole at her mind, veiled it, shut it down.

Snuffling. A small tongue against her cheek. She was instantly awake and sitting upright.

'Bingo,' came a woman's distant urgent voice. 'Come here, Bingo.'

Bingo was a whippet, now cringing several yards away from Annie, a hunched and shivering beast, little more than a skeleton in skin, but one that could outrun the wind.

Annie made soft kissing noises and rubbed her thumb and finger together as if offering food. Nervously the dog crept towards her, allowed itself to be stroked gently under the long sharp jaw.

'I'm so sorry,' said the woman as she panted onto the scene. 'He's only a pup.'

'It's okay,' said Annie, 'I like dogs, don't I, Bingo?' and she ran a finger down the dog's spine, the ribs like a toast rack.

* * *

A copy of *The Press* lay on the bus seat and on the front page a picture of the leaning central city hotel, under the headline, 'What am I bid?'

The proceeds from the auction of the right to press the plunger would go to the mayoral fund. And a raised stage would be backed by a temporary grandstand on the riverbank near the Bridge of Remembrance.

The bus was virtually immobile on Riccarton Road. Annie took the cell phone from her Santorini bag and while she waited for it to power up stared idly out of the window. The pavements teemed. The mall car park was packed and a dozen vehicles toured it on the off chance, like opportunist predators. The quake had done nothing, it seemed, to diminish the urge to consume.

She turned a page of the paper and there was Vince. He was neatly dressed, his shirt open at the neck, posed for the camera, half smiling and cornily holding his old school photo, under the headline, 'Best friend sought after 40 years.' Inset into the photo and hopelessly blurred was a blow-up of Vince and Richard in the back row with their 1969 hair, and just visible in the air above them the wind-thrown magpie. Though the text made no reference to Annie, she felt within her gut a worm of unease.

The phone came to life with a series of bells and squeals. Though Annie's year of birth fitted her just within the generation that the advertisers considered 'tech-native', she did not see herself that way. She could manage the hardware, could intuit her way around a screen, but she would never love the stuff for itself, nor would she ever consider it fundamental to her life, a part of the way she lived. Her two-year-old phone was already considered retro by some of her friends, as if by retaining it she were making a statement.

She scrolled through the list of messages. Vince had repeatedly tried to get in touch. Jess twice. There was a text from Paul and one from, oh Jesus, her mother. As she brought it on screen Annie felt a gulp of something close to dread. 'Call me,' it said. That was all. Though Annie knew that there would have been an exclamation mark if her mother had known how to type one.

Later would be soon enough for Mum. She brought Vince's number up, then decided not to call. She wasn't sure enough of how she felt. She brought up Paul's text. Though technologically astute, Paul wasn't known for using the medium's communicative potential. 'Hi, Annie. Mother on tail. Good luck. P.'

And Annie felt suddenly like a schoolgirl, back on River Road, polite, deferential and scared.

Chapter 25

'But he had every right to do it,' said Jess. 'I don't see what your problem is. Your dad *was* his best mate, and he hasn't seen him for forty years. And since the quakes Vince is not the only one to feel that time may be shorter than we think and that if you want to do something, now's not a bad time to do it. And he's kept you out of it.'

'Yeah but...'

'But what, Annie? Are you scared that he might actually find him? Is that it?'

'Don't be ridiculous.'

'Then what's the problem?'

Annie wasn't sure. It was partly, she knew, the appropriation. This was *her* cause, her mission. She didn't want it diluted. A shameful selfishness, but there was no denying it lurked within her. But there was another reason for her unease at what Vince had done, something to do with its public nature. It simplified and coarsened what was a purely private quest. And then, of course, as Jess suggested, the publicity did bring a greater likelihood of learning what it might be easier, in the long run, not to learn.

'I just wish he'd asked, that's all,' Annie said weakly.

'And you'd have said no. Here, love,' said Jess pushing the bottle across the table, 'have a drink and stop worrying for once. You always were a worrier, you know, even at school. It had its uses, I'll admit. You acted as a sort of handbrake on some of the wilder stuff and you did sometimes usefully see difficulties before they arose. But you specialised in difficulties that were never going to arise.'

Annie smiled and poured what she promised herself would be the last drink of a long day. 'You could have done with worrying a little more yourself.'

'And a fat lot of good that would have done,' said Jess. 'Now shall I be blunt?'

Annie laughed. 'As opposed to your usual subtle and delicate?'

'Thank you,' said Jess. 'Look, there are three possibilities. You could go home without finding your dad, which may be the path of least resistance but it gets nobody anywhere. You could find he's dead. Or you could find him alive. What Vince has done is reduce the chances of the first and increased the chances of the other two and I say good on him. If he unearths some uncomfortable truths, would you really rather not know them? You're a big girl now, Annie. Now if you want some good news read the text I sent you while I fetch dinner.'

Jess swung her legs off the recliner and stood with a grunt of exertion. Annie noticed the bulk of Jess's calves, peppered with a few days' growth of black stubble, and felt a welling of affection for this woman, this friend of so many years. Like Annie she was just past thirty and good at her job and single and childless. Unlike Annie, she had no offer of marriage and children and was in danger of passing the point where either would become unlikely. And if she didn't marry, if she didn't have kids, if she just went on going on, being good at her job, an aunt to some, a friend to others, a forthright nurse who chivvied thousands back to health, was that enough? Or did it simply not matter? 'However you use it, it goes,' she thought.

'Twice-cooked melting pork belly,' announced Jess. The smell of spices brought a place to mind that Annie couldn't quite identify.

'You spoil me, Jess,' she said.

'Oh for God's sake,' said Jess. 'I like eating and I like cooking and you give me the excuse to do both. So shut up and eat. I hope it's okay. I saw it on the telly and my mouth watered so much I almost drowned. If you don't like it, don't tell me.'

Then it came to Annie: Gerrard Street, Soho, main thoroughfare of Chinatown, where the red ducks hung by their hundreds in the windows, their necks coiled like question marks.

At the touch of a knife the melting pork melted, the meat fibres drenched through with fat and spices. They gorged in silence for a while.

'You haven't read the text I sent you, have you?' said Jess. 'I'll save you the trouble. Karl's asked for you, Karl Hamilton, you know, all banged up in orthopaedics.'

'Why?' Annie looked up from her plate in surprise.

'Search me. But he wants you to visit without the dreaded Denise. Or Vince, for that matter.'

'Did you go up and bully him?'

'Perish the thought, sweetheart, I have my standards. No, Jenny from orthopaedics was talking to him after you'd gone and she knew I knew you and well, that's what he wants. I said you'd be sure to pop along tomorrow morning. Did I do right?'

She'd done right. As Annie was taking plates to the kitchen her phone rang. 'Mum,' said the screen. Annie let it ring. It was too late in the day and Annie had heard too much from Ben for it not to affect her attitude, her tone of voice. And she did not want an argument. Annie never wanted an argument. Even so as the phone rang its eleven rings she felt ill at ease. Blood was blood. Mother left no message.

The phone rang again over coffee. 'Vince,' said the screen. She wasn't sure that she wanted to talk to him either, but she reasoned that she would have to at some stage and now was as good a time as any.

'Annie,' said Vince before Annie could say any of the things she had a mind to say, 'I'm sorry. Your mother's on her way.'

'On her way? What, here? Now?'

'Tomorrow. She's flying down tomorrow.'

'She doesn't know I'm here, does she?'

Annie heard the hesitation. 'Shit,' she said. Behind her on the sofa she heard Jess laugh.

*　*　*

'One of her friends, apparently,' said Annie as she poured the coffee, 'saw Vince's thing in the paper, and let Mum know. And she put two and two together, rang her darling daughter in London, and got an evasive boyfriend on the phone. So she rang Vince, saying only she was an old friend of the family and she knew Richard had a daughter and suggested Vince went looking for her, whereupon Vince of course spilt the beans and there we are.'

'When does the eagle land?'

'Tomorrow afternoon.'

'Are you going to see her?'

'I don't have much choice, do I?'

'Sure you do. You're a free and independent adult.'

But even as Jess was speaking Annie was shaking her head. She knew she could no more not go to meet her mother than she could rob a bank. It was baseline morality, first principle stuff. The right thing. Where it came from didn't matter. 'Well,' said Jess, 'I'm a free and independent adult and she's not staying here.'

'Oh, I wasn't...'

'I didn't like her when we were kids, Annie, and I'm not going to give her the chance to start making a better impression on me now.'

Annie said nothing.

'Oh, for God's sake,' exclaimed Jess, bursting into laughter, 'it's only your bloody mother. And you're thirty years old. Come on, sweetheart.'

Despite herself, Annie smiled and then she laughed.

* * *

At three Annie woke. The night was stuffy, oppressively humid. Her head ached, her mouth was dry and she needed the bathroom. With a sigh she stood up. Jess's bedroom door was open. Rich, reverberant snoring. Aspirin, a glass of iced water from the fridge, and feeling the need for some uncontained air, Annie unlocked the back door and stood in her nightdress in the garden as a mad woman might. Light, fast-moving clouds streamed either side of an almost full and almost orange moon.

A noise to Annie's left and she swung around to glimpse the cat slithering over the fence. How different was the world at night, in Hornby, in Turnpike Lane, in Malawi, anywhere. We are so firmly day's creatures, putting such faith in our eyes, that when the light fades our other senses overcompensate and prickle our skin.

As Annie got back into bed she thought of her mother arriving. And that was that for sleep. Thoughts swelled in the darkness, rolled around and around. Annie lay on her right side, her left side, her back, her front. She kicked the duvet off her legs. She thought of birds flying, of open places she'd loved, of the Mackenzie Country where the tussock waves like skinny wheat and the roads are lined with lupins, images that she had used for years as tracks to follow till they faded into the different landscape of sleep, but nothing would do. She tried telling herself that it really didn't matter, that she could cope, would cope, that under the gaze of the moon it was a nothing, a triviality, that people were dying in a thousand places as she lay there and fretted about meeting her mother, that a week from now she'd have forgotten about it, would be astonished it had ever concerned her. But the pillow grew hot, the bed itchy, and the nightdress ruched around her flesh.

At five she gave up, lay on her back open-eyed and tried to think it through. It was guilt. She had deceived her mother, had come to New Zealand without telling her. She'd been wrong to do so. Annie rehearsed the arguments for the defence: that she was here on a mission that her mother would despise, that she was here only briefly, that she was in a different part of the country, that her mother had deceived her about her father's fate, that her mother was manipulative and selfish, that she, Annie, was over thirty and had been dutiful all her life. But though they all made sense they did not begin to outweigh the simple fact of her own wrong.

She heard Jess's alarm go off, followed a few minutes later by footsteps to the bathroom. Daylight cruelly fringed the curtain. The toilet flushed. The next thing Annie knew it was nine o'clock.

Chapter 26

The scaffolders had finished work on the stage. It stood skeletal on the parched turf of North Hagley, rock-concert size. A breeze picked up and dust devils flickered round the base where the turf had been worn to a crumble of earth. Men were now at work fitting plywood flooring and stretching vast blue tarpaulins to form the arch of a roof. Others ran spools of electrical cable out of vans full of electronics and laced them through and under and tied them to the metal frame with little plastic straps.

Stretching out in front of the stage, the space for the crowd, the congregation, was huge, several football pitches worth of sun-browned grass. The paper had speculated that fifty thousand or more would attend, one in eight of the city's population. But it did not suggest why. Was it a sense of community, a religious hunger of some sort, a need for consolation, or just a free concert with celebrities to gawp at?

Ministers of the Crown would be there, up to and including the prime minister, ministers of every faith from

Islam to Mormon, the ubiquitous mayor, leaders of the armed services, of the rescue services, of the police, pop musicians, classical musicians, all had been asked and all had said yes. And validating the whole strange exercise, poor Wills, condemned to a life of just such strange exercises, to playing a role from here to eternity. 'What very strange creatures we are,' thought Annie.

Across the river, she identified the balcony where an old man had sought to flatter and deceive her. But she could see no sign of him.

When she stepped into the ward Karl saw her immediately and smiled and beckoned her with his good arm. He seemed less tense, more mellow, though still strung up with and screwed into an array of medical paraphernalia.

'Are you allowed chocolates?' said Annie, pulling packages from her Santorini bag. 'There's fruit as well, though. Just in case. How are you feeling? It was good of you to ask me back. I'm sorry we...'

'Annie.' As he reached out his hand to take hers, she realised she had been gabbling. 'Thank you for coming. Denise doesn't know I've asked you back. Yes, I know you went to see her and I can imagine what she said. I asked you here just to apologise. In my current condition I've become more emotional but that's no excuse. No, no, Annie, let me finish. I owe it to your dad. He meant, he means, a lot to me. Though before you ask I don't know where he is. But I'll answer any questions you've got. Tell me what you know.'

When Annie mentioned Ben, Karl visibly relaxed.

'I wasn't sure how much you knew. That makes things easier.'

Karl had met her father at art school in Auckland. It was the early seventies and teaching representative drawing or indeed formally teaching anything was considered Victorian and repressive. 'We learned nothing,' said Karl. 'To pass the course you just had to keep breathing for three years. Rich just about managed that.'

As Annie had noticed before, when old friends spoke of her father, they bathed in the memories, smiled at them, seemed to shed the burdens of age. But then again, perhaps that was true of all reminiscing. The memory is a kind editor, compressing yesterday into a wad of rich experience, squeezing from it all the tedium and the routine, all the stuff that today seems crammed with. And though memory doesn't dump the bad stuff, it draws the sting from all but the worst of it and plays it for laughs.

Short of money like all students, Karl and Richard had formed a sign-writing company, jazzing up shop fronts. 'There are still a couple of places on K Road that are a Hamilton and Jones design circa 1971. We both had ideas but your dad did the painting. He had a brave hand. At his best, a few strokes of the brush and he'd be done.'

After art school, qualified for nothing but fearing less, they'd gone together on the more or less compulsory OE, shared a flat in London with an ever-shifting cast of young Australasians, and even done design work on a few shop fronts on the Earls Court Road. A Kombi van took them round Europe and Asia Minor at a time when it seemed so much easier to go from place to place. 'Though today's kids will probably be saying the same thing forty years from now. The older I get, the more I think the world changes less than we do. To the young the world is always full of promise, don't you think, Annie?'

Annie said something noncommittal, not wanting to break the narrative.

They'd parted ways for a while. Richard had spent time in North Africa but both had ended back in Christchurch the following year, where they founded an official business entity, Hamilton and Jones, Graphic Designers. 'Your dad was no businessman. I handled that. But he could draw, and he had a knack of fitting the design to the customer. He read them better than they often read themselves and drew the stuff they hadn't known they wanted till they saw it. And we were young enough to be seen as magazinish, trendy, cutting edge.'

Business went well, they hired staff and Karl married Denise. Richard would have been best man but he and Denise had clashed from the start. For a wedding present he gave them a drawing of a cat melting over a fence, done with half a dozen strokes of a charcoal pencil.

'I told Denise it was from an aunt in South Africa. She loved it, hung it in the hall at home. She often shows it off.' Karl chuckled strongly enough to rattle his metal girdle.

A nurse looked across from her station. Karl waved.

What had this big, soft man ever seen in Denise? She must have been a demanding wife. But people walked into marriage with their eyes open. Had Karl wanted someone to control him as clearly as Denise would have wanted to do the controlling? Annie didn't know.

'If your father had a weakness, it was sex. Nothing odd about that in a man, of course, but Rich seemed to need it. And he loved to walk on the wild side, as it were. You want me to go on?'

Annie nodded.

'When we were at art school it was still illegal to be gay. Can you believe that? Jesus, back then gay still meant cheerful. But if you knew where to look it was all over the place and Rich knew where to look and he actually seemed to enjoy the danger of it.

'He was like that for as long as I knew him. And when we got to London he just dived right in. He'd try anything. Some of the stories he told, honestly, a conventional chap like me could hardly credit them, and I doubt I got to hear a tenth of what actually went on. He settled down a bit when we got back here and went properly into business – he'd had a bit of a scare in Morocco, he told me, and besides he wasn't quite so young and reckless any more – but still, when he walked into the office one Monday morning and asked if I'd be his best man, it came as a shock. I met Raewyn that same week. She was a stunner, your mother.'

Annie had seen the photos – androgynous, skinny, waifish, frayed jeans, the defining late-seventies look.

'She was pregnant, of course, with you, several months gone.'

Karl paused, and looked at Annie enquiringly. She nodded.

'Your dad was never in love with Raewyn, but with you it was love at first sight. He'd bring you to the office for the morning as soon as you could crawl, and we had a little playpen built for you. And he did some great work when you were little. It was his creative peak, I think. We did so well, thanks to you, we had to move into new premises.'

'With tall windows,' said Annie.

Karl smiled. 'Yes, sash windows. They gave wonderful light. Happy times. Then he met Ben. He told me about it from the start. That was another thing about your dad – I never knew him tell a lie. It was as if the idea of lying didn't occur to him. He said he was in love and he was going to tell Raewyn. I begged him not to. I was pretty sure how she'd react. I got him to hold off for a week or two. I thought the affair with Ben would fade. All the others had.'

And here Karl faltered. Annie heard the catch in his voice, looked up and could sense the emotion welling inside him just as it had the last time she'd been there. She took his hand.

'It's all right,' she said. 'Take your time.'

She could see Karl doing battle within himself, fighting down a surge of distress, the mat of hair on his chest heaving as if alive.

A nurse padded over, straightened a sheet. 'Everything all right, Mr Hamilton?'

Karl smiled at the nurse. The way she had addressed him, as if he were a vulnerable child, seemed to make him pull himself together. She moved on.

'I told Denise,' said Karl suddenly. He looked straight at Annie, as if he'd overcome some hurdle and wanted her to see it. Annie looked back at him, puzzled.

'I told Denise about Rich and Ben.'

It was only then that Annie grasped what he meant. She shook her head in surprise and squeezed Karl's hand. 'It's all right, Karl,' she said, 'it's all right. Raewyn was bound to find out. If it hadn't been Denise, it would have been someone else. Besides, if it was anyone's fault it was Dad's. He had the affair.'

Karl looked at her directly. 'Denise couldn't stand Rich. He was too dangerous for her. She's a very conventional woman. She'd have seen it as her duty to tell Raewyn. I should have known.'

Annie wasn't so sure about duty. She imagined Denise phoning, or even coming round to River Road, pulsing with the excitement of being the bearer of bad news. And that would have been the day she remembered with such clarity, the day from which she dated the rest of her life, the day when she'd come home from school in her summer cotton uniform of green and white check.

She saw again from her bedroom window her mother feeding the bonfire at the foot of the garden, seething with anger, unapproachable, unappeasable, dragging clothes from the house, a brown jacket being flung onto the fire and assuming in midair the shape of half a man, its arms outspread, then landing on the flames and flaring within seconds, to be followed by trousers, socks, shoes, books, everything tainted with the touch of the betrayer.

'It's all right, Karl,' she said. 'It's not your fault.'

He closed his eyes but held on to her hand. And he sighed, heavily, a couple of times. She squeezed his hand again. 'I'd better go,' she said. 'I've tired you.'

His eyes popped open. 'Don't even think of going,' he said.

Chapter 27

He plaits three bathrobe sashes into a rope. It takes him half the morning. He tests the rope for stretch, then ties it to the mannequin arm. He knots two napkins together at the corners, his gnarled left hand a hindrance in this finer work.

'Here, boy, here, Friday,' and the dog, with a touch of wariness, comes to be stroked and whispered to. He tells the dog to sit before he lifts a front paw and slides it through a slit between the knotted napkins. Then the other paw through the same slit. The dog does not feel constrained, does not struggle.

The man takes the free ends of the napkins and ties them together over the dog's back. With a little persuasion the dog accepts this and the tying of the free end of the sash rope to the napkin harness.

'Okay, Friday, let's go.' Richard stands and shuffles towards the middle of the room. The dog comes at his side and he keeps a hand on the dog's neck and the strain comes on. 'Come on, boy, come on,' he whispers, and as he hopes the dog braces a little against the broad napkin harness stretched across his chest and the rope does not stretch as the one sash stretched, and he urges the dog on with encouragement and he adds his own puny strength to the dog's and there is a noise and the mannequin shifts in its shelving, balks as if wedged and then both the mannequins come free together, the arm of one wedged invasively between the legs of the other in a parody of intimacy. They clatter to the floor and the dog looks around in alarm, but Richard calms and whispers and soon the dog is happy to haul the two entwined figures across the expanse of carpet to the centre of the room and the place settings.

Richard rewards the dog with Tux. He drags his seat across to where the mannequins lie together, head to toe, the female arm between the male legs. He sits beside them, and as gently as he can he eases them apart, lays them side by side on their back. Both are slim and svelte and bald, with smooth bumps where crotch or breasts would be.

Chapter 28

'Rich never held a grudge. He knew what had happened but he didn't reproach me. It was a while before he even told me that he'd been kicked out, that he'd moved in with Ben. He wanted my advice on what to do about you.'

'About me?'

'You were his only reason for ever staying with Raewyn and now he couldn't see you. Raewyn had screamed at him to leave, calling him every name under the sun, threatening to tell you you had a pervert for a father unless he just went away and stayed away. He wasn't sure what to do.

'I didn't know what to say. And besides, I had enough on my plate at the time. Business was way down. Several big contracts had fallen over, all at once. It was as if the town had turned against us. We had to lay off staff. Money was tight. And Rich was distracted. It didn't help. It was the lowest time between us. And he started to drink. He'd always liked a drink, but this was different. Lunchtime too. In the early days we'd often drunk at lunch, just for the hell of it, because we could. And sometimes we'd do great stuff in the afternoon. But this was different. This wasn't celebration. It was joyless. It was drinking for the sake of drinking.

'He could still draw, of course, but there was less and less call for his sort of stuff. Computers were just coming in and the industry was changing but he didn't want to know. He wasn't interested. One afternoon I told him not to bother coming in next time he drank at lunchtime. He'd had a bottle at least. He didn't get angry – I don't ever remember him angry. He just said, "Sorry, Karl," and walked out.

'After that he only stayed till lunch each day. I probably should have done more but I had young kids and I was worried about the business and Denise didn't always make things easier and, well, things slid. And then of course there was, well, you know about the accident.'

Annie nodded and listened as Karl told how they'd tracked her father down in hospital, how broken in spirit he'd seemed.

'Was it an accident, Karl?'

Karl didn't look at her. He paused, looked at the far side of the ward, looked down at his hands, at the medical devices that held him in place. He sighed. 'I don't see how it could have been, Annie. It seemed so precise and cruel. And the story of the hit and run seemed unconvincing. But in the end I just don't know. The police seemed satisfied and what was I supposed to do?

'The curious thing was that business picked up after that. It was as if the city suddenly remembered we existed. Not that

that was any use to Rich. Of course he still owned half the company but he made it clear even with his jaw wired up in hospital that he wanted nothing more to do with it. I argued for a while but in the end I bought him out. It was a substantial sum of money, paid in instalments while you grew up. Almost all of it went to Raewyn by direct debit. The lawyers set it up.'

When she looked back Annie could see there had always been money around. Raewyn had only ever worked part time but the car was often changed and always newish. Decorators came in one year, new carpet in another. They hadn't gone without.

Karl was clearly tiring. His injuries were severe, worsened when he was dug from the rubble in Lichfield Street and lifted onto a stretcher. He would limp, apparently, for the rest of his life.

'Just one last question then I'll leave you in peace,' said Annie, glancing over at the nurse, seated at her desk engrossed in some sort of paperwork. 'That was, what, seventeen years ago. Have you seen him since?'

Karl nodded. 'I think so, twice.'

'You think so?'

'It was hard to be sure,' and he felt for her hand again, whether to reassure her or to comfort himself Annie wasn't sure. 'Once in the Square, by the old post office, and I called out to him but he went off down an alley onto Hereford. I followed him but he was gone.'

'Did he see you?'

'I'm not sure. But the second time he did. On Cashel Street this time, on the corner with High, where the kids hang out and skateboard. And I'm sure he recognised me and deliberately went away. This time I didn't follow.' Karl paused. 'He looked old, Annie, seriously old. Older than he was.'

'How long ago was that?'

Karl looked up. His eyes were full of distress. 'Two years, maybe three. He wasn't well, Annie. Honestly he wasn't well. If I were you, well, perhaps that's not for me to say. But I'll tell you one thing: he'd be bloody proud of the way you've turned out, Annie. He'd be so bloody proud.'

Annie kissed Karl on the forehead, promised to return before she flew home, waved a bright goodbye to the nurse and got down the corridor and comfortably out of earshot before she withdrew into a little window alcove, turned her back on a passing orderly and, as unobtrusively as she could, burst into tears.

* * *

'I'll go,' said Vince. 'You don't have to. It's my fault.'

'But she's my mother.'

'Look, Annie, oh shit, can I get you a drink? Something really nice.'

Annie nodded. She seemed to be living on booze these days. But soon, she told herself, she'd be returning to her safer, simpler life. Ample time for detox then, and she suddenly had

an image of the little flat in Turnpike Lane and Paul being tall
in it, Paul stooping in the bedroom, cramming himself into the
shower, the breadth of his shoulders. And a feeling came with
it that she tried to pin down – pleasure? Relief at the familiar?
– but it was gone as fast as it came, and she was back in a
restaurant on Clyde Road with dapper Vince. He was wearing
a short-sleeved shirt of duckling yellow, perfectly pressed.

As soon as she'd found the restaurant she knew that Vince
had brought her there to apologise. It was twee, expensive and
self-consciously French. The tables were decked out in red and
white gingham. A notice announced that it had only just re-
opened after the quakes. There were hanging baskets and two
wickerwork cockerels by the front door and also a pair of live
poodles tethered to an old-fashioned boot scraper, white very
Parisian poodles straight from the groomer, with bobbles of
fur at each ankle like Elizabethan ruffs. Annie presumed that
they belonged to a customer rather than being some cruel form
of branding. Even so, they were nervous beasts and they had
managed to twist their leads around each other, shortening
them. As she passed through the door Annie had briefly
considered untangling them, but then thought she'd just tell
the waiter.

'Important stuff first, Annie. I'm sorry. I shouldn't have gone
to the paper without asking you. I was...'

Annie raised a hand to cut him off. He didn't need to plead.
She had already thought it through. It wouldn't have made any
difference if he'd asked her. She'd have said yes. Her mother

had never been much of a reader, of books, newspapers, anything really. And she was 250 miles away. The risk would have seemed negligible

'Forget it. Look,' said Annie, fishing her phone out of the Santorini bag, 'here's the text she sent this morning. "Arriving ChCh 3.35pm, NZ5472."'

'Is that it?'

Annie nodded.

Vince laughed, then bit it back.

'No,' said Annie, 'you're right. It's brilliant.'

The moment she'd seen it Annie had acknowledged its miniature excellence. There was the implicit criticism of Annie and the implicit assumption that Annie would be at the airport to start the process of contrition. And behind it lay the cruel tactic of acting the bully while playing the victim. It was vintage Raewyn, devastatingly effective. Of course, it all depended on Annie feeling guilty but the mother knew her daughter. Annie did feel guilty. Or at least a part of her did. It was not a part she was proud of but that didn't make it go away.

She had not yet decided how she would handle her mother. It depended, she realised, on whether she went on the attack. If she did it might make things easier. If she didn't, well, Annie would find out.

'May I order?' asked Vince.

Annie nodded.

'Good, because I already have.'

The waiter brought two violet-coloured drinks, faintly bubbling.

'Cheers,' said Vince, raising his.

'Excuse me,' said Annie to the waiter, a young man in white shirt and black waistcoat and a ponytail. 'Those dogs out there. Do you know whose they are?' And Annie pointed out the tangled leads and added that perhaps they might enjoy a bowl of water.

'Sorry,' she said, to Vince. 'Cheers.' The taste was sweetly festive.

'Kir Royale,' said Vince. 'Two of these at lunch have got me through many a tough afternoon.'

Annie watched the waiter cross to a pair of trim middle-aged women in three-quarter-length trousers. She was grateful that he did not appear to point her out to them. A minute later he carried a bowl of water outside. But he did not untangle the leads and the women did not leave their table. Annie tried to put it from her mind. Snails. She should have guessed.

'I know,' said Vince. 'But I happen to like them. Or at least I like what they come with.'

Watching and imitating, Annie gripped a shell in the pincers provided, used the two-tined fork to winkle out the shrivel of meat, and popped it, with only the slightest hesitation, into her mouth. It was nothing, a texture only, a substance to carry the rich twins of garlic and butter.

'In case your mother tries to kiss you,' said Vince.

She ate all six of her snails and tipped the shells to her mouth to drain the liquor and mopped the plate with slices of baguette as the waiter brought a bottle of pinot noir.

'Not from Blenheim,' said Vince as he poured. 'I thought that in the circumstances...'

And Annie smiled. An hour ago she'd been weeping for her father in a hospital corridor, but the twin effects of booze and cheerful company were potent. She felt herself submitting to the present tense, the pleasures of the food and drink and Vince's company.

'I've learned a lot,' she said, 'in the last two days.'

'Let me guess,' said Vince. 'Your father had an affair with a young man from a powerful local family.'

Annie stared.

'Oh, look,' said Vince, 'our mains.'

Over sizzling little entrecôte steaks and shoestring fries and an oil-drenched salad of leaves and tiny tomatoes and half-blackened shards of roasted red peppers Vince explained how the story in the paper had winkled out a former draughtsman for Hamilton and Jones.

'He remembered you, even,' said Vince. 'He called you Rich's little princess.'

Annie was growing used to the signature notes her father left behind. The draughtsman remembered his deft drawing, his geniality, his calm. But also in the latter stages his drinking, and the grim state of the business before his departure.

'And after Karl bought him out?' she said. 'Do we know

anything? Karl reckons he may have seen around town a couple of times, but that's it.'

'I was going to keep this,' said Vince taking his cell phone from his pocket, 'until we'd finished eating.'

An aftershock rattled the restaurant and kept rattling it. A strong one, a floor-shifter. Everyone looked up, senses alert for how long, how strong. The poodles at the door erupted, flinging themselves away from the building only to be pulled up short by the twisted leads and flung back against the window glass. And suddenly, awfully, they were fighting, the pair of them biting, screaming, a single ball of fur and terror, throttled by their own panic, blood spattering the glass. Annie dashed from her seat and out of the door but could find no way to intercede between the flashing jaws and claws, just didn't dare, just knew they'd blindly bite and tear her flesh, stood hopelessly by as one dog ripped at the other's ear and more blood spurted and the dog screamed. And the owner, too, had run from the restaurant and was screaming at the dogs but they were deaf with terror and fighting for life and Annie looked around for something to force between them when a sudden wall of water drenched the dogs and they stopped.

The ponytailed waiter laid aside the pitcher, placed a leg between the dogs, bent down and unclipped the lead from one. Both dogs shook themselves. The owner checked them over. Their wounds were superficial.

'Bravo,' said Annie to the waiter. The rest was none of her business and she went back inside.

The pinot trembled a little in her hand.

'You all right?' said Vince.

She nodded, but it had been unnerving, horrible. There was still a brown smear of blood on the window of the restaurant. The dogs' owner did not appear to thank the waiter, but just waited outside with the dogs, her back turned to the restaurant, while her friend settled the bill.

Only when the women had gone, the dogs trotting side by side on their leads in the tiptoe style of poodles and seemingly the best of friends, was Annie able to return her attention to Vince.

On his cell phone was the image of a rambling three-storey weatherboard house, one that looked to have accreted over the years like a coral reef, rather than ever to have been designed. The place was painted a generic cream and the spouting bled with rust.

'He lived here?'

Vince nodded.

'How do you know?'

Vince paused, sighed slightly, involuntarily. 'The manager of the KFC in town saw the story in the paper.'

'KFC?'

'Rich had worked there part time, cleaning up, you know, collecting the trays, wiping the tables, sweeping the floor.'

'When? Recently?'

Vince nodded. 'The lunchtime shift. After lunch he "wasn't reliable".'

Annie tried to picture her father, aged sixty, in the jaunty branded cotton smock they dressed their workers in, shuffling from table to table, dragging a little trolley, clearing away the casual leavings of the young, the soiled detritus of greed and grease. The kids would have looked right past him, through him.

'"Nice and quiet" was how the guy described Rich. And that was all. He didn't pretend to know him well. Just wanted to help if he could. And he'd checked his records, gave me the address of this place. It's a boarding house of sorts.'

'Of sorts?'

'You wouldn't call it exclusive, Annie. Basic, more like. I did a bit of research and found the landlord. About a dozen men lived there at any one time. Sort of one step above the street.'

Annie spread her fingers over the screen to magnify the image. She tried to imagine her father stepping through the concrete nothing of a front yard, up those little steps to the shingled porch, opening the front door. But she struggled. She had no image for him. Probably bearded, drinking, and surely alone, or he would not have been there.

'I want to go and see it.'

Vince shook his head. The place was inside the cordon on Madras. He'd got the picture off Google Street View.

'The landlord said Rich kept himself to himself. Paid his rent in cash. And drank. That was the sort of place it was. Everyone drank, he said. The building's munted, is going to be demolished. He seemed pretty pleased about that. I suspect it was a bit dodgy tax-wise or rent-act-wise or whatever.'

Annie could think of nothing much to say. It was as if she'd been hauling in a net and as more and more of it had come in over the stern of the boat it was becoming clear that the final catch would be negligible, a wretched disappointment, barely worth putting to sea for. Annie felt at that moment, ground down, oppressed by circumstance.

'I suppose I'd better start making tracks for the airport.'

'I'll drive you,' said Vince.

She had expected him to offer and had made up her mind to decline. She needed to confront her mother alone.

'Are you sure?' she said.

Chapter 29

It takes a while to find the clothes he needs. He refuses to skimp or make do or accept second best. He drinks as he goes for strength, for numbness, but sparingly, hoping to keep his judgement long enough, his discernment. Too much, he knows, and he will err, will make choices he'll regret. The dog finds the exercise of no interest, but tags along.

He is easier to clothe – jeans and a white singlet. He lays them on a chair in the corridor. For her he wants the simplest summer dress, a young woman's shift. He tries a dozen rooms but he finds only complicated stuff, stuff cut to hide the flaws of older wealthy women, stuff cut to flatter the fat, to mask the damage done by time, by chance and by excess. The old have all the money. The young have only flesh and hope.

He has to climb to another floor and then another before he finds a wardrobe holding two simple dresses, one grey, one crimson, sleeveless, light, plain, cut from the silkiest stuff. They weigh almost nothing. To choose between them he needs daylight. He drapes both over his arm and heads outside to the roof of the car park. The corridor still smells of bleach, and he shudders at the memory, skirting the damage to the carpet, careful to keep the dresses from dragging.

The brightness of the sun is briefly blinding. His eyes water, are slow to adjust. But as his vision clears he notes the smooth elegance of the dresses against the gnarled flesh and then that the dog has stiffened, is looking away towards the sea. And even as he swings his gaze to look he hears the thump of the helicopter.

'Here, Friday, come,' he calls, taking shelter under the concrete overhang. The dog is reluctant to relinquish its view, but he calls insistently, puts sternness in his voice and the dog comes. They have hidden several times thus as choppers toured the central city, carrying who knows what dignitaries or gawpers, all getting their fix of ruin. He unscrews a miniature vodka, a blaster, a hit.

The helicopter comes ever nearer, the pulse of its engine changing nature and tempo, becoming just noise, ever greater noise, noise to shrink from. It is hovering over the building. The downdraught sends scraps of rubbish swirling on the roof, fills and flutters the dresses on his arm, would steal them if he didn't clamp them down. The noise is head-filling, maddening and the dog is barking furiously. It escapes from his grip on the collar and dances out to the heart of the car park, barking up at the belly of the machine.

'Here, Friday, here,' but the noise is too great and the dog is defending their world and unbiddable with instinct.

And as if warned off by the dog, the chopper takes its noise a little further away, tours around the building, it seems, as if inspecting it, and when Richard judges from the noise that it has reached the far side he emerges from under the overhang and hurries as best he can across the rooftop, still with the dresses on his arm. The dog follows him through the door and waits while he leans heavily against a wall, panting.

The noise pulses through the building, threatening it with violence by vibration, as if to carry on the work the earthquake started, where noise and movement and violence are all part of the one destructive thing. The helicopter stays hovering around the building. Richard withdraws into one of the still untouched guest rooms, closes the curtains, drains a Scotch and lies on the bed, curling foetal, pulling a duvet over him. He gestures to the dog and it leaps up beside him and sits and pants but even though he lays a calming hand on the dog's shoulders and says soft words the dog will not lie down, will not relax and curl. Richard buries his head under the pillows. The noise and movement still find a muffled way through.

And then he hears and feels a further noise, and it takes a moment for him to recognise that he has heard and felt it before, knows what it is. They are drilling again, drilling deep into the walls of the building. Only now the drill is above them, and not far above, perhaps three floors above.

He feels a growl surge in the dog's throat, like the purr of a cat but swelling with threat and the will to fight.

'Shhh, Friday, shhh.'

His mind is racing to make sense of drilling both below and above.

'They're drilling at our bones, dog, they're drilling at our bones.'

And then he does make sense of it and it's like a short, hard punch.

'Oh, Friday,' he says, 'oh, Friday.'

They drill on three sides. It does not take long. The drill stops and soon the helicopter engine changes note and sheers away and quiet seeps back into the building like a balm.

'You'll be all right, Friday,' whispers Richard, in the new-found silence. And still on the bed he chucks the dog under the chin. 'You'll be just fine, I promise.'

And despite everything he feels his throat swell with feeling and his old eyes blink and he gulps twice and then he rolls onto his side and he lays an arm over the dog's shoulder and he buries his wet face in the dog's neck and his body heaves like a child's. But it does not last long. And soon he is asleep.

Chapter 30

Entry to the domestic terminal took Annie through a knot of smokers, between a brace of fiercely fragrant lavatories and past a bronze plaque to some forgotten minister of transport before leading her to the narrow sloping concourse and a seat to await her mother's flight.

A four-year-old stared at the arrivals gate through which, Annie guessed, he was expecting to see his mother come. A woman who had to be his grandmother stood behind him, her expression strained, her manner suggesting she would not be overwhelmed with grief when the moment came to give the child back. Suddenly, the boy shot forward with a noise like a wail and a broad-hipped woman of thirty-something, arriving in a stream of passengers, knelt when she saw him and those behind her had to step around her as her darling flew into her body and wept with relief. Grandma kept a reserved distance, her face a mask.

Sitting next to Annie, a woman of perhaps fifty glanced up occasionally at the gate and then back to a word-finder puzzle in a cheaply printed magazine that consisted only of puzzles. She sucked at a blue Bic ballpoint. Then, without any outward display, she slipped the puzzle into her bag, stood and fell into step with a passing man of a similar age. They did not touch. He wore a fawn zip-up jacket and trousers so neutral they were barely even fawn. He towed an overnight bag. Annie watched the couple's backs as they disappeared towards the luggage claim. As far as she was able to tell, they did not speak.

They had to be married. Such apparent indifference, such complete disregard of the other, could stem only from long familiarity, from the habituation of partnership. Perhaps it betokened the sort of loving trust where nothing needed to be said, where two had become one, where they were fused at the emotional hip and had achieved a sort of Zen-like calm together against a hostile world. But it hadn't looked like that. It had looked, Annie thought, like the very antithesis of loving trust, like weary resignation. As if each embodied for the other the essence of disappointment. The bad choice that had hardened, through hope, and habit and self-delusion, into permanence. That was it, for ever, for them both. They'd make do with it somehow. And besides, there was no point in trying to start again at their age. I mean to say, who'd be interested?

A light on the board indicated that the Blenheim flight had landed. Annie went to stand half hidden by a coffee kiosk, without quite choosing to do so or acknowledging her desire to see before she was seen, to gauge mood and manner. She wished, momentarily, that she'd brought Vince with her rather than accepting his offer to wait with the car.

Her mother's sunglasses were ornate, her jeans stretchily clinging, her boots expensive. The loose white top was well chosen to mitigate a minor hoop of middle-aged fat. All in all she didn't look bad.

'Hello, Mum,' said Annie, stepping forward.

'Darling,' she said, and she let go of the little bag she was towing and delivered the sort of hug that Annie had seen several times in the last fifteen minutes, the half-hug, the apparent hug, the self-conscious event in which the arms reach around and the heads go to one side of each other but the hips hold back for any of a hundred different wordless reasons.

'Such a surprise.'

That Annie had obediently come to the airport? That Annie was in New Zealand? Either way the line was drenched in manipulative irony. Annie felt a stirring of revolt that she quelled with the ease of long practice. It was easier just to ride it out. Though she had more or less made up her mind not to apologise. Or at least not to begin with an apology.

They followed the procession to the baggage reclaim, a low and underlit hall where the newly reunited stood in awkward limbo, between the greeting and the welcome busy world beyond.

Annie almost asked about the weather in Blenheim then bit it back. The conveyor belt did its warning bleep and little orange lights flashed and then it jerked into scaly life. She and a hundred others stared at a single bag left from a previous flight as it rounded the hairpin bend before disappearing through the heavy plastic flaps.

'So how's it going?' Her mother spoke with a breezy brightness, suggesting not only that she knew she held the cards, but that she would enjoy playing them in her own sweet time.

'Well,' said Annie, 'it rather depends on what you mean by "it".'

'Oh God, here we go.'

Annie sighed. 'Why are you here, Mum? I mean, what have you come down for?'

'Isn't it enough to want to see my one and only darling daughter?' And she turned to Annie, her eyebrows raised theatrically above the sunglasses.

Annie turned back towards the hatch that had started to spew luggage.

'Of course, if you'd rather I hadn't come. If you'd rather I went straight back to Blenheim, you've only got to say. Don't worry that you snuck back into the country without telling the person who gave birth to you and brought you up singlehandedly. I'm sure there'll be a plane back tonight or tomorrow morning. I wouldn't want to get in the way of your search for the darling daddy who loved us so much that he left us for another woman. I mean, it's fine by me if you want to go raking up the past but it does feel a bit rich when I spent ten years bringing you up on my own...'

'I know about Dad now, Mum.'

Raewyn took off her sunglasses. 'Oh, you do, do you? So that dirty little cat's out of the bag now. Fine. Are you pleased? Do you think that somehow justifies everything? And have you considered for one moment how it might have been for me twenty years ago, when I was just about the last person in town to learn that my husband was having a fling with some rich little nancy boy half his age, some pretty...'

'Mum, can this wait?'

Half a dozen people were staring in unashamed delight, and twice that number were listening.

'Oh, I don't see why it should. You brought it up. And of course the little pervert had to come from one of the most prominent families in town, as you've no doubt uncovered in your grubby little researches, which made it just about the juiciest bit of gossip going in certain circles. No one gave a thought for the deserted wife, though, did they, nor a thought for what she did to keep any word of it from her daughter's ears. Oh no. And I can't see myself being thanked for any of it at this late stage, even though every single thing was done with you in mind so that you could have as normal a childhood as possible despite the way that bastard had betrayed the pair of us. That one there.' She was pointing at a hefty Samsonite case in light blue. And in unthinking obedience Annie stepped forward and heaved it from the belt.

'Thank you, darling. Where to from here?'

Annie stared at her mother. Did she really expect that accommodation, transport, an itinerary had been arranged?

'Oh, for God's sake. The look on your face, darling. I wouldn't dream of imposing on you or interfering with your little muck-raking expedition. Just show me the bloody taxi stand and I'll get out of your hair. No, no, give it to me. I'm not too old to pull my own suitcase.'

Taxis snaked for a hundred yards, their drivers trained to stand by the bonnet and smile for the newly competitive market. Her mother walked past the two Indian drivers at the head of the queue, who both smiled at her and said 'Madam' while gesturing towards their empty cars like butlers, and handed her bag to a short white man in a black V-necked sweater that had given up the fight with his gut and hung around it in inelastic folds like the valance round a bed.

'Oceanview Terrace, Mount Pleasant,' she said.

'Are you staying with Denise?'

'Oh, listen to Madam Detective. And your point?

'No, nothing.'

'Denise and I happen to have remained friends. Is there something wrong in that? As a matter of fact, she was the one who gave me the idea of coming down, darling. She very kindly suggested I might enjoy the show.'

'The show?'

'You know, darling, the memorial thingy, in Hagley Park. We're going together. They've got some very big names, and Wills, of course, not that I expect such things will interest you now you're so sophisticated and international. Anyway, darling, I'm sure you've got more important things to do than stand chattering with your dear old mum. You have my number. It's been such a pleasure to catch up.'

Brilliantly she leant forward for another half hug. Annie acquiesced. As he got into the car, the driver grunted at the compression of his gut.

Her mother's window came down.

'Oh and darling, there's more to bringing up kids than drawing a few ducks. As I hope you're about to find out. And if you do manage to find him, by the way, I'm told he may not be in the best of shape. But, ah well. Reaping and sowing and all that. Mwah, mwah.'

Chapter 31

Something seems to be happening at the far end of Cashel Street, near the Bridge of Remembrance. But from the car park roof it is hard to know.

Climbing to the penthouse to look takes half the morning. He is aware of waning energy and tries to harbour it. The dog has long since reached the top and waits for him there, its head flopped over the top step, dozing but from time to time opening an eye when it hears Richard sitting heavily to rest, or pulling himself back to his feet with a gasp of exertion.

As he gains the last step Richard smiles at the dog and lays his good hand on the skull, and massages the bone through the skin. But he is feeble as a newborn, drained of all strength, light-headed with weakness, and inside the penthouse he all but falls into the window chair and his eyes close and he lets a sort of nothingness come over him, not sleep but a sort of withdrawal of the senses, an absence.

He is not sure how long he drowses but when the dog pushes against the side of the chair and up underneath his dangling hand it is as if the senses switch back on slowly one by one, like an old television taking a flickering minute to get its valves and circuits running. His thighs ache from the climb. He drinks a little water. It prompts a craving for anaesthetic booze, for the sense of it seeping into sore tissues and blurring past and future into an out-of-focus present. He pours a fat slug of vodka, adds a slightly smaller slug of Kiwi Spring water. The surface of the drink has a swirl of iridescence. He sniffs at the glass. Even the smell is good, relieving, purging the channels, clearing the way.

The first sip spreads and melts over the tongue and says yes and good morning to the back of the throat. It cannot be bad to like something this much, to be so grateful for it, to it. He turns to the window and now he can see what is happening there at the far end of Cashel Street, by the Bridge of Remembrance, just beyond the fence. They are building. Workmen shrunk to toys by distance are clambering over scaffolding. As he sips Richard watches the grandstand grow. There is no mistaking the way it is facing.

'A day or two,' he says to the dog. And he smiles at the dog's delight in his voice and its wise ignorance of anything that might be happening in a day or two.

'You are a good boy,' he says, and as he speaks he feels as happy as the dog.

Richard makes himself eat. He needs energy to do the few things that he has to do. But the square of chocolate sits heavy on his tongue, its sweetness clashing with the vodka clarity of his palate. He is scared he might gag, and if he gags he'll cough and if he coughs he fears it might trigger worse because cough and guts and bowel seem all connected within this ruinous frame of his.

The chocolate has softened on his tongue. He sluices it down with a sudden fling of vodka. It stays down. He does not cough. Nothing happens.

'We'd better go, dog,' he says. 'Things to do.'

*　*　*

He chooses the grey dress. It seems the simplest, the most innocent. The material is silk-like in its softness and fineness. Wool? Synthetic? Some exotic animal fibre? He does not know but is pleased by the way it slithers over the head and arms of the mannequin and hangs from the shoulder, gathers slightly just below the waist like a flapper's dress from the twenties, then flares again, but subtly. When the dog brushes against the dress the material sways before settling. How good she'd look in a breeze. Propped on a chair back, Richard blows at the skirt but his breath is thin and weak and the material hardly moves and he knows that if he blew harder the cough would come. But the dress is good, a dress for a young woman, for a slip of a girl all sinuous and lithe and bright with hope, before the world has got to her. She goes barefoot.

Both mannequins have only a suggestion of facial features, the merest bumps and mouldings in the buff material to indicate that here a nose would be and there the eyes. This pleases him. It lets him see what he wants to see: the puckish nose, the bright-lit eyes.

Fitting jeans on the other mannequin is less dignified. The legs don't flex at the knee so Richard bunches the jeans on the floor as if they'd simply been undone at the waist and allowed to fall. He lifts the naked form upright and snuggles the feet into the piled legs of the jeans and raises the cloth up over shins and thighs and crotch while struggling to keep the figure standing. Once, when it slips against his shoulder and lurches to one side, Richard says sorry.

The jeans he chose are wrong. He has to scour another half a dozen rooms for others, is cursed again by the age and girth of hotel residents. But he persists and a pair he finds on the floor above are just the thing, tailored by age, faded at the knee from flexion and wrinkled at the crotch. When he has slid them up the legs, the waistband nestles on the narrow hips. And as with the dress, the cloth does not hug or cling, but lies on the sweet bulge of the buttock then falls below all perpendicular and good and soft, like a stage curtain. The look has the erotic simplicity that he hoped for. He tops it with a singlet, a simple cotton vest, quite new and brightly white, and rich to the touch of fingertips. He can remember when his groin responded to such tactile cloth, to the promise of the flesh beneath.

Neither mannequin has joints. This will be a standing party then, though later his guests might recline. It does not matter. He removes the chairs from his feasting place. Now, in the centre of the banqueting hall, the three tables stand like a plush and polished island, laid with the crockery and the cutlery and the array of glasses to which he's added three synthetic roses from the cupboard and a silver-gilt candelabrum with five white candles.

And the dog now has two bowls by its bed, one already primed with Kiwi Spring, the other to hold, albeit briefly, a dinner of Tux.

Back out on the car park roof, Friday fossicks while he lies back with late-afternoon wine. Somehow the dog finds interest in what seems a barren world. Though it is only hours since they were here and nothing can have changed, the dog tours with intense attention the concrete walls and buttresses, and the parked cars thick with settled dust.

Richard drowses in the warm afternoon. How long has he been in this building? He is aware that he has quite lost track and he is equally aware that it doesn't matter.

An arch of cloud lies over the city, the nor'west arch. Beyond it the sky is a pale blue-gold. In the silent city the air is late-summer heavy. When the breeze comes as it comes now it is with near tropical warmth on the skin. And on it Richard catches a strain of something, of shouting is it, or music? He rouses a little, looks at the dog but it seems to have noticed nothing untoward, nothing to impinge on a dog's consciousness.

Again a waft of breeze and again a snatch of noise borne across the city from the direction of Hagley Park. The crackling of big loudspeakers, a gout of rock music, and then, absurdly clear as a gust of wind comes, 'Testing, one, two, three.'

Chapter 32

Jess had gone to work. *The Press* was on the kitchen table, two faces looking up at Annie. One was nine years old, freckled and beaming, an ideal front-page image, a heart-warmer, hope-giver and paper-seller. You had to read the text to learn that the child was suffering from a degenerative condition. Unless a miracle occurred, divine or scientific, in a dozen years he'd be imprisoned in a body that didn't work. He wouldn't be able even to smile. Another decade or less and he'd be dead. But for now he was as happy a little boy as could be found in the city: he had the job of pressing a plunger that would bring down a building on a Sunday morning, just a few hours before Annie flew home.

The other face was the royal one, the prince they called Wills, pictured at the airport being greeted by the usual suspects, the men in suits, and the women in hats who never usually wore hats. How many hundred thousand hats bought specially for the occasion and never worn again would greet Wills in his official lifetime?

How was it that the magic dust of royalty continued to work in the twenty-first century? For it did work, clearly and indisputably. Even the crudest rock musician whose success was founded on defying, or at least appearing to defy, every sexual, social or narcotic convention, became a smiling yes-ma'am puppy dog when asked to the palace to have some sort of decoration pinned to his ageing chest.

The last time William had been to New Zealand it had been with his fairy-tale mother. How many times had even Annie, who was three at the time, seen the picture of him playing with a Buzzy Bee on the lawn at Government House, Charles looking awkward in a suit, and Diana looking overblown and eighties-ish? Since then he'd undergone the sort of intensive training that a guide dog undergoes, and he'd become his office.

That morning he would be taken on a greatest-hits disaster tour, consoling selected victims as he went. Then he'd be shown around the red-zoned central city, before his appearance at the memorial service in Hagley Park, where he would act as proxy for his grandmother, the highest of high priestesses, whose juju was the greatest juju of them all. We might scoff at credulous medieval peasants who sought the king's touch to cure disease, but what was the royal presence for in Hagley Park if not to do its bit to heal some 80,000 shaken souls (including, admittedly, some starstruck but unshaken ones like Annie's mother)?

The rest of the paper, which Annie read with a bowl of muesli, reflected a growing discontent. A few weeks now since the big one and the excitement of the trauma had worn off. Most people to the north and west of the city had resumed a life that didn't diverge too widely from the one they led before. Their suffering was little more than inconvenience. But where the quake had raised and lowered land, had snapped the spines of homes, had buried suburbs under tons of silt, had shattered pipes and rendered streets impassable, it seemed that the authorities were overwhelmed, insurance companies cynical and nothing much was being done to make things any better. The letters to the paper were no longer expressing wonder at resilience, or gratitude for the kindness of strangers, but were beginning to grumble.

Annie felt a twinge of guilt. In the time she'd been back she'd done half an afternoon of shovelling silt in Brighton and that was that. She'd shunned the damaged areas, been preoccupied with her own affairs. But then again, she reflected, she was probably typical. Most of us find enough difficulty with what is in front of us.

Her phone rang. 'Annie, it's me, Ben.'

Annie was surprised by her surge of pleasure.

'I'd like you to meet my kids,' he said. An image of them rose in Annie's head, swarming round Ben's car in Glandovey Road, grinning like the boy on the front page. 'They want to go to the thing in the park this afternoon. Prince William's the drawcard, of course. Would you like to join us? Please say yes. We're taking a picnic. And no, before you ask, Steph won't be there. But yes, I've told her and she's fine with it. So what about it?'

Annie could just picture the look of earnest entreaty on Ben's face.

'I'd be delighted,' she said.

And she was also rather keen to see Prince William.

Chapter 33

It is not going to happen today. Something else is, and it is not hard to guess what. From early in the morning guards, soldiers and men in dark suits have been touring the empty, ruined streets below. From the car park roof Richard has watched them, the distance lending a sense of absurdity to their scouring of a world too large and various for them ever to render it safe.

Two sniffer dogs on long leads are being shown down High Street, the dogs' tails raised like masts, their noses assessing doorways and rubble piles in moments, reading the brew of the air as fast as thought and finding nothing of interest, and moving on, towing their handlers. A man in a boiler suit raises the manhole covers in the road for the dogs to sniff down and dismiss.

The suits and security look up at the hotel and other streetside buildings but send no one in to sweep them room by room, aware that the task is vast and the risk small. But once a stretch of street has been gone over by the men and dogs a squaddie with a gun is posted at either end to do what soldiers have always done, which is to stand and wait. There's one now at the rubble-scattered corner of High and Cashel by the entrance to the Westpac bank.

Richard withdraws under his overhang, and the dog curls beside. A gap in the concrete railing lets him see along the route to Cathedral Square. He drops a hand to feel the dog's rough fur and has a strong sense of nowness, of a good sweet morning and his own frailty within it. And he feels a mild curiosity to see the size and manner of the dignitary party. The dogs and soldiers and thoroughness suggest importance, head-of-state importance even.

To add to the sense of occasion, music has been wafting from the direction of the park since mid-morning, gusting in intensity with the strength of the breeze, recorded music, tunes Richard recognises, the sort of anodyne standards that might keep a crowd vaguely anaesthetised while they await some live event. Richard, too, feels drowsy. There is less difference now for him between sleep and wake. At night he lies on his back and is aware of time passing, of the dog breathing in and out beside him. Yet during the day he often sits and drifts into filmy racing dreams with other rules of time and space and consequence.

The noise of wings opens his eyes now, wings beating and then settling. The pigeon is back, lurching across the bright-lit concrete on its clenched left stump. The bird's tail has lost a snatch of feather. Two wing feathers hang at unaerodynamic angles. And between the wings, above what are effectively the shoulder blades, there's a patch of bare skin, bereft of feathers, yellowish grey and dotted with blood. Richard senses movement to his left and a gull lands on the parapet and settles its wings, a meaty black-backed gull, its chest like a Viking prow, its yellow bill a pruning hook.

Richard reaches out to where he keeps his supplies of booze and Tux and snack food, and the pigeon flaps its wings and half hops, half flutters away in alarm. The gull, too, flaps its wings as if to take off but then resettles.

Richard crumbles a biscuit and scatters it on the concrete between himself and the pigeon. Again it retreats in alarm and does not come forward to eat. It looks uncertain, weak on its one good foot. And then it topples. It falls to one side and lies, hopeless, down. The gull cocks its head, assessing, then hops lazily from the parapet and comes towards the pigeon on great webbed feet. Feebly Richard lobs the rest of the biscuit at the gull. It falls well short. The gull hops briefly into the air, then stands and studies Richard. The pigeon lies on its side in the sun and does not move.

'Hotel California' wafts across the city. The gull stands and waits. The pigeon looks dead. The dog gets up and lollops over to clean up the scraps of biscuit with a prehensile tongue. The gull takes three steps into the breeze and rises onto the air, flaps huge wings once, twice, thrice and is suddenly riding the sky, twenty, fifty feet up, twisting its head to peer down at the man and the bird and the dog. It circles and watches, and then with a rippling tilt of its wing-span it arcs and flies back down. As it nears the parapet it pulls up against the air till it all but stalls and it lands as lightly as a leaf.

The dog noses the pigeon. The bird comes weakly to life, flapping its wings but unable to get itself to its feet. It shifts on its side, like a swatted fly.

Voices, and they are on the way up High Street, a party of a dozen or more in glowing orange vests and hard hats the colour of daffodils. Token clothing, worn not as protection against the destructive forces of the world but in propitiation of them, a charm against disaster.

From seven storeys up Richard can sense deference in the way the people are arranged around and behind the focal figure. That figure is clearly being led through the scenes of destruction but is required by status to appear to be doing the leading.

The pigeon is lying still, one wing outstretched in spastic uselessness. The dog has lost interest. The gull has not. Again it has left the parapet and is waddling towards the dying bird. Its intent is unmistakable. Richard makes to stand. There's a spear of pain, a new one, just up under the ribs on the right. He groans and jack-knifes forward, his right hand shooting to the point of pain, kneading it, pressing in towards innards, organs, who knows what. The pain comes in waves. Richard is absorbed by the pain. There is room for nothing else in his world – birds, dogs, nothing.

The waves weaken and recede. He breathes, nervously, relaxes, winces, relaxes more, unfurls a little, opens his eyes.

The gull is stabbing at the pigeon with its hooked beak. It pierces the flank and the pigeon flaps a wing.

Richard tries to rise but sits back down. He shouts at the gull. The dog looks up. 'Friday,' says Richard and he waves towards the gull and the dog looks at him but not at the gull. There's a wine glass beside his chair and Richard flings it and it shatters and the stem skims across the concrete at the bird. The gull grips the pigeon by the neck, spreads its wings, walks into the breeze and up onto the air. But after ten strokes of those vast wings the weight of the bird proves too much and it falls from the gull's beak onto the bonnet of the Audi and lies still. The gull circles. The dog looks at Richard, unsure of the nature of this game.

With an effort Richard rises to his feet. His head swims. When he looks up again the gull is about to settle on the Audi. He shouts and waves his arms but he is too far away and the gull eyes him without alarm. The dog seems not to understand. Richard sets off towards the car, feels himself swaying, is afraid he'll faint and drops to his knees. The dog dances and fusses round him, eager to play.

From down on the ground he can see the gull on the car's bonnet. It ducks its head and comes up with a beak full of fluff, which it leaves to the wind, and then ducks again and again and again. Richard crosses the car park on all fours, the dog beside him. Richard is panting. The old skin of his left hand has torn on the concrete and blood is seeping from a knuckle. He uses the car's front bumper to get himself back on his feet. The gull takes off.

The pigeon flutters one wing but its guts are exposed and ruptured. Richard covers the bird's head with his good hand, holds the body down with the other and stretches the neck till he feels the click of the separating spine. The bird gives a single, weak convulsion. Richard lays his head on the car's bonnet, feels the warmth in the painted metal.

Strength of a sort returns slowly. He looks at the dead bird in his hands. Blood has matted the breast. He strokes the tip of his index finger down the ruff of feathers at the bird's neck, parti-coloured and soft and light as thistledown. He stretches a wing, admires the fan of feathers, the articulation of thin and hollow bone. The bead of the eye, the one good claw, so wiry, scaly and reptilian, the other bunched and useless like his own. He takes the corpse to the parapet and lets it drop. With one wing half-extended it scythes in the air and swings away from the building's flank and then back, as the circling gull swoops lazily down towards it.

A ute is parked down there. Two men in blue overalls are studying a plan or something on the bonnet. The pigeon lands some thirty feet away. Neither man appears to notice. They fold the plan and fetch some gear from the back of the ute and walk towards the entrance of the hotel.

At the other end of High Street the guided party is standing in a semi-circle behind the central figure. Richard washes his hands with a bottle of Kiwi Spring. The PA system in the park plays 'Stairway to Heaven', ebbing across the city on the breeze.

Chapter 34

'My mother's here somewhere,' said Annie. 'She came down from Blenheim specially. She sees it as a free concert, I think.'

'So do the kids,' said Ben.

Annie smiled. The kids and her mother were right to some extent. It was billed as a memorial service, but there was an atmosphere, if not of festival, at least of picnic. Lovely early-autumn weather and thousands had come from all over the city with rugs and baskets and were now sitting on the bleached grass listening to the Woolston Brass Band, smart in their uniforms, striking just the right note. They stood for military reassurance, the triumph of order, the continuation of old Christchurch, values so much more substantial than the froth of mere entertainment. But they were still entertaining.

Ben's kids had accepted her with simplicity. 'Rachel, Clare, Hamish,' Ben had said, 'this is Annie.' And they'd chorused 'Hi, Annie' on cue and that was that. No 'Where are you from?' or 'Why are you here?' Just 'Hi, Annie,' and if Annie proved to be good company then Annie proved to be good company.

The girls treated little Hamish as a sort of doll or mascot. They fussed over him, held him a lot, dragged him about. He seemed devoted to them. He was a skinny thing, the muscles on his arms like knots in string and the skin that covered them abnormally translucent. 'Can we get Hamish some ice cream, Daddy?' said Rachel. 'Please, he's hot.' And they pushed him towards Ben like Exhibit A.

'Okay,' said Ben, 'but just for Hamish, mind.'

'Oh Da-a-ad,' the girls exclaimed together, stretching it out into three delighted syllables of mock admonition. Ben grinned and handed over money and the girls whisked Hamish away between them.

'I know, I know,' said Ben, 'I spoil them.'

'Nonsense,' said Annie. 'And they're lovely.'

The significant people were massing around and on the distant stage, their movements projected on vast screens to either side. When the search and rescue team crossed the stage to take their seats some spectators stood to cheer and clap, and others joined in until the whole crowd was on its feet and the ovation had acquired a self-swelling momentum. In one way, Annie reflected, they were an understandable subject of applause – they held no political office, were merely ordinary people doing an extraordinary job, taking risks to save lives. What could be more virtuously worthy?

At the same time, it was like applauding traffic cops or Inland Revenue. They had only done what they'd been trained to do and were paid to do. But still, it felt good to stand and clap and cheer. It felt like a positive assertion of something.

As did the flags. The place was thick with them, the red and black of Canterbury predominating – most plastered with the word 'Crusaders' – a few examples of the national flag, which no one in London could distinguish from the Australian, and on a hundred makeshift banners a phrase to be found nowhere else in the former British Empire. 'Kia kaha,' the flags said in big letters painted or sewn onto bedsheets.

A military helicopter swung in over the park and landed back beyond the crowds, who then turned to the screens to see the hatch on its green flank open and Prince William step out. A minute later he walked off the screen and onto the stage. The applause swelled.

A lone piper played a lament and the crowd stood and fell silent.

'Do you know,' whispered Ben, 'I think this is going to work.'

The screen showed a video of the central city. The crowd watched in near silence, gasping at the images, the recognisable facades half fallen, the interiors exposed, the familiar buildings lying as their constituent parts, the space they'd held within their walls now open to rain and sunlight. When the soundtrack sank and the screen faded to black, the whole of city, it seemed, was silent for a while. A priest of some kind stepped to the microphone. His words were apt for the occasion but the intensity of the moment fell. And children leaked steadily from the crowd towards the ice cream van and the swings and an even more remote but still eminently visible bouncy castle.

'Happy birthday, Annie,' said Ben. She turned to him in surprise. 'It is today, isn't it?'

She nodded.

'I didn't get you anything. I'm sorry. But I'm really glad you came. To Christchurch, I mean.'

'So am I,' said Annie.

The priest reached the end of his time at the microphone and a murmur of excitement started through the crowd and spines stretched as the people craned to see. And when Prince William began to speak there was silence.

He talked of the world's awe at Christchurch's resilience, and the crowd accepted the flattery. He quoted his grandmother in a line that was clearly designed to make tomorrow's headline. 'Grief,' he said she said, 'is the price we pay for love.' And in the kiwi-feather cloak that women had looped around his shoulders he said 'Kia kaha' in the accent of an English public school and then sat down. It was a model of how to do it.

Politicians and others trooped to the microphone and said brief considered things, but the job of the service had been done.

Annie didn't feel the urge to sing along with Dave Dobbyn but quite a few of the crowd did, in a way that they rather noticeably hadn't with the hymns.

'So what have you got planned for the rest of your birthday?'

Annie shrugged. She hadn't really thought of it as a birthday. Paul had rung her that morning. Her mother pointedly hadn't. And she had not expected anyone else to know.

'It was sweet of you to ask me along. I might have moped,' she said, though she was fairly confident she wouldn't. 'There was one thing I'd have liked to do, though,' and she told Ben about the hostel on Madras where Richard had lived.

'I wish I could have gone there.'

'You should.'

'But it's in the central city, the red zone.'

'So?' said Ben. He looked suddenly boyish. 'Why not? You'd be doing no harm. What would Rich have done? You know how he felt about authority. And besides, what's the worst that could happen?'

'But I wouldn't dare.'

'But I'm coming too,' he said.

'Daddy, Daddy.' The kids were back and more seemed to have happened to them in the last ten minutes than happened to an adult in a week and it was all of paramount importance, the narration only pausing when Hayley Westenra stepped up to sing 'Amazing Grace'.

'She's beautiful,' said Rachel, and the girls pointed Hamish towards her and held him still. 'She's beautiful,' he duly repeated, though Annie wasn't convinced.

At the end the screens showed Prince William leaving the stage and stopping to talk to the bereaved and the broken, bending solicitously over wheelchairs, saying the right things, and by taking frail old hands in his young strong ones maybe curing a disease or two.

The crowd seemed satisfied and cheerful as it drifted towards Deans Avenue, not wrung out by emotion, but not thwarted either, not feeling short-changed. The organisers seemed to have got it about right.

'Yoo hoo, darling.'

Annie wasn't the only person to look up but she was the only person to recognise her mother and Denise. Denise turned away when their eyes met, but Raewyn was heading through the crowd like a yacht cutting across the wind.

'Shit,' she said to Ben, 'my mother.'

Before Ben could speak Raewyn was among them.

'This is Rachel, and Clare and Hamish,' said Annie and the kids chorused hello. They were standing in a knot, an island around which the crowd flowed. Raewyn seemed oblivious to the obstruction they were causing.

'Wasn't Hayley nice?' she said and she looked from Annie to the kids for corroboration.

'I'm the father,' said Ben, stepping forward with his widest smile, and he introduced himself using his full name. Raewyn took the proffered hand, then registered his identity.

'I see,' she said, 'I see. I'm so sorry to have intruded. Happy birthday, darling.'

And she was gone.

'Bloody hell,' said Ben.

'You're not supposed to swear,' said Rachel.

Chapter 35

At dusk he lights the candelabrum, creating an island of light in the centre of the room, animating the faces of the two dressed mannequins, glinting off the cutlery, the long array of glasses, the cellophane wrappers on the biscuits, the chocolate's silver foil. And the margins of the room are lost in the murk, might as well not exist. Richard smiles at the effect, at the little oasis of festivity and commemoration in a wide dark world.

He sits between the mannequins and pours a beer on his right, a white wine on his left. For himself, a hard, sharp, anaesthetic vodka. His guts are not good. The pain keeps stabbing him like a narrow heated blade, then slowly melting. He raises his glass in silent pledge and drains it, feeling the good and necessary warmth.

The dog has played his part, has curled on the pile of duvets at their feet and is dreaming already. His paws are paddling the air and his chest and cheeks inflate to emit the strange, endearing whoops that pass for barking when a dog's asleep. And as the dream progresses the candlelit fur of the dog becomes ever more animated, more frantic, the barking coming faster and more desperate until Richard stretches out a slipper and lays it gently on the dog's flank and though the dog does not appear to wake the contact calms him slowly, as if it lanced the dream and drained it of its fear and conflict. Soon the dog's breathing is as deep and calm and orderly as the in and out of waves on a beach. Still with his foot against the dog's live flank, Richard sits very still. He can hear the candle flames burning with the faintest hiss. Beyond the margins of their light there might be only interstellar space.

He breaks the seal on the pinot noir with a dozen tiny and all but simultaneous metallic clicks. In the island of silence they are great noises. So, too, are the glugs of air through the thick liquid as he pours three glasses, huge balloons that chime when touched together like frangible bells. He swirls the wine as the tasters do and breathes in the autumn fruit of it, the sense of bottled ripeness. It evokes something he cannot quite find the truth of, a memory perhaps, a flash of sun and water somewhere. But he cannot hold the image still to see it, to know the time and place, and the more he tries to do so, the more it fades.

'It doesn't matter,' he says aloud, and he puts down the glass and lays a hand on the cold hard hands of the mannequins to either side. 'It doesn't matter,' he says again. 'Cheers.'

The wine on his tongue sparks the same vague image of a high country lake and sunburnt grass, but again the memory blurs and fades. 'Cheers,' he says again in the here and now.

He sips. The taste is less intense, the memory a little further off. He's sinking. The dog is snoring. 'Friday,' he says, 'Friday,' and an eye opens and its brown depths catch a gleam of candlelight. 'Friday,' and the tail beats the duvet, which is all Richard wants and it almost makes him cry. But he will not cry. He will try not to cry. There is no call for crying.

'Here,' he says to his left, to his right, and he wrestles to remove the plastic cap from a tube of Pringles, and then the paper seal, and he is surprised by his own weakness. When he has the tube open he has to pause to regain breath and clarity of mind. Fatigued, undone, by a tube of chips and he snorts at the thought. The snort becomes a cough that bends him double, his forehead pressed against the cool, thick tablecloth.

When he can trust his breathing again he opens his eyes. Just beyond lies a Christmas cracker. Without thinking he feeds one end of the cracker into his claw and grips the other with his right and pulls, but he is not strong enough.

He lays the cracker on the table and with a knife he cuts through the bands that bunch the wrapping at either end. The thing unrolls to reveal an explosive strip, a roll of orange tissue and a joke on a curl of paper. He holds it to a candle, squints up close. 'What's green and hairy and goes up and down? A gooseberry in a lift.'

He unrolls the tissue paper and it becomes a flimsy crown. He tries to place it on the dog's head but the dog paws it away. He puts it on his own head and giggles. 'I am the king, Friday,' he says, 'I am the king.' But even as he speaks he is aware of a great weariness, can feel a stupor creeping up on him. As host he decides that the end of the party is now. He pours port into thimble glasses, then taps a knife against a wine glass to get the crowd's attention.

'Ladies and gentlemen,' he says, standing between the mannequins on whose plastic flesh the candlelight throws little whorls and gleams. He leans on the table for support. 'Ladies and gentlemen.' From the pile of duvets the dog looks up at him with a single mildly curious eye.

He pauses. He is not sure of what to say. He looks around at the mannequins, the dog, the bottles and glasses and at the distant margins of the room all lost in gloom. 'A toast,' he says.

His voice has thickened. Collecting himself, he raises his glass to his right and to his left. 'To Ben,' he says, 'and Annie.' He drains the glass and holds it for the last sweet drop to drip onto his tongue. And he waits to see if more words will come but they do not. 'To Ben,' he says again, 'and Annie.' And then he sits and pours another glass of port and drains it as he drained the first.

His eyelids are heavy with sleep. He gets down on his knees and awkwardly he lies beside the dog and flips a fold of the duvet over his legs and torso and rolls onto his side and reaches out with his good right hand and lays it gently on the dog's shoulder. The beast stirs and shifts a little, stretches all four legs out simultaneously as if to rid them fully of the day's exertions, sighs with deep finality and sinks to proper sleep. Richard draws his knees up slowly till they enfold the dog's haunches. The candlelight flickers on the dog's rough fur.

'Good night,' he says, 'Good night.' And he lets his eyelids fall. He can smell the dog's warmth.

Chapter 36

'Do you think we should Nugget our faces?'

'No,' said Annie. She was not feeling brave. For all Ben's talk of virtuous intentions she was scared. And it was so hard to fake innocence. As she and Ben walked up Fitzgerald Avenue after leaving the grim little pub on St Asaph Street she felt as if she had the word 'criminal' stamped on her forehead. When they passed soldiers on patrol she was surprised they didn't immediately train their guns on her.

The gin she'd drunk had not lived up to its courage-inducing reputation. Had they had no criminal intentions she'd have smiled and said hello to the soldiers and shared a joke with them. But now it was all she could do to walk. It was as if the sense of guilt got between her and her autonomic functions. Even breathing became forced and self-conscious.

'Shouldn't we wait till later? Till two or three, maybe.'

But they'd been through all this in the pub. The best time was when the pubs shut around eleven. That was when there would be most people about and they would be least obtrusive. And also when the soldiers were most likely to be occupied by the antics of drunks, who were sure to find a fence they weren't allowed to climb and soldiers with guns protecting it an irresistible combination.

North of Cashel they shrank into the shadows and became officially furtive. A police car passed and a foot patrol of soldiers. Annie wanted to giggle. It was like bad television. But she was pleased to be doing it with Ben. 'I owe a lot to Rich,' he'd said in the pub. 'Including the courage to do something like this. He always said doing the right thing was easy, so long as you were sure it was the right thing. This is the right thing.'

They were skulking among cheap native shrubs now, by an outfit called Shox 'n' Lube.

Annie felt Ben's hand reaching for hers in the darkness. 'You all right?' he asked and by the light of a passing car she caught a glimpse of his teeth and hollowed eyes and cheekbones that stripped him of half his years.

'Yes,' she said and they dashed together across the first half of Fitzgerald Avenue, paused a moment under the trees on the median, heard and saw no reaction and dashed again. At the fence, as planned, Annie jumped to hook an arm over the top while Ben boosted her from below and all but threw her over before vaulting over himself and together they ran the last few yards out of the range of the street light and crouched beneath a tall brick wall. They were in. Panting in the inky dark, Annie felt the thrill of trespass.

'Come on,' said Ben. They had two blocks to travel, had agreed the route, poring over a map on the sticky pub leaner. A man with a stained pioneer beard had asked if they were planning a bank robbery and Annie had been grateful he'd been too intent on his own wit and too deep into his third jug to notice her awkwardness.

They edged down the lanes and the sides of buildings. They were beyond street lights now. The high half-moon cast faint shadows, like ink stains washed into a shirt. They were not far from River Road but Anne knew nothing of this warren of buildings and dingy businesses. It was spectacularly quiet. They both started as a cat dropped over a fence. It landed on a sheet of corrugated iron. They heard the soft thud of the paw-pads, the tiny scratch of the claws.

It was as if they were the first people there, a post-industrial Adam and Eve. They passed a yard of dead engines with the smoko room wide open, cups smashed on the concrete floor, the battered cream-coloured Zip still bolted to the wall like a boiler from the *Titanic*.

Ben was deft. He led the way down black alleys, made gates swing silently. He'd have made a good burglar.

At Barbadoes Street they were like shy forest animals on the edge of a clearing, peering out from the shadow of an alley to look up and down the expanse of road. Fallen facades still blocked the pavement, fanning out like scree slopes. A parked Mercedes had been half flattened by masonry, its long sleek nose jutting out of the heap but its boot and back wheels buried, as if stamped on when trying to flee. And there was less than nobody about.

On the far side of Latimer Square the charred spine of the CTV building stood as an awkward memorial to over a hundred dead, cordoned off by high fences while the authorities sought to lay blame. But whoever that blame was laid on, the dead were dead. The paper told stories of people who had nipped out for a sandwich that saved them.

Ben and Annie went north, keeping to the dark fringes, skirting any spaces. Some buildings had already been bulldozed, the materials that shaped them now heaped and jumbled. Annie feared that the hostel, which seemed so rickety in the photo, would have gone too, her father's last home dragged down by hydraulic pincers to be dumped without thought on the back of a truck. But when they rounded the junction with Armagh Street there it stood, sprawling and unlovely. Weatherboard stained by leaks in the spouting. Ancient metal fire-escapes, their last flight hauled up off the ground against burglary. The building filled most of the section. The rest was given over to drains and concrete and weeds that grew skinny and dusty.

A temporary fence had been slung up around the hostel but it was token only. Ben lifted a section aside and they stepped onto the porch. On the door were scrawls in aerosol, the graffiti code of search and rescue. Plastered over that, a red sticker of condemnation. It was an offence even to approach it. There was a combination lock on the door but someone had smashed the frame, and the door opened to a push of fingers. In the dark hall, a smell of rats. Just doors to rooms, some of them broken open, and stairs presumably to more.

'Do we have a room number?'

Annie shook her head. 'Upstairs, the landlord thought. That's all he could remember.'

As their eyes widened to the gloom they climbed the stairs to find a communal kitchen with a toaster and a microwave the size of a tomb, a stove with a frying pan still on it, and a tall old fridge. Annie pulled open the fridge door, then slammed it shut again. Even in that fraction of a second she'd noticed that it was divided into a dozen or so compartments, each with its own hinged door and clasp to which a padlock could be fitted.

A corridor to the right was lined with windows on one side, half a dozen doors on the other. At the far end a door marked 'WC' and another 'Shower'. In the corridor the ends of the floor boards had been painted, while the middle remained bare and blond where a strip of carpet had never been replaced.

Ben pushed on the first door. A free-standing wardrobe. A crudely plumbed sink. A small chest of drawers. A bed on which an unzipped ancient sleeping bag lay scrunched in the position where it had last been thrown off. No sheet. At the head of the bed a stained pillow. On the chair beside the bed a small ceramic elephant, its trunk curled back in trumpeting defiance. Beneath the window half a dozen empty bottles. Dom Pedro Ruby Port.

Annie looked enquiringly at Ben.

'I don't think so,' he said, but he opened the wardrobe. Two thick jackets on hangers. What might have been trousers thrown in below. Ben pulled out a jacket, held it up.

'No,' he said.

The next door had been kicked open, presumably by search and rescue, shattering the flimsy jamb. Another narrow bed and dark old wooden wardrobe. Beside the bed what seemed to be a seventies radiogram-cum-dressing table, though the mirror had gone. Annie pulled open a drawer of wood veneer. In the drawer a couple of notebooks. She took them to the window sill and the thin light of the moon. In the notebooks pencil drawings. Of birds and animals. Of Ben. Of her.

Chapter 37

He wakes before dawn. Though he does not move he knows the dog has sensed his waking, but it, too, stays where it is, breathing with the deep rhythm of the night. From where he lies he can see a narrow line of gallery windows. And framed in one of them a bright half-moon. And with sudden clarity he remembers lying one night on the bank of the Tekapo River, the smooth stones at his back still warm from the day's sun, and the moon seemed huge and clear, and he could make out the pockmarks of the craters, each one a testament to chance, the random collision of stuff with stuff out there in the bowling alley of the cosmos. He loved the thought then, as he loves it now, of things happening to happen on such a scale, in the great belittling emptiness. 'It doesn't matter,' he whispers to the dog, and is rewarded with a single swing of the tail against the duvet.

'Good boy,' he says and he tries not to think ahead, not to think to the morning that is coming, but rather to lie here and watch the moon as it slides now towards the window frame and inch by inch is eaten by the wall. He watches it for half an hour and it is gone, is just a hint of a glow in the dark glass corner.

He drowses, letting himself for once drift backwards on little puffs of memory, drift backwards to the dangerously golden moments. He pauses before waking his daughter, pausing to gaze on her impossibly unblemished face, unpocked by the collisions of chance and time, faultless of skin and composition, so innocent, so vulnerable. He watches her as he watched the moon this morning, gazing at time passing on her flesh. And then gently wakes her and sees her face still folded with sleep, and she is entirely trusting, casting her arms around his neck and letting herself be lifted from the bed, her head lolling on his shoulder. And as he scoops his arms beneath her he feels the warmth of the bed, the warmth that she has left upon the sheets.

And lying broken on the floor of a broken hotel, side by side with a dog, he smells his daughter, feels again the texture of her flesh.

Enough. He rolls and reaches out and tips half a miniature of Stolichnaya onto his tongue. And soon it works as it has always worked and he drifts.

He is at the river again, a different river, under trees, and it is afternoon and they are lying on a blanket laid on sparse grass and sand. Ben's on his back, looking up through half-closed eyes at the dapple of light through the leaves. And he is lying on his side and watching Ben in profile, his hair and eyebrows, nose and lips and chin. Ben's flesh is tanned honey brown from the bicep to the hand. Richard sees again the prominent veins on the forearm, the taut curve of muscle above the elbow, the swell of the chest, the barred butterfly of the ribs shielding heart and lungs and then the soft concavity of the milk-white belly and the arch of the spine that rises to meet it. A little line of glistening blond stomach hair stretches from the belly button to the waistband of his shorts.

Ben knows that he is being studied, turns once to look across and smile. Richard fetches a notebook from the tent and sits on a camp stool. He doesn't know how long the drawing takes, knows only that he draws with a certainty of line that doesn't often come. And when it is done, in pencil, it is done and he has held something of that random spot of place and time for ever. Or whatever is for ever for a man.

Chapter 38

A window had been left open. The room did not smell strong. But there was so little there. A single bed, an ashtray, a bin liner of clothes clean from the laundrette but overdried and scrunched into a bundle, two op-shop jackets as worn by dead husbands, a pair of battered training shoes, another of grandpa slippers, the heels on both worn in at the same angle. The radiogram had no plug, the ancient wires just ripped from the wall in some hotel refit. In the wardrobe half a bottle of vodka of a brand Annie didn't recognise. In the ashtray, a dozen long-dried butts of thinly rolled tobacco.

Annie tried all the drawers. Ben looked under the bed, on top of the wardrobe. Nothing.

They sat on the bed. No sheets. A striped and hollow mattress. A shiny purple eiderdown. The pillows, a pair of floral sofa cushions.

They flicked through the pages of the notebooks. One was mainly pictures of Annie. Another mainly Ben. Ben sitting, lying, standing, sleeping, clothed, naked, showering.

Annie looked around the barren nothing of a room.

'Come here,' said Ben. His neck smelt of soap and wine. Annie felt the silence of the city centre. Over his shoulder she could see the half-moon low in the corner of the window. Next door was a yard full of second-hand whiteware. A twin tub gleamed in the moonlight.

'Shall we go?' said Ben.

'Do you think we should take these?'

'Yes.'

'And if he comes back?'

'The place is coming down.'

'We'll leave a note,' she said. And she looked for a pen or pencil, found nothing, went to the next room along, and returned with a ballpoint.

She tore an unused page from the back of the one of the books. 'Dad, Rich,' she wrote. 'We came to look for you. We took the drawings. We love you.' She added her name and contact details and Ben did the same. And then she folded it in half and wrote 'FOR RICHARD JONES' on the front and underlined it and placed it prominently on the derelict radiogram under the corner of the ashtray so that it wouldn't blow away.

Chapter 39

Summer has ended. The night takes longer to dissolve into day. Richard watches the window lighten above him, through shades of grey to almost white. Light reveals the mannequins, the candelabrum, the bulbous stalactites of wax, the remains of drinks and snacks, the opened cracker.

Richard rolls onto his side and then, with some difficulty, kneels. He is woozy with weakness and he stays a while on all fours, his head hanging. The dog waits and watches, used to the slow progress, the long moments of pause.

Like a mountaineer taking on the next pitch of rock, Richard lifts his head, seizes the edge of the table with his good hand and hauls himself to his feet with a grunt. Pain stabs at him in half a dozen places but pain is a known companion. It is the weakness that troubles him. He has to make it to the car park roof.

On the stairs he puts both hands on the rail, and lets gravity take him down a step at a time. His thighs seem to have become absurdly weak, like the spindle-legs of a newborn colt.

To keep himself going he counts off the twelve steps in each flight. There are six flights. The dog is all patience. Richard talks as he goes.

'You're to go, see? Do you understand, Friday?' says Richard, speaking in bursts between breaths. 'You're a good dog and you're not old. Okay? Do you promise now, dog? Do you promise?'

From the landing below him the dog looks up and cocks its head to one side.

'Where are the rabbits, Friday? Find the rabbits. Find the warm hearts. Ahhh,' as he half misses a step and his ankle buckles and he has to cling hard to the rail as his hip swings into it. The shock spears through him and a fierce new pain erupts in his haunch.

But they have reached the car park floor, the corridor of catastrophe, the bleached carpet and the door propped open, framing a slice of parapet and sky of thrush-egg blue. The dogs bounds for the outside world, pisses prodigiously on the first concrete buttress and Richard again feels wonder at the creature's patience. He lurches in the dog's wake, supporting himself on the wall to ease the weight on his hip.

It is early yet. He lowers himself into his seat, ginger with the pain and weak from the descent, and takes a Gordon's from his pantry. He drinks straight from the miniature bottle, urging it to the bits that crave it.

Through the parapet he can see down Cashel Street to the Bridge of Remembrance. Despite the hour people are crawling about the temporary grandstand.

The dog tours the rooftop as diligently as on the first day, asserting its own presence, scouring for sign of others, as if this concrete floor hoisted fifty feet into the air were its wild and vital territory. The dog does not tire of its own way of being, and not for one second does it doubt. Richard feels a surge of envy and of admiration and of love and he calls the dog who looks up in slight surprise then pads across.

Richard sits forward to stroke the dog and the pain flares in his hip. He cries out and the dog starts at the noise. But Richard swings his legs together and sits up straight and the pain recedes and he puts out an arm and the dog comes in close and lays its head on his lap and looks up into Richard's eyes.

And Richard sighs and runs his hand repeatedly down from the dome of the dog's skull along the ridge of its neck and between the softened shoulders and as he does so the dog shuts its eyes and Richard talks in a whisper and then he places his head against the dog's head, skull of a beast against skull of a beast, and he stays that way for some seconds and then he kisses the dog on the top of its head, his lips pressed against a few of the billion shining hairs. And Richard takes a Tux from the pocket of his dressing gown and the dog takes it gently in those jaws that can crush bone and with an effort that makes him groan Richard stands and lurches towards the door into the hotel.

The brass pot that holds the door open has weathered and dulled, the soil dried and shrunk, though the rubber plant seems as synthetically glossy as before. By pulling on the plant's stem Richard tilts the pot till it falls and rolls away. He leans back against the door to stop it closing. The dog has finished the Tux and is standing in front of him.

Richard has no more biscuit. He reaches out and strokes the dog's head once. 'Sorry, boy,' he says, 'but sit. Sit, Friday, sit.'

Puzzled by the tone and the oddness, the dog lowers its rump slowly to the concrete, eyes on Richard. When Richard starts to withdraw inside the dog makes to follow him but 'Sit,' says Richard again and the dog stops. Richard closes the door between him and the dog.

He slumps against the wall in the corridor and sinks slowly to the floor. He is affected with a grinding sense of dread. He meant to climb to the penthouse, to sit overlooking the city and to drink himself to sleep. But he isn't sure he has the strength for the climb. And here's as good as anywhere.

There is a pane of toughened glass let into the middle of the door. But he doesn't have to stand and look through it. He knows the dog is still there.

For the first few minutes the dog is silent. And Richard too. He all but holds his breath. Then comes the first faint whimper. He tries to shut his ears. The whimper feeds upon itself and grows in volume like the sawing of some mawkish violin, before collapsing into the silence of disappointment, of betrayal.

The silence then is as bad as the noise. Worse. After perhaps a minute, Richard catches the first mouse-squeak of renewed reproach and again the whining builds like a self-sustaining wave. When he hears the scratch of claws on the door Richard almost cries out. But he wills himself to stay quiet. The dog must lose hope.

The scratching becomes a frantic two-pawed scrabbling at the door. Richard can hear the claws tearing through the surface of the paint. He jams his hands over his ears but still feels as much as hears the scratching and the whining, which again subside to little, then to nothing.

Richard feels as quietly as possible in the pockets of his robe. Half a vodka miniature. With infinite caution he unscrews the cap and places it so gently on the bristle carpet and he tips the little bottle to his mouth and feels as much as tastes the vodka on his tongue and throat and suddenly he is coughing, bent over and spluttering, and even in his gagging distress he can hear the claws against the door again, their redoubled effort, and the whining that's as clear as speech.

The cough fades. Richard levers himself up onto his feet, groaning as pain licks through his hip. The dog is frantic at the noise, rasping with its claws, half whimpering and half barking at the barrier between them.

Richard staggers down the corridor and through a smoke door into the stairwell. In a room beyond he finds an unplundered mini-bar and stuffs the pockets of his robe and falls onto the bed and lies there, face down. And he realises that he is listening. That he is straining to hear the dog. He can hear nothing. He is unsure what to do. Some nameless emotion that is neither despair nor fear is grinding at his heart.

He rolls onto his back, sits up against pillows, drinks a Scotch and listens. He is too far away to hear the dog but he listens. He waits. He catches a glimpse of himself in the mirror, haggard, attentive, on his head a crown of orange tissue paper. His mind is out there on the car park roof. He wonders how long he has. He urges himself to stay where he is. The dog will up and leave, he tells himself. It will. It must.

He sits on the bed and drinks at intervals for he doesn't know how long. His hip aches fiercely and he tries to concentrate on that, but every time he lets up in his vigilance he finds his legs swinging off the bed, being drawn towards the car park and he has to force himself to stay by an act of will that he knows will buckle in the end.

And it does. Back he goes, numbed by drink. He stops short of the closed door and listens. Nothing. He creeps the last yards, hunched and leaning on the wall, straightens, counts to five, says 'Please', and looks through the inset pane. The dog is not at the door. It is not where he told it to sit. The dog has gone. It is as he hoped. And he has never felt so alone.

The dog is by his chair under the awning, its nose aligned to the door and its eyes open and it has seen his face at the glass and its ragged plume of a tail has swung with joy and the dog is up on its feet and coming to the door and Richard's heart surges with forbidden feeling. He leans on the handle and the door swings open and he stumbles through it and falls to the floor and the dog is all over him, licking his face and whimpering with joy.

'Friday,' says Richard, 'Friday.' And he is laughing.

Chapter 40

It was Vince's idea to go to watch the hotel blown up.

'You know you want to,' he said when he picked her up. And Annie acknowledged she was curious. Would it be formal, with a front row of dignitaries in suits, or would it be merely an entertainment for the ghoulish masses, a violent flip side to the memorial service?

Jess had been on night shift and was not to be woken. Annie felt mean for feeling relieved. But it was so much easier to leave a written note of thanks than to hug and say goodbye, even with her oldest friend. No dithering or awkwardness, no lapsing into dishonest formulae.

A fence-lined corridor had been let into the cordon, from Rolleston Avenue to the river. The crowd walking towards the Bridge of Remembrance seemed in a festival mood. It consisted mainly of fathers and kids, all clearly excited by the bang to come. An ice cream van had managed to get to the Durham Street corner and was doing good business in the Sunday sunshine.

The grandstand soon filled up. Importance was attached only to the theatrically mounted plunger and the little dais beside it. The kid in the wheelchair was already there, being wheeled about and greeted, his grin a slice of the purest joy. A man who was presumably his father pushed him up a ramp towards the grandstand and he waved like a film star to the crowd and those who were looking were delighted to wave back. Some called his name.

Most of the hotel was plainly visible, and the angle it was leaning at. Would it fall in on itself as the World Trade Center had done? The planes had flown out of just such a sky of late-summer blue as this one. On that extraordinary morning, now a decade past, Annie had spent hours in front of the television, held by something awful in the heart, the same thing as had drawn this happy holiday crowd to watch a demolition.

Between the grandstand and the central city the Avon came as a slight surprise, its shallow, spring-fed burble just going on its way regardless, ready to take the punts of finger-trailing tourists on whatever day they happened to return.

The doomed boy, still beaming, had been wheeled to his position. A local radio personality was calling the countdown to midday. Annie felt a nudge in her side. Vince was pointing to the end of Cashel Street, where a mongrel had appeared inside the fence. Others had seen it too. There was a slight buzz of chatter on the bleachers.

The dog was a safe distance from the explosion but Annie's heart still went out to it. The noise would terrify it. Perhaps an official would fetch it out, or one of the security guards. But no one seemed to be moving. Then the dog went back up Cashel Street, disappearing behind rubble.

'One minute!' cried the radio personality.

Annie half stood up but Vince put a hand on her arm. 'It's a long way away,' he said.

Those in the crowd who'd seen the dog seemed already to have forgotten it. They snuggled in towards the climactic moment, grew quieter.

'Thirty seconds.'

Annie wasn't looking at the hotel. She was scanning the fence for the dog. And there it was again, behind the fencing like a zoo exhibit.

'Twenty seconds.'

The dog barked, one, two, three times. Annie heard the barks clear above the swelling countdown. No one else seemed to.

'Fifteen, fourteen, thirteen, twelve.' Perhaps a thousand people were calling the numbers.

'Eight, seven, six.' The dog looked across the river at the grandstand then it disappeared up the street again. The kid had both hands on the plunger, his little stick elbows raised in readiness like bat-wings, his face a mask of concentrated joy. Annie couldn't see the dog.

'Three, two, one,' and the kid all but lifted himself from his chair with his vigour. Down went the plunger and innocuous puffs burst from halfway up the building, like bullet pocks. A second or so later came the noise of the blast. The building teetered, ruptured at base and waist, was held airborne by the habit of inertia, then down it went in one accelerating rush. And it had gone, disappeared behind other buildings, a devastating conjuring trick. In its place rose a seemingly self-generating cloud of smoke and rubble dust, a brown and swelling bloom.

The dog was back against the fence, fear-struck by the blast, its ears flattened against its head, its tail whipped between its legs. The crowd was no longer looking. The radio celebrity thanked everyone for coming, announced how much the sponsored demolition had raised for medical research, said kia kaha and goodbye and people were gathering things and filing down the planking steps, talking excitedly. Annie stood and let them pass, as a squat security guard in a yellow jacket crossed the Bridge of Remembrance and Oxford Terrace.

'We should get to the airport,' said Vince.

'Hang on.' Annie watched as the guard unhitched two segments of fencing and knelt in the gap to attract the dog. The dog came cautiously but when the guard went to take its collar the dog withdrew. The guard followed.

'Hang on,' Annie said again.

Moments later the guard ran back into view, talking urgently into the radio on his lapel, and beckoning as he did so and a pair of paramedics appeared from under the grandstand and went running across the bridge, their medical bags swinging. They followed the guard through the fence and out of sight. No sign of the dog. And almost immediately they heard the siren and other security guards were clearing the fencing off Oxford Terrace to let the ambulance through and it drew up with fierce theatricality at the end of Cashel Street just as a paramedic emerged through the fence. She spoke to the driver of the ambulance. And though they still unloaded a gurney from the back and wheeled it up Cashel Street and out of sight, they did so without any sense of urgency.

* * *

A bright and frosty morning, and London sparkled as they flew in from the east down the silver worm of the Thames. In the Terminal 3 arrivals hall Annie picked out Paul almost immediately. She waved. When he saw her he performed a sort of comic shrug, his palms facing upwards at shoulder height, his head cocked slightly to one side, his eyebrows raised in unmistakable enquiry.

Annie smiled.

Acknowledgments

Finlay Macdonald and Jim Gill for their faith, and Anna Rogers for her peerlessly tactful editing.